Born in the 60's, Dancing in the 80's

Dear Kay,

With love & Sam xx

(AKA Mandy Sellers)

Tovu Jenkins

ISBN: 9798651552306

PublishNation
www.publishnation.co.uk

Overview

It's 1985, the year of Live Aid, earthquakes, the birth of the World Wide Web and the year they found the wreck of the Titanic. Technology is not accessible to the masses as it is nowadays, but it is an important year for IT; the only way to communicate for the majority of people is on a landline, letter or face to face for the majority of people. Microsoft publishes version 1 of Windows and Ernie Wise makes the first mobile phone call with no idea of how technology will revolutionise everything in the future. Margaret Thatcher is the Prime Minister of the UK and there are riots in Brixton that shake the country. The mid-eighties music is arguably the best of the best and the nation's awareness of the issues in third world countries heightens. There are tragedies and celebrations, including terrorism and the birth of Prince Harry.

It is the year that I finish my student nurse training and became a staff nurse in a mental health day unit. I am 24 years old and by my own admission still growing up. People say I am attractive. 'Pretty' some say but my sisters are beauties and they completely outshine me. I lack confidence and I know I am overly sensitive at times, but also people say I am funny and creative with words. I think my story will relate to all females who grew up in the eighties and by their mid-twenties, still didn't feel like an adult should feel. I am still innocent and gullible, but I try to be caring, respectful and treasure my friends and family even though they can drive me crazy. I am hopeless with men and attract 'the wrong sort' and I desperately want to find love.

So do my two sisters and two best friends. Can we achieve it in this incredible year?

This year is eventful, there is never a dull moment, so I do hope you read on and enjoy it.

Chapter 1

Larissa is nervously eying up the scruffy Welsh barman who is asking her about local music venues as he only recently moved to the area. Her bright blue eyes dart between him and the exit door and she blushes as she explains she isn't from around here either. She dashes to my side and hands me a glass of cheap white wine and starts to sip at her own. I am so hot, the pub is stifling and I am dreading the news that Larissa is about to land in my lap. Beads of sweat are forming on my top lip and I dare not take off my jean jacket because I only have a white tee shirt underneath that not only states on the back 'I love Marc Almond,' but will show seriously foul sweat stains. Goodness knows what aroma is cooking up in those armpits. I ask her what's happened. She only ever calls me to meet her for a drink when she wants to pour her heart out. She sweeps her hair up with one hand and plays with it on the top of her head;

"Oh nothing much, I just wanted to catch up!" she says in her sing song voice. I am not buying it and say, "Give me the dirt Larissa, what's going on?"

She stops playing with her hair and responds with the dreaded words;

"Can I just stay with you a little while? I can't go to mother's she drives me nuts".

"So, what's happened?" I ask again. Then she lets it all flow out.

She tells me about her job being stressful, a young man she is working with keeps biting all the staff, the latest boyfriend has dumped her, and she has run up debts amounting to £2,000 and needs to pay it off. I patiently get her to give me the details and we consume a bottle of wine whilst she never stops to take a breath or ask me how I am. The best bit of her story this time was about her now ex- boyfriend; it shouldn't have been funny, but we couldn't stop laughing when she told me what she did as revenge. We will call him Ken; it wasn't his name but I used to call him it secretly because he was skinny and plastic. Larissa in an uncharacteristically angry state took the scissors to his clothes and delivered them to his mother's house whom he had got to do the dumping for him. The bin liner was full of shredded ties, socks, pants and work shirts that he used to leave with Larissa for when he stayed over with her. The look on his face had apparently been priceless, as reported by his younger brother who had told anyone who cared to listen.

We walk round from the pub to my 'Nurses Accommodation', of course we are not supposed to have people stay at all. They do spot checks but so long as they don't find a body physically there, they don't say anything. Voluptuous Becky who lives next door to me often has a half-naked man wandering around looking for the loo. I play Soft Cell loudly on many evenings to avoid the sounds that come through the walls. Fortunately, she loves Marc Almond too. Larissa sleeps with ear plugs in. She has few possessions to move in, it will be fine from a practical view, but I like my space and I like my quiet. She also reminds me of our childhood and how I shared a bedroom with her always. The stark reminders of dad's temper and mother's lack of confidence in all areas, apart from knitting and keeping her children out of sight as much as possible. I took refuge in my bedroom until Larissa was sent there for her frequent misdemeanours. We used to lie on our beds silently hating each other for different reasons and yet loving and loyal, bound by ties that would never break. Now we are the best of friends.

Drunk from the wine we crash on my bed, top and tail and talk about the family; the focus ending up on our brother Landon. We both adore Landon; most women do and like us, even knowing his playboy ways doesn't get in the way. We despise his girlfriend Jaynie for it though; she should leave him and take better care of herself. She is borderline anorexic and whilst most ballet dancers look it, we think she is also suffering at the hands of our dear brother and heading for illness. We giggle for ages about the time she joined us for one of mum's famous Sunday Roasts and had two small carrots and three pieces of broccoli. Mum could barely contain herself and kept looking at Landon as if to say, 'tell her, tell her to eat some meat and potatoes and then some apple crumble and custard or she'll die'. Landon just ignored it and told us about a man he sold insurance to that week who had a Charlie Chaplin moustache, who actually tripped over his own feet when he left the office.

In the morning I rush around looking for a my nurses badge; I know I put it in its usual place and then I remember I didn't, it was stuffed in my duffle bag when I changed to meet up with Larissa. She is looking like a rag doll in her sleeping bag on the floor. Crumpled and pink cheeked.

"Leave the door unlocked when you leave!" I shout at her as I rush out to catch the bus to the day centre I am working in.

I have to take the bus as I have little money for petrol and I'm still a bit nervous driving. I am early as always, but for most of the journey I am imagining the bus is going to break down and I will be late. People stare at me a lot; I don't know why. There's a man in a suit watching me, I can see him in the reflection of the bus window. I can't wait to get off the bus. He gets off at the same stop, what's a man in a sharp suit doing on the bus anyway? Could he not have got a taxi?

I'm starting to sweat again and then he says to me;

"Umm, sorry but did you know your cardigan is inside out?" I am mortified. Shrug my shoulders and give my thanks before rushing off.

I see Helena walking into the day centre; she is in a good mood because she is wearing green. Her happy colour. The joy of being a mental health student is that you don't have to wear a uniform all the time like a general nurse does.

We greet each other and head for the kitchen to make a cup of coffee as I take off my cardi to turn it the right way out. Charlie and Jim join us and start talking about last night's match; we leave the kitchen quickly and grab a seat in the office ready for the morning meeting. Neither of us are fans of rugby.

Vanessa the manager bounces in with a huge smile;

"Good morning everybody, don't you all look sassy today?"

She bounces back out again; we call her Tigger.

"Oh Tovu, can you come up to my office after the morning meeting please?"

She's bounced back in, delivering me a request that sends me spiralling into thoughts of what I could have possibly done wrong.

Yes, my name is Tovu, often pronounced Tofu and misspelt, more often than not. Helena shrugs and tells me not to be daft when I try and bring her down into my anxiety spiral and I am so hot now I think I might just internally combust. She diffuses me for a moment and before I can reignite it; Charlie and Jim walk in with Debbie who calls us to order to plan the day ahead.

I get to run the Women's Support Group with her, I love it. A group where I feel at home and pretty much more sorted than

4

everyone else in the room. This is a rare feeling for me. Then this afternoon it's the craft group which is a joy. My favourite person attends the Craft Group. Uma, a survivor of sexual abuse who is always asking if she's done something wrong, it's almost as though she vocalises what I think. Aside from that, she is warm hearted, generous to a fault and a funny woman whom I think the world of.

I remember to go up to see Vanessa and knock on her door; she calls me to enter and I sit in the chair next to her desk and wait for my telling off. Instead she beams from ear to ear and says she'd like me to consider working here permanently when I finish my training. She starts to feedback all the good reports from the team but all I can think of is how I am going to have to pass my exams now and qualify. I smile and nod and tell her I would be honoured, and she dismisses me as her phone rings. I contain my excitement because I don't want to upset Helena who loves the day centre but isn't getting the same offer, and I get on with the day's work.

Later, I find Larissa sat on the floor of my room and the sleeping bag wrapped around her shoulders painting her toenails with my favourite nail varnish. She looks up guilty as I come in and I wonder what else she has 'borrowed'. I strip off my tops and head for the shower asking her to put the kettle on and make me a cuppa. She has a little moan about it and scuffles off down to the shared kitchen. When we both return, we decide on junk food for tea and just as we set off in search of carbs, Jay appears and says there's a phone call for me. Jay is a bearded hippy student nurse who has a thing for Larissa, so he blushes when he catches sight of her. I leave them to exchange pleasantries and head off to the phone. I am then subjected to a brief conversation with our mother who reminds me we must attend Uncle Sid's

5

60th tomorrow afternoon and could I pick up cousin Deedee, the posh one from London. My heart sinks but I agree, and she puts the phone down. No 'I love you', that's just not the Jenkins way.

Larissa looks relieved when I re-appear and saying goodbye to Jay we walk out and find our fave fried chicken place. Larissa has done nothing on her day off today; she is wallowing. This annoys me but I understand, and I try not to lecture her. I become irritated though when she completely takes the wind out of my sails by commenting on my work news with;

"You just have all the luck Tovu or does your boss fancy you?"

Bloody cheek, she can fuck off I think to myself. I just smile and affirm I am indeed sleeping with my boss, even though the thought of it makes me laugh. I am definitely heterosexual, not that I haven't considered it and once I dreamt a very raunchy time with a fellow student nurse I am friends with.

My love life is a joke, I haven't much luck with men. Anyway, just as I am pondering my loveless fate, who should appear but Greg. Greg the junior doctor who turns everyone's head. Tall, dark, swarthy and just plain gorgeous. He nods in recognition and gives us the hugest smile. Larissa is completely in love and wants to know all about him. I tell her he is off limits because Nadia the Irish junior doctor who has a model figure and the confidence of a Giselle that beats everyone in a race with grace and speed. Greg is meeting his brother, who is just as handsome but rough around the edges. Mike is allegedly an alcoholic who is unemployed and depressed. I feel instantly attracted to him.

They join our table just as I am chewing my sweetcorn, making a huge mess and with bits already stuck in my teeth. Deep joy! No wonder no one is ever going to love me! Larissa is blushing and chuntering on about why she could never be a doctor. I see Mike lusting at her across the table, I am resigned to letting them get on with making a date to meet up. I know it's inevitable. Greg is paged and leaps off to get to a phone. I declare myself to be the best gooseberry ever, the sort that disappears. I say I have to leave as I am meeting up with friends. I don't, I just want some alone time whilst I can. Larissa will reappear much later I am guessing by the way they are chatting and getting closer and closer to each other.

Alone in my room I put on some Simple Minds and attempt to tidy up. As I'm dancing around, I am interrupted by a knock on the door. Another phone call. It's Mary wanting me to go over to see her. I renege, I am a 'please person' and I do as I am asked. Mary is a brunette with molten brown eyes who everyone loves because of her humour. She is bubbly and energetic. Always positive and forgiven for being slightly chaotic. Her family are like a second family to me; I often sought refuge and slept over with Mary when we were younger. Her older brother Frank and I used to have sneaky liaisons of the sexual kind. We never dated but good friends. Frank is funny and looks a bit like a cartoon character with overly big features and spiky hair. It is he who lets me in when I arrive at their welcoming home; which is full of trinkets and antiques their father Frank Senior enjoys collecting. He greets me with the words.

"Look what the cat dragged in, any pillow punching lately? Mary's in her room, go on up."

The reference to pillow punching is because I told them about a Drama Therapy Group I had to join last week; and to help someone express their anger we did an exercise where we had to punch pillows imagining them to be someone who had wronged us in the past or was annoying us in the present. The family

7

Brownlow think this is hilarious; I don't understand why; it was really good. Frank squeezes my bottom as I pass by him, I give him a withering look and then we both grin at each other.

Mary cannot wait to tell me about our mutual friend Belle's latest scheme for getting into the Guinness Book of Records. Belle is a feisty, fair haired, and a hazel-eyed beauty who is always looking for a challenge and drives everyone to distraction with her latest idea for getting notoriety. Mary tells me that the latest attempt she is making is for the 'most spoons balanced on a human body'. She is aiming for 50 to make it into the book. Now Belle is curvy and has a fair bit of skin she could use, but we are doubtful. Watching her attempt this feat will be amusing though. We agree it will be perfect for her to try her first attempt very soon, so long as we can watch. Mary produces some spoons and suggests we now try placing them on our bodies. She plays hurt when I tell her the wooden and plastic ones won't work and would not be counted. We attempt it though, for a good ten minutes laughing so much it brings her mum to the bedroom door. Gracie has her hair in rollers and a green quilted dressing gown covering her from neck to toe; she peers at us through colourful rimmed glasses which are her trademark.

"What are you two up to?"

She catches Mary with two spoons balanced on her cheeks, one on her left thigh and three on her right. I have three on my left arm, one on each knee cap and one on my nose. She starts shaking her head and then says,

"Don't tell me, this is the latest fashion for pulling boys?"

We try and coax her to have a go and she retreats hunting down her ever elusive husband. We give up and Mary produces a bottle of Asti to share and encourages me to consider staying the night. I daren't stay for fear of Larissa using my bed with or without a man in tow.

"Well I managed more spoons than you" Mary says, and I tell her that's because she is more hairy. She then reminds me of the time I used Immac on my sideburns and came up in a horrible, painful rash. Gosh that stuff stank. We then titter about Marion Morris who had pubes down to her knees; we know because she joined us sunbathing one time and we witnessed her long, tendril like ginger pubes. We both turned into fervent pube shavers ever since and we definitely don't use Immac on them.

Mary puts on some Kate Bush and we whirl around her bedroom singing with abandon, very badly and cry laughing.

'So spill the beans on Larissa" Mary asks me

I tell her what I know and then feel the need to dash home to check up on her. I ask Mary to say goodbye to the family for me and arrange to meet up on Sunday after Uncle Sid's 60th so I can tell her the gory details. She attempts to get me to stay a bit longer, but I am resolute in getting home and make my way home on the bus.

The bus is packed, I seem to have chosen pub kick out time to leave Mary's and I sit next to an oriental looking lady who is dressed in a gorgeous purple coat. I tell her this and she smiles not understanding what I am saying and turns back to staring out the window. I feel a tap on my shoulder, what now? I am thinking, is my jacket on inside out? I glance over my shoulder and see a hairy bearded man with the lightest blue eyes looking at me and he asks me,

"S'cuse me love but are you that woman off TV?"

I am not sure what woman off the TV he is referring to but guess he means Heather Lockyear off TJ Hooker, I apparently look a lot like her. I shake my head and say,

9

"No I am not". He doesn't leave it there;

"Well you look like her, I really fancy her on Dynasty, all that hair!"

People are now staring at me, even purple coat lady who seems to understand English all of a sudden. He doesn't stop there;

"I love her feisty cop role too, what's it called that show?"

He asks his fellow seat neighbour, who seems a bit drunk; his head lolling about and shoulder slumped against the bus window. I really need to get off this bus, thank goodness it's my stop next. I get up to make my way to the front of the bus and hairy bearded man hands me a piece of paper and says,

"Call me".

I most certainly will not and bin the piece of paper when I am out of his sight.

Larissa is nowhere to be seen and no evidence of her having been back to my room, I am annoyed but go to bed with an Asti woozy head. There's nothing I can do and I am sure she will turn up by the morning, she has to 'be at the 60th' too. I drift off to sleep dreaming of chasing bad men through the streets of Los Angeles.

Chapter 2

My orange mini called Bertie is struggling to start, I haven't driven him for days and he is grumbling but thankfully gets going. I am dreading driving today, I have a slight hangover but am mostly just tense and sweaty. Larissa is sat next to me nursing her hangover and because she has already updated me on yesterday and her doings with Mike, is quiet. They had spent the night together, a night of booze and sex and no plans to meet up again after. Larissa was descriptive about his sexual abilities and preferences; she warns me against getting off with Greg because they apparently share a penchant for anal and dogging. I am lost in thought wondering if this story is just to put me off them both so she can carry on seeing Mike in secret or in fact a true story; when she turns to me and asks me if we can stop off at a pharmacy because she needs the morning after pill. Sometimes she tests me! We are now going to be late for Deedee, I am fuming but have to agree. Larissa is not ready to take charge of a baby, she's still learning about caring for herself and far too chaotic.

10 minutes later we are back on track and may not be late for Deedee after all, apparently getting the morning after pill doesn't take much time at all. Good to know. We get a bit lost though and I've missed the turning to the right road twice now. I am getting more sweaty and panicked. Deedee will be cross with me if I am late, Larissa is getting cross with me too and I just want to go home. Finally, I get it right and park outside the right guest house and ring on the doorbell, to discover that Deedee has decided to go by taxi. I am fifteen minutes late, she could have

waited. No doubt she will tell everyone at the party how useless and ditzy I am and they will all smile, nod and agree. Larissa is too hungover to join in my rant and I just know she will not take any responsibility for our lateness.

We get there the same time as Landon and Jaynie who are with Evan and Jan my other brother and his wife. Evan is 32, blonde, blue-eyed. He left the air force after one week because he couldn't cope. He is now a social worker for people with physical disabilities. His wife Jan is also a social worker and they have two sons; Lucas 3 and Joshua 5.They are excitable and full of energy, Jan believes in letting children grow in 'their own way'. This sometimes exasperates Evan as his upbringing was much more regimented. Thankfully they have left their riotous sons with Jan's mum for the day. We say hello and as a group go on a hunt to find Faye our youngest sister. Faye is 17 and also blonde with green eyes like Landon and always confident about everything. She is adored and she knows it. She is spoilt and she knows it, but she is beautiful inside and out and loves her family. We find her surrounded by our boy cousins who are hanging onto her every word. She squeals when she sees us and rushes over to hug and kiss us. Faye is the only member of the family who is publicly affectionate and does the whole kissy huggy stuff. She even gets away with calling our parents mum and dad. I must try harder to be more open with my feelings; Uma is always coming in for a hug with me and she often says these wise words,

"I like to give love so that I get it in return."

I really need more love in my life. What I am thinking at this time is, 'Fuck, wank, shit, bollocks!'

All my siblings together in one place is a joy, we don't see each other, or talk to each other loads but when we are together, we are as a whole. Catching up with each other is often so much fun. Mostly we tease each other and reminisce about our childhood at our parent's expense. Mother's cooking and father's temper give us lots of content. Evan says,

"Do you remember when mum made that pie that had a thimble in it? It was supposed to be metal but she only had a blue plastic one and it melted all inside the pie rendering it inedible?"

Landon joins in with,

"Oh yes and then that time she made those cheese scones that were so thin and hard we decided to call them cheese biscuits?"

Faye tells us about a recent cooking disaster involving corned beef, garden peas and mash potato but forgot the gravy, thus the 'corned beef hash sec' was born. It was so dry and claggy much of it ended up in the bin and Faye went for a walk to the chippie to get something decent to eat. My mother appears and tells us all to go find our tables because Uncle Sid wants to make some speeches. No, 'hello darlings, how are you? Don't you look well?' from my mother, just instructions. Father is different depending on his mood, he seems to be in a good mood today and talking animatedly with Auntie Helen whilst holding her hand, palm faced up. He's reading her palm, it's his favourite party trick. He catches us looking over and raises his free hand and waves, then continues with his reading.

The tables are organised so there are six places around each; guess who is left out of the table seating with my brothers and sisters. Apparently, I must sit with the young cousins as I am so good with children, right now I hate them. Well no I don't, but it makes me feel the outsider from my siblings.

"I am not swapping before you ask, I will forget not to swear and you never swear!"

Larissa quickly tells me. I bloody well do swear, just mostly in my head.

I have to entertain four children aged 6 to 14 years old with my cousin Freya's boyfriend Dan who is a puppeteer, so of course he is the other choice for this table. Freya is not pleased, Dan is not pleased and I am not pleased. I suggest Freya and I swap but she wants to sit with her family, she's so selfish I think. Dan turns out to be quite entertaining we gossip about people we mutually know in code.

"Felicia and Dana Ascot went to my school, everyone knew them because of their infamous dad the rank bobber,"

He tells me. I work out what he's done with rank bobber, so does Emlyn the 14 year old.

"Wait, you know the Ascot family, Geoff Ascot was framed wasn't he?" he enquires, he tells us he has been reading the book about the local bank robbery of two years ago. I don't know too much about it, they are my friends, I don't pry and they mention it hardly at all.

"Can I go pee Tovu?"

Tilly the 6 year old asks me, I have to take her and glance over to her mother who is knocking back the wine at a rate of knots. Who should be in the queue for the loo but Deedee, "Oh Tovu, I thought you had gotten lost so I took a cab. The cabbie was horrid, he stank of cigarettes and body odour."

"Oh well, in my car you would have had stale alcohol breath and armpit stink, so not much different!" I say and laugh.

She scrunches up her nose at me and says,

"Oh Tovu you are a joker. You go ahead of me, Tilly looks desperate to go."

Tilly is jigging up and down, so I agree and we make it just before she has an accident.

Deedee is in the other cubicle when we come out, so I hastily get Tilly to wash her hands and leave. Only to bump right into Jaynie who looks close to tears, pale and listless.

"Ouch!"

"Oh it's you Tovu, sorry I was in the way!"

I want to talk to her but Tilly is pulling me by the hand hard.

'Sorry, sorry. I will try and find you later after the food." I am dragged away by a persistent Tilly.

Back at the table Dan and Emlyn have stopped talking about bank robbers as it started to upset the others. Emlyn goes off to find his parents for some reason and Dan turns his attention back to me; wanting to know about Larissa. Freya has filled him in about most of her breakup but apparently his friend Andy has told him about Mike. Andy knows Mike from AA. Andy knows Dan from football. I ask him what he knows, he tells me pretty much all I know. Wow, Mike is a dick. He has squealed big time. Poor Larissa. Dan then tells me that Mike told Andy that really he had wanted to ask me on a date but Larissa seemed much more up for some fun. I despise him now. I tell Dan that he likes anal and dogging so probably is gay, with the intent that this gets back to Mike via Dan and Andy.

The speeches start and I am called to read out my poem. Yes, I am the family Poet Laureate, every occasion I have to stand up and read out a poem. Sometimes someone else's work and sometimes my own. On this occasion I decide to read out The Tyger by William Blake;

"Tyger! Tyger! Burning bright, in the forests of the night. What immortal hand or eye. Dare frame thy fearful symmetry?"

I finish the poem by saying,

"Uncle Sid is a Tiger, a fiercely proud and protective father with the smartest coat in the family always. Three cheers for Uncle Sid!"

Uncle Sid is a very dapper dresser and always wears the most colourful attire. Everyone claps and cheers him and he takes an exaggerated bow. I sit down, job done, and I can go hide away for the rest of the afternoon. Dan is telling me I am clever, and he enjoyed my reading, he is starting to accidently on purpose touch me; first my hand and then a boob graze and his eyes are looking flirty.

I decide to get some air and leave him to the kids. I don't want to fall out with Freya and I don't fancy him in the slightest anyway. He wears clothes that are too tight and too short for him; just look at those ankle swingers. I signal to Larissa to join me outside; she'll be dying for a fag. I tell her what Dan has told me about Mike's indiscretion and also Dan's inappropriate touching. We are gone so long we miss the rest of the speeches and the queue for the buffet. Slim pickings left but after several fags we don't have much appetite. We feel someone will have noticed our absence and any minute someone is going to tell us off, so we hunt down our parents to get it over with. They have been forced to sit together and I can see the signs that really the pair of them need to go home; dad is drunk already and mum is sat tight lipped playing with her rings with the saddest of expressions. As the sober, sensible one I ask them if they want a lift home and they decline because dad wants to dance. This means they will have to stay much later. Mum is so upset with dad she has forgotten to rebuke us for nipping out, so we go in search of our siblings again.

We discover that Landon has already left with Jaynie because she felt unwell and Evan tells us he has to go soon to pick up the boys. Faye has returned to the group of boy cousins. We feel we could also make our exit, only Deedee appears again and says,

"Oh Tovu, you will take me back later won't you. Oh hi Larissa, how are you, you look unwell?"

Damn my cousin Deedee. We are stuck with her talking at us for a full fifteen minutes before she tires of us and flounces off to find another victim.

"She can get a bloody cab back for sure!" Larissa exclaims.

I am pretty clear on that too and agree; if only I could have some wine right now. Dan appears, Larissa abandons me to him saying she needs the loo.

He asks me if he can pinch a fag but it had to be secret because Freya would kill him if she saw him. We find a secluded spot behind the car park, behind a large oak tree. I go to light his fag and he presses himself up against me; I am now sandwiched between him and the tree. He takes the fag out of his mouth and puts his head towards mine. I manage to turn my head so he doesn't get my lips and because he has me pinned now I can hardly breathe. I can smell his hot breath, it reeks of pickled onions.

"Get off me Dan, what are you playing at?"

"Oh come on Tovu you know you want some, you've been looking at me and flirting with me all afternoon."

I have not!

"Stop it, it's not funny!"

He pins me more tightly. He grabs my right boob and tells me I am a slag. I ask him to stop and I am crying now. He's now trying to get up my skirt and pulling at my knickers. I yell at him,

"I will tell Freya and you know how strong her dad is."

That makes him stop, he moves away;

"Fucking hell, you prick tease! Don't you breathe a word to anyone or I'll break you!"

He threatens me. He lets me go and sneers,

"You ain't worth it anyway, thought you seemed desperate for some though slag".

He slaps me across the face and strides away with those white socks flashing with each step like a rabbit's white tail.

My knees nearly buckle in relief when he leaves, I feel sick and vomit all over the roots of the tree. I must look a right state now, I cannot go back in, people will know something has happened. Now what do I do, Dan the puppeteer is a nasty piece of shit. I must somehow warn Freya and his workplace without them knowing it is me. I just know I will get blamed for it if I am the one telling the story. I have to find Larissa and leave this place.

I'm shaking now, I have a fag and wander across the car park. I find my little orange Bertie and get in the driver's seat. I could maybe just wait for Larissa here and hope that she is telepathic to know where to find me right now. She doesn't come, I am tempted to just leave and leave her. She can get a cab with Deedee. Surely, she will come look for me surely, she will know I would take refuge in Bertie. I am trying hard not to cry now, and I decide to leave. No- one will notice anyhow; I don't leave a huge hole when I leave a group.

Back home, I get undressed, chuck my dress and knickers in the bin and study my face for a bruise. Although the slap stung, he hasn't left a mark. I wonder if he has practiced such a slap. Then the tears come, rolling down my cheeks again, the gulps come in waves and I am sobbing. I dry my face with my towel and the water droplets keep coming, I can hardly breathe. I tell myself it could have been worse; I tell myself I maybe did lead him on and it was my fault. I tell myself I can tell no one because it just proves I am a loser and a slag.

Eventually. I stop crying and I make myself presentable enough to endeavour to get to the kitchen for a coffee and then the bathroom to wash, I feel dirty. No-one around which is unusual, that's lucky. I manage to get sorted and into bed within twenty minutes. I wonder if Larissa will appear soon and then kick myself for not warning her about Dan, maybe he will try it on with her as well. Now I am worried and can't get to sleep, where the hell is she? An hour later of restless tossing and turning, Larissa appears.

"Where the hell did you get to Tovu?! I looked for you for ages and then had to get a lift off the Barrett's, you know how boring they are".

The Barrett's are ex-neighbours of Uncle Sid who now live near me. I am relieved she is here and I start crying again. I can't tell her what happened and I beg her to tell me about anything that I might have missed leaving early. She dishes the dirt and it cheers me up. She doesn't say anything about Dan or Freya. She does tell me about a fight that broke out and Aunt Geraldine getting drunk and dancing on the tables, then slipping and having to be rushed off to A&E. They think she's broken a hip. Aunty Geraldine is Uncle Sid's wife and is a large lady with a large personality. She has one of those chests that look like a shelf you could perch your cuppa or side plate on.

Larissa becomes concerned about me again and I struggle to stop myself telling her about what happened; instead I settle for a hypothetical scenario for her to consider in her experience in care.

"So I was talking to a friend of mine and she told me this guy came on to her and she wasn't interested but then he got her alone

19

and tried to force himself on her. This friend knows this guy's girlfriend and he is in a really responsible job too. Should she say something to the girlfriend and report him to his work?"

Larissa does not put two and two together, she immediately says,

"Oh my God yes they should so report him the fucking bastard."

The reaction I thought I would get from Larissa and the one I wanted too.

"But what if they are scared of them and don't want them to know it is my friend that tells on them and will they be believed?"

She is sometimes quite sensible and suggests that my friend sends an anonymous letter to the girlfriend and the guy's boss. Even if they are not believed it may sow a seed of doubt that could germinate and achieve the desired outcome. I tell her I will pass on her advice and close off the conversation about it. We then go on to talk about our brothers until we can't stay awake any longer. Both of us have work in the morning. I feel better, maybe it isn't a bad thing Larissa is staying with me after all.

That night I toss and turn and have my childhood recurring nightmare; it sounds daft but I am being pursued by large thumbs. It is terrifying and so upsetting. They never quite catch me, but they are there, waiting for me, chasing me, pressurising me and now one of them has Dan's face. The rest are faceless, the Dan one is the biggest and closest one. I just know tomorrow I will feel and look like I have Flu. Larissa is snoring and oblivious.

Chapter 3

I am sat in a hot stuffy room, there are green glass bottles decorating the window sills which are full of faded silk flowers. I am running over in my mind the morning and the relief of having other people's heartache and issues to focus on. Uma gave me a poem she wrote for me because she knows I am leaving soon and will be going to another placement on the acute ward. It touches my heart and she asks me to write her a poem back because she knows I write them too. The room really is unbearable, I look for a window but there is only the glass door which I manage to wedge open to let some air in.

I hate waiting, my mind wanders too much. I am trying so hard not to think about yesterday and Dickshit Dan as I will now refer to him as. I am tired and want to leave, I wish I hadn't opened my mouth and agreed to be part of this project. I always do it, say yes and then regret it. The clock ticks loudly, suddenly the manager walks in and sits opposite me in his grey suit and moleskin shoes. His deep brown eyes rest around my chest area for about five seconds and then he peers at me through silver framed glasses.

"Tovu, hi! I am Tom, the service manager for the acute service and you are interested in the practice development project I am leading on is that right?"

He smooths down his unruly long, dark, curly hair and smiles the most white smile ever. I feel shy and smile back nodding my head yes. I am not listening very much, distracted by the sweaty armpit feeling I have and lost for words when he tells me we should go for coffee sometime. I nod again in agreement because it may give me the chance to find out what he just told me about the project. He doesn't seem very much in a rush though, closes the door commenting on fire policy and starts asking me about how my training is going. He asks where I'd like to work when I qualify, if my interest in the project was sparked by any particular experience at work to date, etc. He nods and smiles at me when I start to talk about myself. The conversation turns to music somehow and he makes me feel very limited in the music I listen to. He tells me to listen to JJ Cale, John Martyn and Morrissey. Tom is an interesting man and that makes him attractive. I try to concentrate a bit better on his words and join in with the odd question I manage to extract out of my brain. I eventually escape and practically run out of the hospital because I am late for Mary.

Mary arrives five minutes after I do, and I was ten minutes late; we had chosen our fave pub to meet. It is quirky and small, adorned with 1960s memorabilia and an old, broken juke box stands at the far corner of the bar. It is quiet and the old barman Rick never hassles you even if you sit nursing the same orange juice for three hours. He always has a smile and an inane joke to tell you, but then he leaves you alone until you come up to the bar for another drink. It's probable he makes no money from his pub but seems to enjoy it as much as the punters who frequent it. In fact, it's great for getting no hassle whatsoever. Perfect today. Perfect most days. Mary wants to know about the party because she knows with my family some drama was to be had. I tell her about the hideous seating arrangements and mention Dan but not what he did to me. I tell her about the fight and Aunty Geraldine as if I had witnessed it, without saying I had missed it. I tell her about dreadful Deedee and then ask her about her day yesterday.

Her eyes widen and she grins even wider,

"Well you know I have been fancying this guy at work. He asked me out and we went to the cinema and then onto a club."

I squeal at her,

"Tell me more! I need the full description and then tell me whether you are seeing him again."

She almost glazes over in a dreamy way,

"Bob pulled me aside after our morning meeting, I thought he was going to ask me to do some work for him but he just looked at me straight and asked me if I was free that night as his mate had let him down and he had a spare cinema ticket. I didn't even ask him what the film was, I just said yes I could go as my mate was at a family do."

She smiled some more and then told me about a pretty uneventful evening, very pleasant, very easy and then when they finished at the pub he leant in and gave her a deep snog. Told her he had wanted to do that all evening and asked her to go out with him next week sometime. She agreed, she likes him a lot.

She asks me about my day and I tell her about the poem and then the meeting about the acute care project. She tells me that she thinks that Tom was definitely hitting on me. I hate men. I hate Tom and I despise Dan. I am just about to tell Mary about Dan, because we share everything and I feel I can do it without bursting into tears as we are in a public place; when Larissa bursts through the door of the pub.

"Tovu, thank God I have found you! I have been looking for you everywhere!"

My heart is sinking again, what now?

"Jaynie took an overdose and is in hospital, Landon is beside himself and wants you NOW!!"

Mary wants to come too, I secretly wonder if it's just to see Landon. We get a taxi and arrive at the hospital twenty minutes later. Landon is pacing outside the entrance and we can see some nurses ogling him. He is relieved to see us and feels all clammy when we hug and smells of Kouros aftershave and fags.

"Hi Tovu, Larissa and Mary. The rescue party has arrived then? I am sorry to bring you out here but I just don't know what to fucking do. I can't believe she would do this to me. I am so angry!"

He is clearly suddenly very irate and proceeds to swear and rant about how selfish she is and how he wants nothing to do with her but knows that would be really bad form. Jaynie has had a stomach pump and a psychiatrist has assessed her and said she has to be admitted to the mental health ward that I am just about to be placed on. However, they don't have a bed so she has to stay on the medical ward for the night. Landon wants me to go and talk to her; she is refusing to see him and in his current state that probably is a good thing. I let out a massive sigh and head off to the medical ward alone.

When I get to the ward a snooty nursing assistant tells me that Jaynie is resting and cannot be disturbed. I am about to head off when Doctor Greg appears;

"Oh hi Tovu, what are you doing here? I have just been doing an assessment".

I tell him that it's my brother's girlfriend he's probably been assessing, and he confirms it.

"I just prescribed her some sleeping tablets, she can't have anything until her body has recovered but she needs observation. You go in and see her and I'll find out if they can get a 1-1 for her overnight. Good to see you Tovu, sorry about Jaynie, your brother must be worried sick."

He doesn't ask where my said brother is, but as I enter the dorm to see Jaynie and I am wishing he was doing it instead.

Jaynie is laid on her side, more pale and fragile than I have ever seen her and that is saying something.

"Hey Jaynie"

I say as I approach. She glances up, her huge eyes pools of sadness.

"Tovu, how is Landon? Will he ever forgive me? I can't live without him, he's not going to dump me is he?"

I suggest she calms down a bit and take each question one by one.

"Landon is in shock. I don't know what he is thinking right now, I thought he dumped you and that is why you took the overdose. Why don't you tell me what happened?"

Jaynie, looks down at her bedsheet and then almost whimpers as she tells me how Landon had told her after Uncle Sid's party that he thought they should have a break as she was not happy, and it was maybe best they have some space. She said he was worried about her weight and told her she needed to get some help. I listen to her some more and nod and repeat back to her things she says to me like a good counsellor should and then an hour later Mary appears to rescue me.

Jaynie is drowsy now and almost asleep. We whisper our goodbyes and she begs me to come and see her tomorrow. I say I will try and think about the irony of her being admitted to the ward I am starting on tomorrow.

"I had to come and get you; I knew you would get stuck and then that Greg doctor saw me and Larissa and told us how great you were to be so supportive to Jaynie. He is so scrummy that doctor; I said I would relieve you but she's going to sleep now. Let's go, I am really tired too."

Mary is right, we need to go home. I find Larissa and Landon having a fag chatting to Greg and we all agree to have a nightcap at Landon's flat as its walkable. I would rather go home but don't want to break everyone up as they are all so keen to carry on chatting. Greg seems to want to tag along and Mary latches onto him. Larissa sniggers in my ear that she had better watch her bumhole. I decide at that point I need wine. Landon asks us what we are giggling about, and we ask him about whether there was another reason he wanted to dump Jaynie, like a new lady on the scene. It transpires there is indeed a new love interest. Poor Landon is always being approached by women but this one he says is not interested in him and that makes her more attractive. The cat and mouse game of courtship, the excitement of the chase. Tia Jones is a manager for a fashion magazine and looking for business insurance for when she expands its reach, Landon is helping with this. Tia is raven haired, slanting brownish hazel eyes, long, long legs and aloof. She walks as though she is secreting rubies between her thighs and talks in a deep and husky way that reminds Landon of Mariella Frostrup. Tia is quick tongued and scathing about almost everyone. Landon thinks she's amazing. I immediately wish I was more like Tia; she sounds the opposite to me. Larissa says,

"I want to be her. Why are we not more like her Tovu?"

Love my sister sometimes, she knows me as well as I know her. Landon uncharacteristically tells us he loves us despite our lack of sophistication and frequent scrapes.

In Landon's flat, which is very monochrome and cool chic for the 80's we crash on his floor which looks comfier than his sofa. Landon is a big Debbie Harry fan and says he was inspired by the album sleeve of Parallel Lines. He gets us beer and wine and puts on some Boomtown Rats and then slips in that he has tickets for Live Aid. We are all completely jealous and ask him who he is taking with him. He hasn't made up his mind but then that is typical Landon. He will have to appraise who will benefit most, who will be most grateful and who he wants to spend the time with amongst thousands of others in a confined space. If you don't know about Live Aid then you haven't lived so I'm not going into it now. Greg suddenly seems more interested in Landon than Mary and they both turn their attention on him. I flick through a magazine and half listen to the friendly banter of 'take me!'

I then catch an article about a woman who was raped at her sister's wedding and it makes me feel sick even though I don't read it all; I read enough. I go to the puzzle section of the magazine to make my brain work again and distract my mind and emotions. Three down, seven letters, 'male relative'. Easy, 'brother'. 6 across, six letters, 'medic'. Easy, 'doctor'. I put the magazine down and try and join in the chat a bit.

The rest of the evening passes in friendly chat and we all go our separate ways home, dropping off from the taxi we get. Larissa and I are the last stop, although Greg kindly paid for it. We don't say much, just do our night time routines and crash. I sleep a restless alcohol induced sleep until 5 a.m. I toss and turn for an hour and then decide to get up and have a shower. I'll miss the morning rush and will have time for a cuppa. Larissa wakes as I step around her, she mutters something about getting up too. I leave her to it. When I return, she is dressed ready for work and has made us both a cup of coffee. She's gulping down hers and then says,

"I better dash, another day another dollar sis! I will see you this evening".

She collects her bag and jacket and exits. I also gulp my coffee and get my bag together and leave for the ward. I am supposed to be shadowing one of the regular nurses today and meeting them on the ward at 8.30 a.m. It's only a short walk away so I have plenty of time but I like to get to work early.

Monday and Fridays are the busiest days for the ward, the nurse I am supposed to be shadowing is having to do an assessment and I am told to join her. She is sat in an interview room with a pale man who is staring bleakly ahead, off to the right of her shoulder. He is dressed in cricket whites, including shin pads and this accentuates his paleness. She is asking him about his childhood and he says in a gloom laden voice,

"I don't remember it much, my father was violent and my mother didn't care about us. My brother was always out with his friends, I didn't go out much."

Sherry prompts him to say a bit more and he says,

"I don't want to talk about it, I want some medication to take away my numbness".

Sherry is undeterred and continues to ask him questions, he becomes monosyllabic and even though she tries hard to get him to open up, she sees she is wasting her time and after ten minutes of this questioning tells him she will show him his dormitory. She asks me to stay with him and help him unpack, get him some water and settle him in. He relaxes a little when he has unpacked and I have taken a list of all his belongings, he declines a change of clothes. He won't even take his shin pads off and just sits on his bed. He asks me to pull the curtains round and then asks for the doctor to get him some medication. I know the doctor is busy with a discharge, I tell him it shouldn't be too long before the doctor arrives and then I try and make small talk. I ask him about cricket, and he tells me he doesn't play. I ask him why he is wearing the cricket whites and he says to confuse the demons, that he is hoping they will think he is someone else who does play cricket. That his voices tell him to wear them and that they are a shield against the demons who want to kill him. I reassure him that he is safe and that the demons cannot get him in hospital. That we will look after him and get him better. I am relieved when an Indian doctor appears from behind the curtain, followed by Sherry. Sherry tells me to go for a break and she will find me after the doctor has finished. I scurry off.

I meet Helena in the staff room and she introduces me to her mentor a large ginger haired man call Dave, he is jovial and chatty. My break goes so quickly and he brightens my mood until Sherry appears and asks me to escort 'shin pad man' over to the Occupational Therapy unit and then help with the clinic room stock take. I ask her if a lady called Jaynie McGovern was being admitted and tell her about the connection. She tells me that she has not heard that name mentioned today. I am hoping Jaynie doesn't need to be admitted, it would be awkward. Sherry tells me I would have to be moved off the ward if she was admitted and work in the ward next door instead. When I return to the ward seeking out the clinic room, I pass the office and see Tom is in there with Dave, they are talking intently. Thankfully I pass by unnoticed and find Helena in the clinic room who has been told to help with the stock take too. Helena updates me on her relationship with Nobby, a bespectacled Adonis who she has known since high school. They are planning to get married next year but he is working in Scotland on an oil rig. At least he won't be meeting many other women there, but she is missing him. We are not making much headway with the audit, so I suggest we focus and get it done. I tell her I will count, and she can record everything.

We just have to do the supplies not the meds today. I start counting boxes of plasters and green needles. We don't take long and realise it must be lunch time when Dave appears to take the meds trolley.

"Good timing Dave, we have just finished. Shall I help you with the meds?"

Helena asks him and hands me the clip board she has been using. She's such a suck up sometimes.

I ask where Sherry is and go and help her gather the patients for lunch. I almost bump right into Tom.

"Hi, I was hoping to see you. Are you free tomorrow afternoon for a catch up about the project?"

I am on an early shift tomorrow and suggest I meet him in the stuffy room from our last meet after I finish. He wrinkles up his nose and says to meet him at 'Martha's Café' in the town. I agree and then tell him I must help with lunch.

I pop my head in the lounge where there are four people sat around the edges of it in high wing-backed armchairs and all staring at the TV which has the news on. They all get up when I tell them lunch is ready and shuffle off to the dining room. I find some stragglers in the female dorm and usher them out. Lunch is chicken casserole with processed mash potato and green beans. I help dish it out on the white crockery with 'hospital property' printed in blue paint around the edges. When everyone has had food, I scan the room and feel sad looking at the patients until in runs Ruth flapping her hands, singing very loudly "fucking food glorious fucking food!" Sherry goes to her and asks her to sit down and be quiet. Ruth does sit down and carries on singing but it is quieter.

She grabs Bertie's cake and scoffs it down and then leaves the dining room with Sherry in pursuit. I have to find Bertie another cake and sit with him until he is calmer. Bertie starts to tell me his take on quantum physics and I smile and nod, losing track of what he is telling me and I hope I am smiling and nodding in the right places. After lunch some of the patients are shipped off to the OT department and we are left with Ruth who is now wailing in her room upset by Sherry for telling her off about the cake. I also have 'Shin Pad' man who is having his physical check, John K who has Korsakovs and wanders, John C who has just come in for admission and Jean a severely depressed lady in her fifties who is threatening suicide and needs close observation.

The rest of the shift goes without too much incident and I am sent home fifteen minutes early. I walk out with Helena and we chat about Nobby again. I tell her a little bit about Tom and the project. She tells me to be careful with Tom because he has a girlfriend and a reputation. I nod and tell her that I had heard this too and will be careful.

Chapter 4

Tom and I have not stopped talking for the last ninety minutes and we have covered a lot of ground. The waitress is now glaring at us to leave because it is closing time. He pays and takes my hand,

"Come on we can walk around the church; I like to look at the gravestones and wonder about people's lives and how they may have died."

I tell him it sounds a bit morbid but agree and like the feel of his hand around mine. The churchyard is well cared for, it is adorned with flowers and bordered by lush, well mowed grass. It has recently been mowed and the lingering smell of newly mown grass adds to the happiness I feel as the sinking sun shines on my head. Tom is studying a new headstone. He looks lost in thought and I study his lean profile, his sensuous, full mouth and then quickly look away as he glances across at me.

"Look at this one, Mary Harrison, she was only eighteen when she died. Look at the inscription, it is truly beautiful 'Mary, Mary never contrary, always lived with heart and loved to the end of time' Wow!"

He then starts to quote Yeats the Cloths of Heaven:

"Had I the heaven's embroidered cloths,
Enwrought with golden and silver light,
The blue and the dim and the dark cloths
Of night and light and the half-light;
I would spread the cloths under your feet:
But I, being poor, have only my dreams;

I have spread my dreams under your feet;
Tread softly because you tread on my dreams."

I am enchanted, I love this poem. I suddenly feel a little uncomfortable and say I need to go; I must be more less trusting I should have learnt from the Dan situation. He accepts this and asks me to meet him same place and time next week as we still have details of the project to sort. I agree and leave him gazing at Mary's gravestone some more.

My tummy is churning a little and I am flushed; I walk quickly home and pray that Larissa isn't in yet. She is; she is lain out on my bed, just where I want to be.

"Hello sis, how was your day? I've had a knackering one, but I have bought us some beans and bread for a slap-up tea!"

I tell her mine was tiring too and thank her for the food. We both agree that an evening of PJs, beans on toast and coffee would be heaven. I find some space on my bed and snuggle up to my sister. She smells of coffee and a slight fustiness, like a second-hand clothes shop. When I tell her this, she explains about the home she worked in today and the strangeness of the elderly couple she had to look after.

Mr and Mrs Pilchard are both in their eighties and have lived in the same cottage since they married in their twenties. They have both got physical health conditions and need a lot of help with their personal care. They don't like accepting help and this makes them very particular about who they have in their home and the way they want things done. They have specific routines and although their home is cluttered and dusty, they refuse help to clean it. Mr P believes that dirt is good for you and owns several collections of books, china, stamps and matchbox cars. There is so much that he has out on display gathering dust. He gets extremely upset if anyone touches any of his collections and needs to remain calm as he has a heart condition. Mrs P has mobility problems and a colostomy bag, she is fragile and only eats toast or cereal for every meal. However, she is fiercely independent and is frustrated that she has to have help; this makes her agitated and she swears a lot during personal care. Larissa tolerates this where other carers do not, they like her more than other carers and want her to return. Larissa was therefore asked to make lots of coffee for them and herself.

I tell her about Tom and how I felt attracted to him even though I know he has a girlfriend and he is a senior manager. She wisely advises me to keep it strictly business but wants me to give her an update on whether things develop.

Later, when we are settling down to sleep, she mentions that she bumped into Freya and Dan in the park she walked through from Mr and Mrs P's. Freya asked us to her birthday party in two weeks' time. I am immediately sent into a state of panic and curse myself for not having written those letters to Freya and Dan's boss. I feel like telling Larissa about Dan's assault of me but say instead;

"I think I am working a night shifts weekend. You will have to go without me if you want to go."

Larissa says she'd rather not as she doesn't really like Freya that much.

Damn it, I can't sleep again. I am worried my nightmares will return and I have wind from the beans. Thank goodness I am on a late shift tomorrow and I resolve to write those letters in the morning. I try and sleep but keep getting flashbacks of being pinned to that tree, of Dan slapping me and calling me a slag and prick tease. I feel dirty all over again. I also start to think that I need to cancel on Tom, his attention is confusing, and I can't imagine what he sees in me. He is in a relationship and if I continue to see him I truly am a slag because I sense he wants more than a working relationship with me and there is a part of me that likes that and a part that just thinks I will get hurt.

Several drafts later, I have written the letters. I decided in the end to keep them brief and type them; I try not to make them too emotive or the rantings of a madwoman. This is what I wrote to Freya:

'Dear Freya, it is with a heavy heart that I need to tell you that I am led to believe that Dan recently sexually assaulted someone. I am sure he will deny this but want you to be aware that he may not be the man you think he is. Regards, a Wellwisher.'

I am nervous to send this, I know there will be repercussions and upset. I feel a responsibility to Freya though, even though we are not close. I wonder if Freya will come to her senses on her own and Dan will show his true colours to her or whether it had been my fault in the first place. I lose confidence and stash the letters under my mattress for now. I don't want to cause upset. I need to talk to Mary about it. Dan will know it was written by me and tell lies about me. I am so torn. Mary will know what to do surely. I call her and arrange to meet up the next day when we are both on a day off. I wonder how I am going to withdraw from the acute care project, so Tom has no excuse to meet with me. I wonder how I am going to get through the rest of the day.

I forget all of this when I work my shift with Jean who I have to be 1-1 with most of the time. Jean turns out to be not only very depressed but very obsessive compulsive and fears dirt of any kind. This means she has now made it clear that she is not leaving her bedroom, she is lucky to have one of the three side rooms on her own. She will not talk to anyone. She is also refusing food, drink and medication. I manage to build some rapport with her and she seems to trust me more and more, so by the end of the shift she has taken some water, some cake and her medication from me. Jean despite all her challenges has a great sense of humour and responds well to my positivity, reassurance, kindness and warped outlook on all things anxiety provoking. One thing causing her great anxiety is going to the toilet; she is bursting to go though. I grab a disposable bedpan and a light blanket and present her with them. Her eyes widen and she looks unhappy; I say to her

"Jean, this is completely brand new from the clinic, the blanket is to cover your modesty and I took it off the trolley that came just now from the laundry all clean and fresh. I have told the staff that no-one is to enter the room and I have put a big sign on the door saying, 'please do not disturb!' I want you to use the bedpan and THEN we can have a game of rummy! Don't think about it just do it. I am going outside the room and you can knock three times when you are done and I will get rid of the bedpan."

Her eyes widen even further and then she gives me a small nod. I leave the room. It takes her ten minutes to do it but then I hear three little taps on the door. Jean has filled that bedpan with large amounts of urine and faeces; now I am wondering how I am going to transport it without spilling any. I give her tonnes of praise and gingerly pick up the bed pan and manage to get it out of the room without accident. Once out, I call for help and Dave rescues me with a commode on wheels and cleaning materials in case of any splashes; his face makes me giggle as it looks like he is going to be sick. We manage together to sort it without making too much mess, clean ourselves up and I am able to return to Jeanie and play cards with her. She looks, unsurprisingly much more comfortable.

Larissa is meeting me from work today and we are walking down via the chippy to the 'The Tap', the pub Mary and I love. She joked that it was better than beans again and my farting. I cannot wait to eat my chips and down a glass of cheap plonk. Unusually 'The Tap' is quite busy and Rick seems to have sunk a few beers because he greets us like long lost friends and introduces us to a crowd around the bar who are a rugby team from Hartlepool on tour. I almost feel he is trying to pimp us, but we are friendly and extract ourselves from their questioning to sit in a corner. Larissa had a pickled onion with her chips, the smell is making me feel nauseous. I tuck thoughts of Dan away in some dark recess of my brain. I make a bit more space between us so I can't smell her breath and we exchange the stories of our day. Larissa has been with The Pilchards again; we agree we should have chosen to work in fashion not care.

A couple of the rugby players wander over to us and offer to buy us a drink; they are both huge men with bulges everywhere, one is fair and one is dark; I will refer to them as Ivory and Ebony because we forget their names as soon as they tell us. Larissa asks them for a glass of wine each for us and allows Ebony to sit between us whilst Ivory goes to get the drinks.

Ebony tells us he is a mortgage adviser and Ivory is an estate agent; we are not sure we believe them and don't really care because we know we won't see them again and have no intention of staying very long in their company. I think about Mary's boyfriend and wonder if he would be so flirty away from his hometown. We let them talk about themselves for a good half hour and then we make our excuses to leave. Ebony is gracious, Ivory frowns and starts to say something, but Ebony says,

"See you ladies, lovely to meet you. Come on mate let's join the team, we have tactics to discuss for tomorrow's game".

Ivory loses interest in us and turns towards the bar. I feel a bit worried about them as I was sure he was going to call us a pair of prick teasers. Larissa just laughs at me when I tell her this and says,

"All mouth no trousers those two. I bet they are married. Come on, let's get back."

There's a man walking in front of us with his white socks flashing as he strides ahead; my heart freezes and then see that he is too tall to be Dan, he is at least 6 ft 4. Larissa doesn't notice. I breath again, which is just as well as we are heading up the steep hill to the nurses' accommodation from the pub.

I am immediately panicked when I see my bed has been made; Larissa has gone to the toilet, so I rummage under the mattress and find the letters from earlier and feel relieved. Larissa comes in and says in a quiet and kind tone,

"So, when were you going to tell me Tovu?"

I flush and ask her what she means because I was sure the letters seemed untouched when I just checked.

"Those letters under the mattress Tovu, is it you that was assaulted and was it Dan because those letters are addressed to Freya and his boss."

I decide in that split second to tell her the truth and whilst I cry, she holds my hand and strokes my hair. She is furious by the time I finish and wants to take the letters and hand post them directly to make sure they get them.

"You have to speak up Tovu".

"I'm scared Rissa" I have retorted to baby speak, I used to call her Rissa when I was little.

She hugs me and tells me she will look after me and convinces me I have to send them. She would like me to report him to the police but understands how traumatic I might find that. I agree to post them tomorrow and she puts on some Soft Cell and tells me about her conspiracy theory about the bubonic plague to cheer me up.

Larissa believes it was the work of an alien race trying to weaken Earthlings before they attack. We can talk about this a lot and the rest of the family just think we have watched too much Dr Who. Her ploy works and it takes my mind off our previous discussion; for all her faults Larissa is a loyal sister. It is however, wearing a bit thin that she is here in my little room. I ask her whether she has heard from her recent ex-boyfriend or his mother and what her plans are. I regret the question as her face falls, and she becomes dewy eyed; I am so insensitive sometimes and I truly thought she was over it.

"He hasn't been in touch at all Tovu, I did ring his office and was told he was in a meeting and not heard from him at all. I even asked after him when I saw Gazza his best friend in the corner shop when I bought the bread and beans yesterday. He said he would pass on a message to him that I was asking after him. Gazza high fived me for the cutting up of clothes, which I thought was a bit strange."

Now it's my turn to cheer up Larissa; I am inwardly kicking myself for killing her previously jovial mood. I tell her about Belle's spoon challenge and ask her if she is free the day after tomorrow as she has arranged to attempt the challenge at the sports centre that afternoon. Larissa giggles with me as I tell her about mine and Mary's attempt.

The days fly by, they blur into each other. I met up with Mary but didn't tell her about Dan, I still haven't posted the letters and lied to Larissa that I had. I know it is shameful, but Freya dumped him last week anyway for catching him flirting with a friend of hers on a night out. I just can't tell even now; I feel too guilty. Later, I find out that Larissa tells her on the QT that she saw him groping someone behind a tree at Uncle's 60th and that she wasn't entirely sure so had kept it to herself but now she knows about his cheating on Freya, feels more sure it was him. Freya told his boss who she knows quite well that he is a cheating bastard, that cheating bastards are generally just bastards and to watch him and sure enough two weeks later he is sacked following complaints from parents that he shouted at a little girl who wouldn't stop talking during one of his shows. We all hope we never bump into the idiot again.

Belle's challenge didn't work, I missed the event due to work and was told she definitely needed more practice. Poor Belle; I so need to see her. I must arrange it with Mary; maybe take a road trip together. We all could do with a break.

Six weeks after Larissa moved in with me, she moved out. I am relieved but will miss her too. She has found a cheap B&B nearer to her work's office and one of her colleagues is also there. They are going to look for a two-bed flat to share together.

Jaynie never did get admitted to the mental health unit, she was told to get a grip by her ballet principle and get back to practice. Landon stayed firm that they were finished but isn't getting anywhere with trying to seduce Tia.

Live Aid generated a community of love and sympathy for the starving children but mostly for us is was a spectacle of some of the best artists out there. So much so we couldn't decide whose participation had the most impact. I had to work that day, but even on the ward, most of the patients and staff watched the concert on the T.V.

It is long after the concert and I have been working on the acute care project with Tom and he has been a complete gentleman and professional since I cancelled on him for the meet in the café and then only agreed to meet him in hospital premises. I am running to meet him now as I am a bit late. The hospital canteen is noisy and smells of sausages. Just beyond it, is a coffee area which is much quieter. Tom is sat there gazing at his pager and then sees me and smiles;

"Hello you. Have you been running?"

I am gasping for air having rushed so much, I really am unfit.

"Oh so sorry I am late, I got held up on the ward!" gasp out.

He gets up gracefully, like he is on oiled castors.

'Sit, sit I will get you a coffee. Milk two sugars?"

I sit down and nod gratefully. I look around and see a couple of junior doctors sat deep in conversation, a small group of cleaners having a break and a lone admin worker eating her sandwiches. I open my bag and pull out the document I have been working on, 'Defining the roles of the acute care team and the right skill mix for the number of patients'.

Tom takes a while before he appears with the coffee, he tells me he got stuck talking to another manager he met in the queue. Probably a leggy brunette I think and thank him for the coffee as I hand him my document. He immediately starts reading it in front of me and I feel flushed and sweaty.

"This is good, really good, well done Tovu." He looks up at me smiling. "I think the next step will be to expand on the role of the multidisciplinary team, how it should interact and complement each other. Often teams work against each other and conflicting opinions can get in the way of good patient care."

I agree and after we chat about this further, he leans forward and whispers to me;

"I hear your sister moved out Tovu, how are you coping?"

I whisper back,

"It's great actually, I have my space back."

"Can we go and see it? I want to see what makes you tick; people's homes help with that."

I am taken a back; I am blushing and am now so much sweatier. I am in such a foul stinking mess that maybe it would be okay to let him see my place as he couldn't seduce me with the stench lying beneath my clothes. Impulsively I agree and he grins at me and says for us to go now.

When I let him into my room, it suddenly feels young, naïve and I am regretting my decision. He eyes the walls with a Monet Poppy Field picture, a photo of my family and a poster with DESIDERATA written across it and below:

crotch and I know I have to give him a blow job. I hope he pulls out before he comes. I decide to **'GO PLACIDLY** amid the noise and the haste, and remember what peace there may be in silence. As far as possible, without surrender, be on good terms with all persons.

Speak your truth quietly and clearly; and listen to others, even to the dull and the ignorant; they too have their story.' Etc, etc.

He picks up the book by my bed and tells me he likes John Irving books, his favourite being 'The world according to Garp.' I am reading the 'Cider House Rules', it is engrossing and evokes feelings of anger, sadness, pity and nagging uneasiness, but I am compelled to read on. He then asks me to put some music on; I put on a Simple Minds CD and he sits on my bed, then as I pass him to get to door he pulls me down gently to him and kisses me. Long, hard and in a way that makes my insides flip, my heart race and my head feel dizzy. He starts to tell me how beautiful I am and how he wants to fuck me, so long as it is alright with me. I only feel lust and he is kissing my neck and then back to my lips. He holds my head in his hands and kisses my face gently all over.

"Do you want me?"

He asks and I nod forgetting my smelliness.

We start to take off each other's clothes, he is gentle and in no rush, I am tingling all over and he carries on kissing me all over. He doesn't touch my breasts until he has my bra off and then he takes one nipple at a time to suck, kiss and lick them. He then traces his tongue down over my tummy and below to make me squeal; and I am in ecstasy, yet something holds me back and I fake an orgasm so he will move on. He does, he places my hand on his hard cock and I stroke it up and down. He pushes my head down towards his mount him after a while of sucking and him moaning and then he rolls me over and fucks me hard. He comes pretty quickly and I fake another orgasm as he comes with a deep, satisfied moan.

Afterwards, I become conscious of my sweatiness and nakedness. He pulls me towards him though and tells me not to get up because he wants to hold me. He kisses me some more and wraps himself around me.

"Did you know that the moon is covered in volcanos? That it has no life form; yet when I look at it, I see beauty and lifetime of secrets? I look at you and I see the same. You are complex and aloof at times and then at others you are a beaming light."

I am feeling like a million dollars and then he says,

"You know I am seeing someone else; it's not working but she is ill and I don't feel I can let her down right now?"

My heart nearly stops, and I am brought back to real life. I just nod without looking at him. I realise he is not mine to keep only to taste. I feel okay about it and think to myself that I can use him as much as he is using me. I don't need a boyfriend right now; my life is busy enough.

When he has left, I feel remarkably content and peaceful. He doesn't make any plans to see me again and I don't mind. It was just the loveliest sex I have had ever. He is my secret. I am his.

Chapter 5

Mary, Belle and I are heading down to Dorset in my Mini, it's a squash with all our luggage, we seem to have packed for a week abroad not a little weekend break. Mary and Belle are arguing about the route we should take, and I am concentrating on the road ahead. There's a lorry ahead of me, lit up like a Christmas tree and going a steady 60 mph; it's a safe one to follow and I keep my distance behind.

"Tovu it's the next turning off to Bournemouth on the left and so you need to take the right hand to Bridport."

Mary directs me. I check in my mirror and move off to the right and the illuminated lorry goes off to the left. The road is pretty clear and Belle starts singing along to the radio which is playing 'Madonna I'm Crazy for You'. We all join in:

"I'm crazy for you
Touch me once and you'll know it's true
I never wanted anyone like this
It's all brand new
You'll feel it in my kiss
I'm crazy for you, crazy for you "

When we get to Bridport we find our B&B pretty easily as it's tucked off the main road running through the town centre. The thatched cottage sits in a large garden full of abundant flowers and bird tables. The whitewashed fence frames it and the pathway to the door is shingled and crunches under our feet. We are shown our room, a large, beamed floral bedroom that welcomes you with an old charm that makes you smile. It's 8p.m. and we are hungry; the lovely little lady dressed in a baggy overshirt dress tied with a gold ribbon, who is our hostess for the weekend has brought us a hot chocolate and digestives but it's not enough to fill us up. We ask her for directions to the nearest pub and head down there giggling about our bed situation. Two of us have to share a large, creaky four poster double whilst the other has a small single pull out bed. I get the single because I apparently am the smallest. Mary is grumbling about Belle's habit of slinging her leg over anyone she shares a bed with. Belle retorts that Mary snores and talks in her sleep.

We decide large glasses of wine will help us sleep. As we step inside the pub the six people at the bar turn around to stare at us and it has gone quiet.

"Oooh "ello we have totty in the town, welcome ladies, what can I get you?"

The barman is beautiful, dressed in a dress with a full made up face but undeniably male. Everyone else has stopped staring and returned to their previous conversations.

"Call me Cha Cha, tell me all about yourselves, you have to be more interesting than this lot!"

He sweeps an elegant hand around the room to show he is referring to everyone there. We order a bottle of wine and chips to share. Cha Cha wants to know all about us and then he tells us about a recent trip to Vegas where he met other cross dressers and a group of drag queens at some sort of convention. Most of them were American and had hilarious stories about misunderstandings and sexual liaisons. He tells about one man who tried it on with him, he was just 5-foot-tall, round and pudgy with a shaven head and tattoos of eagles and lions down his arms. His voice was squeaky and he complained about having gout half the night but he was sort of funny and endearing. Cha Cha isn't homosexual though and had to explain he just enjoyed dressing as a woman and liked the attention this brought him, both good and bad. He said that most people were really accepting of him and then there were others like his parents who just didn't acknowledge it and simply refused to see his difference. The ones who were downright obnoxious or threatening he brought down to size with his quick tongue or simply punched them. He hadn't been in many fights but he was always victorious, especially as his opponents underestimated him.

"Just because I wear a frock now and again doesn't make me weak and I work out a lot so I am really fit and strong."

He makes us squeeze his biceps to prove to it. Bella is fascinated by him and engages him in a conversation about feminism.

Mary and I take the bottle of wine to a corner table and I suddenly feel really tired. Mary asks,

"So what's the plan for tomorrow Tovu?"

I suggest we explore the shops and check out the local activity farm. Mary wants to know all about my trip to the zoo with Tom last week. I want to know all about her new job, she hasn't told me much about it and I wonder if she is regretting moving jobs. Belle joins us just as I am telling Mary how Tom held my hand around the zoo constantly, we spent most of the time kissing in front of the various animals. Except for the fish, they looked so bored and miserable we didn't want to upset them further so, we pulled faces at them to cheer them up. Only really amusing ourselves. Afterwards we had hot sex in my room and he left me as seems the pattern, without promise of a next time.

"And what does 'hot sex' involve?

Mary laughs and then says,

"Don't you feel sorry for his girlfriend, isn't it annoying he uses you like he is?"

She is being blunt but the truth of what she is saying is cutting through my heart like a scalpel. I am just thinking that its likely we won't see each other now as the project is coming to an end, when Belle replies on my behalf.

"I think he really likes you Tovu, you should have a heart to heart with him, see if he feels the same. There definitely sounds like there's chemistry from what you say and your smile says it all when you talk about him."

I don't want to date a cheater I say, and they ask me if I don't think I'm cheating too; his girlfriend doesn't know about our liaisons, it's unfair. I kind of agree and remind them we won't see each other now. Even as I am saying it I can feel the linger of his lips on mind the touch of his hand stroking mine.

Mary tells us that her new job is horrendous on account of her new boss who is completely sexist and arrogant. He is also stealing work off her just at the time of completion when she has done all the leg work. Her targets are not being met and he picks on her at team meetings as a result of it. Bob wants to thump her boss on a daily basis. Bob's boss is mates with Mary's new boss so she persuades him it's not a good idea.

We make some suggestions for sorting him out, hiring a hitman, kneecapping him when he leaves the pub on a Friday evening pissed and castrating him in his sleep are our favoured ones. As well as her boss problems she also dislikes the rest of the team who all suck up to him on a regular basis. So much so, it seems to be expected. Giles the mortgage advisor is the only colleague she likes; he is in his forties and happily married with three sons. Giles encourages her to speak up for herself when the regional manager is over. We try and re-enforce this as a good idea.

Cha Cha is clearing tables and wants to know what we are getting so animated about; he loves the story and tells us about a time he worked at a holiday camp and was bullied by most of the other entertainment team. He decided after a week of them picking on him enough was enough. That evening they were all due to do the end of the week big show; he was to play a clown and the others different circus characters. He laced all their drinks at the pre circus sing along shindig. He knew they all liked some 'Dutch courage' before the show, so he put a laxative in each of the beers and served them to his peers. By the end of the evening they were all rather ill and blamed it on the bad beer as Cha Cha was the only one who didn't suffer and the only one who didn't have a beer as a self-proclaimed tee-totaller. He was laughing his head off at their stupidity and left the camp in the morning with a bag full of ladies underwear and make up he stole from some of the girls. He is still so delighted with himself over this we have to laugh with him. Mary doesn't think lacing the team's coffee in her work's morning meeting is going to be a good thing. We suggest she get another job and then do it as a parting gift like Cha Cha did.

The following morning, we all have sore heads, we drank far more wine than we planned; not helped by Cha Cha keeping us topped up and entertaining us so well. The breakfast table is a picture or gingham and farm produce; it looks and smells amazing and we fill ourselves until we are stuffed full. Our hostess provides us with some homemade blueberry muffins to take for a snack later; she is so adorable. Today she is wearing flared jeans with sequins on them, a silky paisley blouse and a white linen apron with the words, 'Glastonbury Rocks' and a picture of the Tor on it. We ask her if she has been to the famous festival there and she laughs,

"I go every year my lovelies, you have to go!"

We are impressed and inspired by this spry lady we are now picturing rocking out in front of the pyramid stage. Belle has been and they chat about how wonderful it is and she says how in the evenings the festival is like a magical dragon emerging from the hills, breathing a life fire that dazzles and inspires.

Belle decides that we all need a make-over; Mary because of her job, me because of Tom and Belle because of her giving up the spoon challenge and now unsure what to do next. We agree and hit the shops, Bridport has got a very hippy chick to eco warrior vibe and we are in stitches at the outfits we try on; from baggy, low crotch, tie dye trousers and hessian shirts to full-bodiced, purple, silk gowns that give us the mystical hag look. After much hilarity we all buy a little summer dress with shoestring straps in various pastel or vibrant colour schemes and straw hats with silk, wildflowers woven into them each. We go on the hunt for a denim jacket to complete the look and turn to the secondhand shops to achieve this, we can't find a decent one anywhere but it's fun looking. Exhausted from shopping we go for lunch at a small café and decide we give up on our image change and go to the farm place I suggested the night before.

By the time we get back to the B&B we have sore feet and look very untidy. The farm was such fun, we had a go-kart race, fed goats and bunnies and zip wired for at least an hour. We have to take turns again to shower and get ready to go out for food and wine again. When Mary is in the shower Belle is doing her make-up and turns to me to say in a hushed voice,

"Did you know that Bob is cheating on Mary?"

I am shocked and ask for more information. Belle knows someone whose sister had met Bob in a club, and they had ended up snogging on the dancefloor. The friend says that she intimated they went back to her place afterwards, but it was not confirmed by her. Two weeks after, the friend actually saw them in a restaurant looking very intimate and gazing into each other's eyes. I am fuming and want to know why Belle firstly hasn't said anything before and secondly, not told Mary. We stop talking because the shower is turned off and we can hear Mary singing. We put the radio on and carry on getting ready, so she doesn't suspect we have been talking about her. I want to tell Mary but don't want to hurt her and Belle warns me against it. I feel confused all over again. What is the right thing to do?

"Oh that shower was perfect, you can go in now Tovu!"

Mary starts towelling her head and turns the radio up louder as she wants to sing along to a Queen song that has just come on.

"We are the Champions........of the World!!!" we all join in and then I get to my shower. It has very powerful jets and it seems to wash away my feelings of unease and worry. Let's just enjoy the weekend I decide. We agree to return to see Cha Cha in the same pub as last night, he had said Saturday nights were a riot and they had a band playing. We all dressed in our new outfits and set off arm in arm towards the pub. We get a wolf whistle by someone passing in their car and someone shouts, 'Oi Oi Beauties!' as they drive past too. We giggle and stride into the pub which is very noisy and packed solid. We can just make out Cha Cha behind the bar, surrounded by people of all ages and all manner of dress. Some have clearly made an effort with a bit of sparkle and tightness about their clothes and others look like they have just come off the farm after a day of ploughing. There is however a jovial spirit to the gathering and a band is playing in

51

the corner of the room with gusto. They seem to be a cross between the Wurzels and Status Quo, great fun.

We manage to get to Cha Cha at the bar, we note that he is in tight satin maxi skirt, split up to his mid-thigh and a frilly blouse and with a splash of guyliner and lip-gloss as his make-up. He seems to be camping it up this evening and looks amazing. We order our drinks; he is pleased to see us and plants a kiss on all our foreheads before getting our wine.

"Ah my hot Totty; so lovely you came back to see me. Let me deal with these reprobates and I will come find you later!"

He winks at us.

"There is a space to dance beyond that crowd there and you will find it most entertaining!"

He turns his attention to some other customers, and we weave our way towards the band with our drinks and manage to nab a small table, some people are just leaving. We enjoy the band, the dancing and singing and join in after our second bottle of wine, until I discover my dress is see-through as it has a pale pink background whilst the others have a black background print and are not see-through. Trust me! I sit down and Mary joins me. Belle is whirling round like a spinning top and a bearded man catches her as she topples a bit.

"Steady as you go Miss!" he holds her around her waist and keeps hold much longer than he needs to.

Belle is dizzy but giggling; "Ooops silly me, thanks for catching me. I must apologise!"

"No need Miss, you go steady now. Can I get you a drink?" he is still touching her arm and pulls her towards him.

We manage to get across to them and Mary extracts his hand off her arm;

"We will look after her thank you sir" She gives him a stern look and he withdraws,

"No problem Miss just trying to help, I see she has enough help with you two."

Belle is dragged off by us and we sit her down to catch her breath,

"Get him, he is clearly ancient and should know better! You pulled Belle!" Mary thinks this is hysterical and Belle laughs at her teasing.

"Oh yes, I attract the mature man alright. Did you know Tom Baker off Dr Who and Prince Phillip all want to date me? Oh and John Noakes off Blue Peter!"

"Well John Noakes isn't that old is he?" I ask.

"He's about fifty Tovu." Mary replies.

"Oh, I thought he was about thirty-seven, that's not too old is it?" Mary and Belle both look at me quizzically,

"And why might thirty-seven be an age you have fixated on Tovu?"

Damn it they have caught me out. Bloody wine gives me loose lips. I feel a little cornered and confess that this is the age of Tom. I had managed to evade answering the question of his age before and knew there would be eyebrows raised.

"No way Tovu, that's too old for you! He is not for you!!" Mary exclaims. Bella says,

"Well hold on, hold on, age shouldn't be the issue." I nod in agreement,

"It's whether he has a large...... bank account that really matters!" she giggles and I playfully thump her on the arm.

"Seriously Tovu, surely you don't want someone THAT old, just think when he's in his sixties you will be bringing up the kids and everyone will think he's the grandfather."

53

Mary has a point but Belle and I gang up on her and try to convince her that age doesn't matter so long as you have other attractive qualities and you love each other. Mary asserts that it just doesn't work long time and that it is bound to end badly. We argue about it for some time and then realise the pub is emptying out and the band has left.

Cha Cha is waving everyone out and comes across to us, when there are just an elderly couple sipping at their brandies in unison, left in the pub. He wants to know what we are debating as he could see us getting a bit heated. We let him join in, he is definitely on Mary's side and tells us about a relationship he had with an older woman when he was twenty; she was thirty and very glamorous. Own house, own car left to her by her late husband who died of a heart attack at fifty. So not only had she been with a much older man she was now involved with a much younger man. Cha Cha tells us she was very experienced in the bedroom department but selfish and vain; didn't want to be seen with Cha Cha as she thought she would be judged even more than when she was dating her late husband. They saw each other for about three months, she fascinated him, but he didn't really like her. He lusted her but when she told him she was taking another lover and he could carry on with her too or not, he chose not. I sat there listening to this tale wondering if that was all Tom thought of me, as a good shag and maybe I just found him fascinating and experienced to be around but actually he was at his core a cheat. Mary puts her hand on mine and looks at me, she knows me so well,

"Maybe we shouldn't upset Tovu about this anymore. Anyway, you said you weren't likely you see him anymore. Come on, let's go, we have to get up fairly early and hit the road back home."

Cha Cha is sad to see us go and makes us promise to keep in touch giving us his phone number.

The elderly couple get up to go at the same time and as they pass us the woman looks up into her husband's eyes and they smile at each other, a picture of pure love for each other. The woman says to Cha Cha,

"Aww your angels are leaving Charles; don't worry you will find a nice lass to be by your side like I have my Graeme."

Cha Cha plants a kiss on top of her head and says,

"If only I was a little older I'd have been after you Margie!"

They all laugh and so do we. Cha Cha herds us out so he can be left to tidy up our tables and get home to bed.

Walking back Mary suddenly says to us,

"I think Bob might be cheating on me."

If ever there was a prompt to tell all, it was now. Belle spills the beans and Mary weeps all night and I feel like weeping and Belle is trying hard to comfort Mary as she knows we'll get no sleep tonight if she doesn't stop wailing.

Mary half believes what Belle told her and half doesn't, she had her own suspicions just based on him being more distracted, losing a lot of weight and being 'busier'. Yet he had taken her out for her birthday and brought her an expensive bracelet, she was sure he wouldn't have bothered if he wanted to finish with her. We wonder if he just had a guilty conscience. We wonder if he is having his cake and eating it. I feel bad for her, but it does seem that something is not right and he is acting as though something IS wrong. She needs to talk to him to be clear about what is going on and tell him how she is feeling. Is it wrong that I am hoping they break up and we can be single together? I think that if I suggest this as a plus right now, she would start howling again.

When we say goodbye to our lovely host she gives us all a hug and hands out a paper bag each, containing, an apple, a homemade cheese scone and a white chocolate and raspberry muffin each. We all promise to return or try and find her at the next Glastonbury festival.

Chapter 6

Autumn is approaching and I am kicking the wet, russet leaves in the park as I am scurrying through it on my way to the day centre. I have a meeting with Vanessa who wants to know if I am going to take up a post with them when I qualify as the results are due very soon. I have written Uma a poem to give to her, in thanks for her poem.

When I enter the day centre the familiar sounds, smells and atmosphere wrap around me as soon as I set foot into reception; I do love this place. Charlie and Jim say hello and tell me Debbie is off sick. Vanessa has yet to arrive and so they make me a cuppa and want to know how I have been. I give them a potted account of,

"Well the acute ward was interesting, hard at times, a lot of 1-1 obs and medication rounds. Recently went to Dorset with my mates and discovered the best B&B and pub with the only cross dresser in Bridport. "

They both want to know more about Cha Cha and think it would be a hoot to go and see him. I am not sure if they want to meet him out of admiration or an interest from a psychological level. i.e. wanting to analyse why he behaves in the way he does and what makes him tick. This is the problem with working in psychiatry, we are fascinated by the human mind and behaviours. Charlie is the spitting image of Prince Edward, a posh psychologist from South London who enjoys vintage cars and opera, he is married with two daughters under 7 years old. Jim is short, ginger, bearded, Scottish and in his forties, he went over to the Philippines to buy a bride. Said new wife is lovely, sweet and obedient. Jim adores her and whilst tight with his money on all other matters, pays out for her many requests for new stuff. She in turn shows her love by taking the mick out of him and promises him she doesn't want children. Jim is far too selfish and self-centred to ever want children and Beth just wants to be spoilt by Jim and keep their house nice. Charlie and Jim together are like an old married coupe that bicker and tease each other a lot of the time but somehow have things in common that keep them the best of friends.

Vanessa bounces in and sits down with us,

"Hello you lovely people! I am so sorry I am late! Nadia is unwell so I had to get my mom to look after her and take her over to Pinnar."

"That's no problem Vanessa, we've been quizzing Tovu here for you. She doesn't want to work with us lot unless you put her on the top band salary!" Jim jokes and Vanessa says;

"I think she's worth it, but we don't want to upset the others now do we?"

"So, are you coming here Tovu? Oh, I should be asking you this in private, ignore me!"

She laughs and turns to Oliver, a patient with schizophrenia who has approached her and asks her if he can see the doctor today.

"Hello Oliver, so nice to see you! I think the doctor is in later so I will ask him for you. You are not booked today but he might squeeze you in. If not we can book you some time as soon as possible. What do you think about Tovu here joining our team?" Oliver responds,

"I, I, I, thank you! Y, y, y, yes! l, l, l, like T, T, Tovu."

He smiles and leaves us. I smile back at him and then say,

"I love it here and I would love to work here permanently. I can't believe you want me."

"Yess!!!"

Vanessa gets up does a little jig and tells me to bring all my documents needed to start next week. Jim says,

"Blimey, you don't have to be mad to work here but it helps!"

Charles, reaches over to shake my hand,

"Welcome to the team Tovu. We will look forward to you starting".

I feel great, I think I have made a good decision and this is confirmed when Uma comes in, gives me the biggest hug and starts to cry happy tears when she read my poem.

"I love it, thank you, thank you Tovu!"

She then proceeds to read it out loud to everyone;

"Have I done something to upset you?..."

Everyone applauds when she finishes, and she is crying again and has to take her glasses off to wipe her face and them clean. We have another hug before I go, and she tells me she can't wait for me to start working in the day centre again.

It's raining when I leave, no coat and no brolly with me. I pray for it to stop and then with a sigh I walk as speedily as I can into town where I am meeting Mary for lunch. I really should have brought my car, or at least checked the forecast and been prepared for the weather. There are other people rushing about with no protection from the wetness, I am not alone in my lack of preparation. Some are trying to shelter under trees and doorways, some like me are walking as fast as is possible to their destination. By the time I reach the café I look like a drowned rat but laugh as I see a dripping Mary at the back of the room. She is laughing at me, the café staff are not as amused at us dripping all over their floor. One of them looks moodily at us and is about to tell her colleague to clear up our mess when Mary takes control and asks them for some paper towel to clean up the drips and pulls out of her bag a large blanket shawl to wrap around us and get warm.

"I didn't want to get it wet because I thought I might need it for you."

I look at her quizzically and then we laugh again. With one thing or another I hadn't managed to catch up with Mary since we got back from Bridport. She tells me that things are working out better with Bob, they had had a good chat and were back on track. The flirtation he had with someone else is over and he says it was really that she was going through a tough time. He thought she needed a friend, but he could see how it looked and that she may have misread his attention and wanted more. Mary has also gone back to her previous job and they are sending her on some training so she can climb the next rung of the ladder. I am so pleased for her. I tell her about the day centre and that I had a most embarrassing evening out with Larissa this weekend just gone.

There's a club in the city which is newly opened and Larissa wanted to go desperately, it is modern and full of mirrors, glitter balls and lasers. We didn't have much money between us so had had a couple of vodka and cokes before we set off and as we hadn't eaten much were both tipsy from the outset. We decide to keep with the vodka and ordered two singles, but then were told it was happy hour so we had a double. As we had gotten there early, we found a corner seat and watched people trickle into the club. It was so noisy you could only communicate by shouting and the smoke machine kept obscuring our view. We nursed our vodkas for a good hour and then the club came alive, people started dancing and the noise level increased. We decided to dance and give up our table, there was no way we could save it if we both left it. As I stepped onto the dancefloor, I was pushed over by some guys messing around. I went full on splayed across the floor with my skirt up and my old school PE shorts I was wearing underneath for comfort showing. Larissa was too creased up laughing to help me up, but this guy did and asked me if I was okay. I had managed to regain some composure and realised I was okay, nothing broken. I am helped off the dancefloor and over to some seats which the guy commandeers telling people to make room.

Mary is stitched up, she thinks it's hilarious and now it's becoming history, I do too.

"Well at least I was wearing shorts and not a thong, imagine that!"

"I know some silky or lacy boxer shorts would have been better but I can't afford them, £30 I saw some for."

Mary suggests I treat myself to some sexy boxers next pay day. She enquires about my saviour and I fill her in on the details of this knight in shining armour.

"His name is Rob, he is a geek, he is 26 years old, he has mousy hair, limpid blue eyes and is an IT data manager."

Mary's grin widens,

"Oh, so you two chatted and got close enough to see each other's eye colour then? And what pray tell me happened next?"

I feign ignorance as to what she is getting at. I confess, yes we did have a slow dance, yes we did kiss, yes we do have a date and no I didn't take him back home with me to have my wicked way with him. Mary is clapping with excitement,

"When's the date? Where are you going?"

We have arranged to go to the cinema on Wednesday to see Back to the Future, his choice but I don't mind.

"Don't forget to wear those PE shorts Tovu, I'm sure that's what he found so alluring about you!"

Mary gets a thump on the arm. When we leave the café Mary suggests we double date some time if it goes well over the next week or so with Rob and me.

"I have a Bob and you have a Rob, what greatness!"

I hug her and we say our goodbyes. It has stopped raining now thankfully but it's a little chilly. Mary wraps her blanket around her and heads off and I pop into a charity shop and find a cheap cardi for a pound. It's a loose weave, grey cardi that is baggy and long, almost down to my knees; it becomes my go to snuggle cardi.

Trudging back to my room in my fusty but oh so warm cardi I see cousin Freya in a shop, looking like she is arguing with the shopkeeper. I put my head down and rush by. I go un-noticed but I am getting flashbacks of the tree, the pickled onion breath and the white socks mocking me. I stop for breath at the bottom of the hill to my room and also to stop myself from letting out a loud fart I have been brewing since I had that cheese scone in the cafe. Damnit the fart comes anyway and I have to make a loud coughing sound to cover it up. Not that there is anyone around at this point. I inwardly blush and get to my room wanting a lie down. When I get there Becky opens her door before I pass it,

"Tovu, you have a dozen red roses! They are in the kitchen sink. I put them there for you. Who's your lover?"

She has now come out of her room and wants to know all about the person who has sent me the roses. I am not sure if they are from Rob or Tom or maybe someone else. There is indeed a beautiful bouquet of roses in the kitchen sink, no water but in the sink. I open the little envelope with the card inside. It says, 'Dear Tovu, looking forward to seeing you on Wednesday, Love Rob xx' I am chuffed to bits, but a little weirded out about the 'love' bit; we have only just met.

I tell Becky the bare minimum about meeting him and the date. I certainly don't want her to tell everyone about my PE Shorts. Becky says she is chuffed for me and then tells me about her latest man, an Italian junior doctor who calls her 'Bambino' and has an impressively long tongue. I blush when she describes something he can do with this tongue and say,

"Too much information! Please warn me when I have to play my music loud next time he is due."

She smiles and says he is coming on Wednesday, thankfully I am out with Rob.

I eventually, after I've dried off and changed my clothes, get to lie down in my room and settle into listening to some Mozart, I feel in a reflective mood. Just as I close my eyes there is a knock on my door. I am truly cheesed off, until I open it and standing there is Tom with a hungry look in his eyes. He says he is taking an 'extended meeting with his boss' and is pleased to find me home. My insides melt and I let him in. He takes me in his arms and kisses me deeply and ravages me for the next hour. I am still faking orgasms but I feel I am getting closer to the real thing. Tom suggested I let him put a finger up my bum because it's supposed to enhance your orgasm; as mine are fake, I decline the offer. He's brought me a mix tape and we've been listening to it. When John Martyn sings 'May You Never', he tells me this is our song and he is my 'hand to hold'.

I forever associate the song to Tom, it's becomes one of my favourites even though it clearly about friendship love not true love. We chat a little and then he leaves. He didn't question who had sent me the red roses now proudly sat in an old coffee jar on my dressing table and I don't ask him about his girlfriend. We have only chatted about music and work gossip. He has however, asked if he can see me again soon. I tell him no. He looks forlorn and then gives me that smile that turns me to jelly,

"Not even a little trip to Brighton?"

I am resolute, I have to see if I can have a proper relationship with Rob. Tom is someone else's, he'll never be mine. Rob has potential. I go to give him a call to thank him for the roses and get an answering machine, I don't leave a message, I hate those things. I will thank him on Wednesday unless he calls me before.

Alex is in the lounge as I return from the phone and I sit with him,

"Hi! How's you?" I ask him.

"Hey, I'm chilled Tofu, I was just going to put on a film about the Amazon Rainforests, my brother got a pirate copy; want to watch with me?"

He insists on calling me Tofu as it goes with is vegan ways. I go and grab my duvet and snuggle up in a chair to watch it with him and he gives me some vegan crisps.

"I love a good docufilm."

He says and I think that he has just made that word up. Short way into the film we realise it's not a documentary at all and a ten-year-old boy gets abducted by a tribe. Nevertheless, we watch it in some horror and some disbelief as the plot winds to its sort of happy ending.

"I am going to kill my brother!"

Alex declares, I am laughing.

"I quite enjoyed it."

Alex sort of agrees but thinks it was indulgent in places. I'm not sure what he means and change the subject and ask him how his current placement is going. He is working on one of the general medical wards and had said previously he wasn't enjoying it too much. The qualified nurses keep playing pranks on him. They once sent him off to get a set of fallopian tubes and then another time to get a melaena stool for the doctor to sit on. For those of you not medically trained, a fallopian tube is in your reproductive organs and a melaena stool is a black tarry poo. Yesterday they asked him to answer the phone and he got a great glob of KY Jelly all over his hair and ear. I'm laughing so hard and he is perplexed but sees the funny side of it. We take some time to think up some ways of getting them back but mostly giggle about stupid phone pranks, like phoning and asking in a fake voice for Mike Hunt or pretending to be the zoo and asking if their keeper Mr Lyons has been admitted. When we've exhausted the options, Alex asks after Larissa and wonders when she is coming over next.

I like Alex and so does Larissa but only as a friend, he has some serious hygiene issues being an eco-warrior and can be both naive and intense in equal measures. I feel slightly guilty for telling him that she is seeing someone now and isn't planning to come over any day soon. Which is not a lie, but his face is forlorn and sad. I decide to cheer him up by telling him about my mishap in the club and get him to solemnly swear not to tell another living soul. It does the trick though and he trundles off to make a mixed bean curry.

Chapter 7

Wednesday evening and I am half expecting for Rob to stand me up, he hasn't rung and I am trying to remember if he said 7 p.m. at the cinema or 7.30 p.m. I decide it must be 7.30 p.m. as the film starts at 7.45p.m. and it would be daft to get there too early. I am generally early, so I arrive at 20 past and see Rob there standing under a neon sign that says 'This way up'. He sees me and instantly grins, I quicken my step and think that maybe I should have been here at 7 p.m. after all.

"Hi, sorry am I late? I thought I was early."

"Oh no, I haven't been here very long, I tend to be early for everything. Come on I have the tickets already. Do you want some popcorn or sweets? Anything to drink?"

I settle for some wine gums and a bottle of water and thank him for the flowers he sent me. He shrugs it off and says he's glad I like them. He takes my hand as we look for our seat in the dark, his grip is limp and slightly sweaty. I guess he is a bit nervous and I always excuse people's sweatiness and wind problems being a sufferer myself. He doesn't ask me where I want to sit and chooses some seats just at the front of the seats behind those that are right in front of the screen. It's a bit close for my liking but I don't say anything. Throughout the film Rob makes strange sucking sounds when he is pondering the plot; this distracts me rather and on occasion he places a hand on my knee. I try not to flinch, oh dear. I tried to focus on the film but have no idea what is going on, even though Rob whispers too close to my ear for my comfort, snippets about what is going on and how futuristic it all is.

After we head out of the cinema Rob suggests we have a drink in a bar just down the road; it is brightly lit and busy with fellow filmgoers. It is noisy and he spends twenty minutes at the bar and five minutes in the gents, so by the time we sit to talk he is looking at his watch and yawning.

"Sorry, had a busy day, I have been looking at developing a programme using Objective C and I can't quite get my head around it. Larry says my extensions and binary binding are all wrong."

He's completely lost me now but I nod and ask what his views were on the mobile phone. Ernie Wise was on the news making the first UK call to Vodaphone HQ recently. I don't really pay much attention to what he says next, I am listening in on the conversation going on behind me. It is more interesting and easier to follow as they are debating the loo seat up or loo seat down preferences of males and females. Rob, must have picked up my disinterest and says,

"Sorry, I get carried away. I don't want to bore you. Tell me about your work."

I tell him about the day centre and whilst keeping confidentiality tell him some of the patients' quirks. He chuckles good naturedly and makes some quite insightful comments. I am warning to him now. The bar bell rings and he looks at his watch,

"We better get off, do you want me to walk you home?"

I know he lives in the opposite direction to me and so I say I'll get a taxi. He doesn't argue with this and tells me he's had a lovely time and would like to go out next week sometime. I agree and suggest he rings me at the weekend to arrange.

He sees me into the taxi and plonks a clumsy kiss on my cheek. I wave goodbye and feel relieved the evening has drawn to a close. It wasn't a bad evening , just not a very good one. I think he's gentlemanly and kind but there is no spark between us. I wonder if the spark might develop. I wonder if he will call me at the weekend and if I will take the call or not. When I get to my room there's a Larissa shaped person lying on my bed.

"Hi! What are you doing here at this hour?" I ask.

"What are you doing being out so long, I have been waiting for you for hours."

I make sure she is okay and that there are no dramas to report and agree for her to stay the night. I pour some wine and tell her about Rob and also Alex and she tells me about her new flat and flatmate who turns out to be a man she works with who has split up from his wife and she is now in a relationship with. It sounds like disaster is written all over it but I hold my tongue. He had gone out with his best mate this evening to see the same film I had seen but different cinema.

Larissa thought it was a good idea to come and check up on me. We establish we are both on days off the next day and some how I have agreed to visit our parents. I'm not exactly looking forward to this, but a duty visit wouldn't go amiss, and it is our mother's birthday next week. Larissa also suggests we see if Evan and Jan will have us over for tea and we can pop in and see them too afterwards. I look at my watch, it's a bit late to call them now so will call them first thing in the morning.

"Can I borrow a top tomorrow Tovu? I bought underwear and a toothbrush but think I'm going to need a clean top."

I agree this will be fine and trudge off to the bathroom to have quick shower before bed and save myself some time in the morning. My dear sister has a wash in the sink in my room whilst

I am gone and has made herself a bed on the floor. We talk about what I am going to do next month when I have to move out of the student nurse accommodation now the course is ending. Janice who works at the day centre has already offered up her annexe for me but I haven't worked out the finances yet. Larissa offers for me to stay with her but it would be a pain getting to and from the day centre from hers. Plus, I don't want to be a gooseberry if she and this 'flatmate' who is apparently called Raj; are going to be romantically involved. I'm not sure he likes Soft Cell. I have two weeks to get somewhere, I'm sure I'll find somewhere I don't have to listen to other people having a good time.

In the morning I manage to get hold of Jan who is happy to give us tea and we agree to pop over before the boys are in bed so we can be good aunties and dine with them and then read to them before they go to bed. This day is going to be such fun I think ironically, and then rebuke myself and tell myself not to be such a grump. Some people have no family and some people certainly have worse family than me. We get going when Larissa has spurned several of my tops and found one she actually likes; it's a plain, bright blue and capped sleeved T Shirt that looks better on her than me. I tell her she can keep it. My mini needs petrol, so we head for a garage.

The counter staff is staring at my chest whilst asking me for my money and asks me if I need anything else. I have already added chocolate, crisps and coke to my shopping and say no thanks. As I'm walking out with my arms laden up with my goodies, Freya walks in the door I am about to exit. I cannot avoid her and so say in an overly cheerful manner,

"Hi Freya, you look great. How are you? How's Uncle Alfred and Aunt Tabitha?"

She smiles and says all is well.

"How about you Tovu, I hear you are nearly qualified now and seeing someone."

I now have to stop and let her in the garage shop and then answer her questions,

"Oh yes just waiting for the results of my exams and yes just started seeing someone I met at a club."

Still laden and trying not to drop anything and feeling uncomfortable emotionally as well, I don't want to spend time elaborating on any of this, especially with Freya.

"I must dash, due at the parents and you know what my dad is like about time keeping. We must get together sometime."

She has already started to move off to the counter and says,

"Yes of course."

I know this is not a genuine reply, we just never really have much to say to each other. I meanly think that the man serving her will not be looking at her chest, she has very little in that department. Larissa says Freya has always been a bit jealous of me, my chest proportions being one of the things she envies.

When I get in my car, Larissa is wide eyed;

"Oh my God, I saw Freya go in and you two talking! What did you say?"

I repeat the conversation and my thoughts on hoping she doesn't spend any time with me soon. She then spies the chocolate haul and immediately, gleefully demands a Twirl and a Curly wurly.

"These are for if mother gives us lunch and it is inedible, we will need the sugar load to recover!"

I give her the Twirl,

"But you can have this for breakfast."

We set off again and just two miles up the road a car comes the opposite way at speed and a stone is kicked up and shatters my windscreen. The noise makes us both jump, it was almost like getting shot at. Fortunately we were only going 20 MPH on account of the roadworks; the little Pratt in his white BMW that ignored the reduced speed limit probably does not care at all that we are now holding up a queue of traffic as we have to stop, the screen is now totally obscured. The man in the car behind us comes to investigate the hold up; he almost runs up to us.

"What the bloody hell is going on!" he shouts in a broad Lancashire accent; then looks in the window, sees two blonde young ladies and the windscreen disaster and his whole demeanour changes.

"Oh, some windscreen problems aye lasses? You're goin' t' need towing to a garage. Shall I 'elp you push it on t' 'ard shoulder? Ya can't leave it 'ere 'olding up traffic."

We agree this would be great and he goes back to his car and returns with two other guys. He tells me to take the handbrake off and steer to the left and they will push. This manoeuvre works well and we leave the car and walk the two miles back to the garage we'd just been in. Larissa moans all the way, saying her feet hurt. An hour and a half later, windscreen fixed and back on the road we pray that our father has decided to go out and mother has decided lunch is not required.

"Larissa, Tovu! Where have you been? I missed a pub lunch for you two and your mother says lunch is spoilt. I had to have a sandwich as I was starving. Go through to the dining room, it's all ready for you. Your mother has taken a lot of trouble over YOUR lunch."

Our father greets us thus and we do as we are told. He is not in a good mood. Neither is mother, she has been anxious and her

71

bedraggled hair spoils the overall look. She tries to push the straggling strands as we come into the dining room and sit down.

"What happened to you girls? You are so late, again. I have made some scones and sandwiches for lunch so luckily nothing to spoil."

She tells us to tuck in and we tell her the saga of the windscreen. True to form the cheap white, thin sliced bread is stuck together with Shippams Paste; I hate the stuff because she used to put it in my school packed lunches and I wished many a time that we were eligible for free school, stodgy meals. Her scone biscuits are very dry but slavered in lots of butter are okay to eat. Our father has learnt to eat most things, he is always hungry so doesn't seem to care about what it tastes like. He grumbles throughout, about all sorts, we zone out and then I am caught off guard when he says,

"So what are you going to do now your training ends. Have you got a job? Somewhere to live?"

I'm bit surprised he's interested and very surprised he knows my situation; in addition to not having been paying attention and chewing a large piece of scone I start to cough and feel like the crumbs are stuck in my throat and also impeding my windpipe. I feel like I can't breathe but manage to calm enough to take some breaths and drink some water mother gets me. Larissa speaks for me,

"She's got a job in a day centre and we talked about options for a place to stay last night, she'll be fine".

When I can speak again, I agree with what Larissa has said and add that I will also do some additional bank shifts on the acute ward. This seems to bore my father as he moves on to tell us that his bank manager is taking early retirement due to a windfall, but he reckons he was pushed out as he is a very heavy drinker that often frequents the same pub as him.

He has retired to his office, probably to have a nap so, we help mother clear away and wash up, etc in peace. As we arrived late, we don't have long before we must leave for Evan and Jan's. Mother does, however, expresses her current list of worries, her health, her friend's sick dog, Evan and Jan making ends meet, Landon settling down, etc, etc. She however has a little surprise for us; Faye bounds in through the door.

"Hey big sisters!!! Sorry I couldn't get here for lunch but I did want to see you. Mum told me you were coming, she walked up to the hairdressers to let me know and they let me get off early so I could catch you."

We all squeal in delight and Faye makes us see her new bedroom makeover she designed herself. This also means we get to gossip out of the ear shot of mother, I can never call her mum, Faye is the only one of us who does. Faye fills us in on the latest about Landon, she had coffee with him a couple of days ago.

"Guess who he took to Live Aid in the end and is now seeing?"

She answers herself before we can speak,

"That Tia, the one who is Miss Hoity Toity and he was pursuing! She hasn't met anyone in the family yet though and apparently only sees him at weekends because work is too busy in the week. He thinks she might be seeing someone else in the week but then so is he. I don't know how he gets away with it!"

We question her about the 'someone else' and she tells us that Landon was tight lipped about the mystery lady. Faye wants to know all about how we are. Larissa, lets slip that Raj has four children, what sort of dad leaves four children? We chat some more but we have to get going or face another host being pissed off about the fact we have ruined their meal.

It only takes 20 minutes to get to Evans from our parents' house; this is forever a contentious issue as they never get a visit from them except mother will child sit occasionally. Father expects them to visit them and is always moaning that they don't seem to bother. I take a deep breath before we enter another mad house. Jan opens their door to us with Lucas bundled under one arm and dangling there crying and Josh holding onto her left ankle squealing;

"Hi aunties, come and play with your nephews while I finish off the food. You came just at the right moment."

We enter the lounge which looks like a war zone, toys and stuff just everywhere, with barely a surface free to sit on. Jan sweeps some toys off the sofa and shakes an ethnic throw and puts it on top of it gesturing for us to sit down; with a nephew each on our backs this is tricky so we have to manoeuvre them to our fronts and plonk down together. The boys think this is great fun and demand for us to tickle them. Jan leaves the room and shuts the door and shuts out the sound of us tickling the boys and their resultant chuckling. We manage to calm them down and snuggle them as I tell them a story about an ancient rock that was very wise and had a cheerful friend called Silo the Seagull. They are listening intently until Evan arrives and flings open the lounge door.

"Hello gorgeous people!" he says with a big smile on his face.

The boys run to him, "Daddy! daddy, daddy, daddy!!!"

He hugs them and then asks what their aunties have been doing with them, "Aunty Tovie was telling us a story about a rock and a seagull and they have adventures. How can a rock have adventures daddy?" Josh says and Lucas nods solemnly, not quite understanding what his brother is talking about.

"Well I think Auntie Tovie can tell you more about them after your baths tonight, what do you think?"

The boys shout in approval and Evan herds them up to the bathroom to wash their hands before tea.

Over the old pine table Evan and Jan seem a little strained with each other; Jan has cooked a lentil soup with homemade bread and vegan curry. The soup already in bowls and curry on the table ready to serve when it has been eaten. The boys are used to this sort of diet and tuck in, Larissa and I try it in trepidation but fortunately it's quite tasty and we cope with the textures. The conversation is dominated by Josh's many questions. We excuse our lack of appetite on the late lunch at our parents. Evan wants the low down on everyone, he looks directly at Jan and says,

"Can you bath the kids tonight and I'll wash up and tidy up with the help of Larissa and Tovu so we get a chance to talk properly.

"Why daddy? I want you to do my bath!" glares Josh.

"Because my dear boy, I need to talk to your aunties and make sure they tell you the best goodnight stories after your bath".

Josh accepts this and asks so many more questions which we don't have many of the answers for. Questions like, 'why does Mrs Baxter have a red face?' Mrs Baxter his teacher at school. 'Why can't I fly a plane?' and 'Why can't Josh wear a dress to nursery?'. Evan and Jan believe in letting children express themselves; I'm not opposed to it, but boy is it tiring.

Washing up in the kitchen, as cluttered as the lounge; Evan asks about us as we dry and try and find somewhere to put things. Larissa in turn, asks him how he is and if everything is alright with him and Jan. He sighs and says,

"We are just tired with the boys and work, we don't have much time to be good with each other. It's always busy, busy and then we collapse, sleep and it all starts again."

We ask him why he doesn't get some help and he shuts down that option quickly,

"We are skint and we don't trust anyone but family. Jan's mum helps a bit and ours a little, but you know we have a certain way of being with the Lucas and Joshua."

We accept his explanation and bite our tongues making it difficult to volunteer some help. He changes the subject and we are dragged away to read the goodnight stories. Larissa reads a couple of Mr Men books, making funny accents up. Joshua demands to know what happened with the rock so I tell the rest of my story and they fall asleep. We can't stay much longer and want to leave them to have some relaxed grown up time as we managed to tidy the lounge as well as the kitchen between us.

Driving back to Larissa's to drop her off, I say to her

"Can we leave it a year before we do that again? I am completely exhausted?"

She completely agrees and is tucking into more chocolate so is looking at me with a chocolate covered grimace. I get her to feed me some crisps as I drive along and we giggle at the family food offerings.

Chapter 8

I persuaded Rob to come for a walk through the woods and he's not very happy because he is cold having worn a very inadequate needlecord jacket. I am in a very warm hat, fleecy, waterproof jacket, have thermals on and fake Hunter wellies. I am snuggly. He tries to cuddle me in order to get himself warmer and I give him my scarf instead. The woods are quiet, damp and slightly spooky; I say as much to him and as I do we hear a twig snap behind us and jump, turning our heads to see if we can see what snapped the twig. I laugh because there is nothing there, maybe a twig just snapped off a tree in the wind. As we walk along the path a gorgeous black and white spaniel appears and is intently sniffing the ground; it's owner rounds the corner and says hi to us. As we get closer, I see it is Dr Greg.

"Oh hi Greg, is this your dog? She is lovely!"

"Hello Tovu, I didn't recognise you in that hat; it suits you! This is Poppy, she's not mine, just borrowed her from a friend as I fancied a walk. It's glorious today!"

I smile and agree and we carry on with our stroll.

"Who's that?"

Rob sounds suspicious and it gets my heckles up as I have been completely faithful to him these past months and believe me when I say I have been tempted. I tell him about Greg and he seems a bit happier that he is with someone and not a doctor who I work with regularly.

We walk in silence and he takes my hand in that limp way of his. I realise I am feeling a bit narked and uncertain whether I like Rob at the moment. It had been going okay, he was always a gentleman and kind to me, always did what he said he would do, but there was something missing. I have tried to inject a bit of fun and variety to our relationship because he is pretty good at doing the usual cinema or restaurant sort of date but not much else. He tends to either refuse or goes along with my suggestion to please me more than anything and seldom seems to want to do them again. I feel I am being unfair. He buys me flowers and gifts on a regular basis and even offered to take me on an all expenses paid trip to Paris. I said I couldn't possibly accept, not just on the basis I didn't want him spending all that money on me but also because I wasn't sure the relationship was going to last.

I break the silence and enquire about his plans for the coming week and he chats about his various projects and clients. I am day dreaming as he talks, it's gone into a blur when he nudges me and says,

"So you can be free the weekend after next for Paris?"

He's studying my face now, so I feel trapped and say,

"Oh yes, that's amazing thank you!"

Damn my feeble, wandering mind! He pulls me to him and kisses me on the top of my head. "Come on, I'm still cold! Let's get back and I'll take you to lunch."

I agree of course and wish he didn't say 'take you to...' as I feel like a child or a pet.

There's a quaint tearoom with a collection of old chairs and tables that don't match or look well cared for; but it sells the best cream teas. It is usually packed in there; the mismatch of tablecloths and crockery in all colours that clash and collide makes it a cheery place. Lucy the owner and front of house hostess is a tall, slender, rosy cheeked lady with the bluest of eyes and an unfortunately large nose and buck teeth; is just the best. Rob doesn't like going there as he starts to stare at her nose, but we find a corner table and he bravely goes to order us a cream tea each. Lucy comes over to see me,

"Hello beautiful. How are you? I haven't seen you in here for ages! Don't tell me you have been hiding from me?"

I tell her how busy I have been and ask after her son who used to attend the day centre.

"He's doing very well, no longer anxious and depressed he has a job and a girlfriend. I really can't thank you enough for what you did for him."

She tells me that he is also completely turned vegan and she is thinking about making her café vegan. I rather hope she doesn't. I hope he's going through a 'phase'! She leaves us to it and Rob says,

"I don't know if I will get used to you being known so much around these parts, you are always being spoken to wherever we go."

I smile and say it's just because of my job. The cream teas come and we sit in blissful silence eating the most sweet and delicious scones in the world.

When he drops me back he makes plans to see me the following Thursday evening so we can plan our Paris trip further. He tells me to check my passport is in date and to write down the details for when we meet. He doesn't come in, we haven't actually got beyond third base. He seems satisfied with this, I worry, does he not fancy me enough?! Thinking about Paris I am assuming he will want to go all the way, I don't know if I do. All these thoughts today I know should tell me to end it right then and there, but I don't. Am I a coward? An optimist? A user because there's nothing better around at the moment? I am surely not the only one to stay in a relationship hoping things will improve.

I have moved into Janice's annexe; she completely leaves me to my own devices and the annexe is perfect. The entrance around the back of her house leads into a galley kitchen and then you are off into the lounge area. The en-suite bedroom is off the lounge. I have a double bed and my inbuilt wardrobe is a dream. The annexe also came fully furnished so all I had to do was move my clothes and me in. I did have to buy a few kitchen bits and the rent is a bit more than my student nurse accommodation, but I am now getting a qualified staff nurse's wage. After Rob drops me there I hear a knock at the door. It's Janice who wants to know if I am around on Tuesday as she has a plumber coming round to look at my leaky shower. We organise that she can pop home to let them in as we are both working at the day centre of course. I can cover her reception duties whilst she is gone. I make a mental note to make sure it's tidy and there are none of my knickers on the floor. Not that I have a habit of leaving them around, you just have those days when you cannot be bothered.

Janice also tells me the new doctors are starting tomorrow and asks me if I can show them around and brief them about the way things work, room booking, appointments, etc. She says all the rest of the team are tied up in meetings and appointments. I agree. I am an agreeable person, I am bricking it! These sorts of things make me feel so nervous, what if I come across as stupid, what if I trip up or make a fool of myself some other way? You can imagine the trauma I feel but don't show. I nearly ask Janice to do it and I will cover reception but that would not be very professional. I will just have to do it and wear extra deodorant as I am bound to be sweaty with my nerves.

When Janice leaves I have a shower in the leaky shower and get into my PJs, it's about 6 p.m. but I am not intending to go anywhere now. I find my book I am reading, 'Women Who run

With The Wolves', by Dr. Clarissa Pinkola Estés; I am loving it. All about female empowerment and power. I am considering my own wild woman tendencies and wishing I could connect to my deeper soul. I am hoping to find this by the end of the book. I put some music on, a little Clannad to chill to. As I am drawing the curtains in the lounge I see a shadow outside. I go to investigate to see if its someone coming to my door. It's Mary, what's she doing here? I am pleased to see her, although I was going to chill. She spies my PJs as I open the door;

"Oh good you are in for the evening. You are alone aren't you?"

"Yes, yes, come in, you look forlorn. What's happened?"

Mary unwraps herself from her layers of clothes as the annexe is warm.

"Oh I am okay, I need to pass on a message to you, you need to get a phone Tovu. It's nothing too bad but your dad is unwell and you mum is beside herself with worry. She rang my mum and my mum promised we'd get the information to you. So here I am; can I stay on your sofa tonight? Have you got anything to eat?"

I grab her a coke and find some crisps in my kitchen. We decide Clannad is too sad to listen to and change it to Madonna. Mary tells me my father has been diagnosed as having a minor heart murmer and needs to live a healthier lifestyle. He is refusing to change anything which is frustrating my mother. The days she tries to get him to eat healthier he gets into a rage and so she has stopped trying. She said that she didn't need the family to do anything other than try and persuade their father to be healthier. When we saw them the other week there was no sign anything was wrong but thinking about it, my father eats far too much red meat, drinks too much alcohol and smokes his pipe far more than he ever used to. I look at Mary and say, "So what else is the matter? This news could have waited until tomorrow, is everything okay at your place? Are things with Bob going well?"

Mary stares off into the middle distance, she then says,

"Bob has dumped me Tovu, he says he needs some space and he feels smothered."

"Wow, you hardly see him and he feels smothered? I think something else is going on."

"Me too, I suspect there's someone else. I feel such an idiot."

I get the Asti out and chocolate. We discuss this further and Mary reflects on all things Bob. I make her laugh about my previous week and several embarrassing farting incidents and the time I came out of the loo at work with my skirt tucked in my knickers and offering a wine to the boss instead of a coffee. I also tell her about Rob and Paris. She tells me to go for it and stop worrying about whether I'm taking advantage of his generosity. She thinks it will make or break us and I think she could be right, but what's the etiquette around finishing with someone after they've forked out hundreds to take you on a trip away? She asks if I have heard from Tom and I tell her that I haven't and then she tells me that's a good thing and I agree.

Monday morning and I have a bad head. Mary and I lost track of time last night and the numbers of glasses of wine we had. Cheap plonk makes your head worse than the expensive stuff. I feel like death. I turf Mary off the sofa and tell her to get in the shower while I make some breakfast. Tea and toast ready, she reappears and says,

"You have a leaky shower Tovu!"

"I know!!"

I say and glare at her and then laugh because I had already told her about it. She gives me a lift in her old orange beetle which just has the best throaty sound coming from it. I always associate beetles with Mary. I decide I can save on petrol, I can walk home as it's not supposed to rain and possibly Janice will give me a lift anyway. Mary arranges with me to have a night out together with Belle on Friday, more local not the trendy club where I showed my PE shorts to everyone and met Rob. She is in a more cheerful mood and yells out the car window when I get out,

"LOVE YOU!!!!"

I run inside.

I nearly collide with Jim,

"Steady on there girl you'll do yourself some damage!"

I apologise and walk into the kitchen. Debbie is there and offers to make me a cuppa. She chatters on about an episode of one of the soaps, I'm not sure which. My mind is on showing the new doctors round. There's just two, a Registrar and an SHO Debbie tells me when I ask later. That's not too bad I think until they walk in together. Oh my, they are very handsome. The SHO is tall, dark, Spanish and makes me feel tiny and insignificant in the looks stakes. The Registrar is a handsome Nigerian, clearly sure of himself, confident and poised. His suit is perfection. I feel a bit wobbly. They are called Phillipe and Ade. I somehow get through it without any embarrassing moments and I'm proud of myself.

All the patients we have met have told the doctors I am the best nurse there. Janice gave me the nod when we walked past reception and I nip to the loo when they've gone into their perspective interview rooms to meet their first patients. As I wash my hands I suddenly notice my jumper is on inside out. I quickly turn it the right way and just pray no-one has noticed.

Phillipe comes into the office, I feel a bit faint.

"Oh Tovu, I need a BNF, have you got one?"

I fetch him one from a cupboard and he thanks me, Janice is also in the office and witnesses the exchange.

"He is rather lush, you will have to watch him Tovu".

I laugh,

"I doubt he's interested in me; anyway I'm spoken for. He is very lush though, makes me quite swoony."

Janice laughs and then as she leaves says,

"Glad you turned your jumper the right way, I was wondering if it was a new fashion thing." I have a group to run in 15 mins but get the teas and coffees done for the team to grab between their different activities.

Sure enough the office is like a busy train station with staff coming in and out, grabbing drinks and biscuits and leaving again. I have a glass of water and then go on up to the activity room to prepare for my Women's Group. I set the chairs round in a circle and check the names on my list to see who is due to be there. I scan the list and see the familiar names. I love this group, the women have been through trauma, loss and disappointments on a huge scale yet really care about each other and have become a crutch for each other. I have been so humbled by their strength and resilience. One of the ladies lost her 8-year-old son from a car mounting the pavement when they were walking back from school, he had run slightly ahead. She is a single parent mum and her only support is her own mum who is also devastated by the accident too. Another lady in her forties has recently left an abusive marriage, her husband used to lock her in their bedroom for punishment if she didn't have the dinner ready on time, or something was out of place in the lounge, or she dared to disagree with him about something. She had learned to be compliant, to be miserable to keep the peace. Her liberation came when someone who worked with him told her in the middle of the supermarket that he was having an affair with his secretary at work.

"Good Luck to him!"

She packed her bags and moved in with her best friend. Her friend had encouraged her to get help to readjust and come to terms with over twenty years of emotional abuse. The personal stories of all the ladies make you see how amazing women really are.

At the end of the working day, the patients have left, the new doctors have left and there is just Jim, Janice and me to close up the centre. Jim tells Janice and me to go as its pretty much done and he can set the alarm, etc. Janice offers me a lift and I gladly take it because I am drained. I know I should have walked but I just wanted to get a shower and have a relaxing night in on my own. I don't have much to eat left in the house after Mary and I raided the cupboards but I don't feel very hungry and a shop can wait until tomorrow. We had had a lot of tears in the group today and one of the ladies shared some details that shocked and appalled us all. She completely broke down sobbing and we all had to give her so much love and support. I also had to arrange for her to go to a place of safety. Janice has been a diamond today and we chat about the day on the way home. She teases me again about the doctors and I say that Phillipe is quite possibly gay and Ade has probably got several wives. Janice laughs. Her husband Darren is a manager in a wool mill and was her childhood sweetheart and her daughter Jilly is eleven and an angel. Her hair is like gold and flows down her onto her shoulders in ringlets. Janice is happy with her life and has nothing to complain about. I envy her so much but know I am nothing like her and maybe I will never have what she has. I am however, living life to my best ability and definitely trying my best to be a good citizen.

There is a pile of post on my kitchen floor, I scoop it up and put it on the side by the kettle. Shower first, then kettle and then look at the post which is probably all bills. When I get to go through my post, I find two bills, two bits of junk mail and then a handwritten letter which looks intriguing. Don't try and guess who its from, I tear it open and read.

"Dear Tovu,

I have been thinking about getting in touch for some time. I only recently found out where you were living; I managed to get it out of Dr Greg, don't worry he doesn't suspect anything. Anyway, I wanted to let you know that me and Christine have at last split up. I keep thinking about you and wishing I could have treated you better. I know that you may have felt used, but my care and affection for you is genuine and I will always feel that for you.

I hear you are seeing someone and I wish you the very best, I can imagine he feels the luckiest man alive. I know I felt that when I was in your company. I don't want to upset things with you and him. I just wanted to say, I love you,

Tom x"

This letter annoys the hell out of me for some reason, I want to scream and kick something. I consider his motivation for sending this and know in my heart that it is an attempt to do what he says he is not meaning to do and get me to go running to him now he is single. I immediately think that that is the last thing I want to do. At least Rob isn't a liar and a cheat, a manipulator. At least I don't think he is. I am now also wondering who told Greg where I lived and when did those two have cause to chat? I am feeling so mad and why tell me her name now? Every Christine I meet I will wonder if she is his ex whom I callously betrayed. I stuff the letter away to show my friends and Larissa.

I put on some Beethoven and try and nap, I have some planning to do for Paris, but I need to clear my mind from Tom. It's a struggle and when I do doze, I have a confusing dream where I am with Tom and Rob is trying to get me off him.

Chapter 9

Seven hundred and four steps to the second floor of the Eiffel Tower, I wonder why we didn't get the lift to the third. Rob is red in the face and is perhaps thinking the same. I think we have about twenty more steps to go, the end is in sight. At the top of the staircase we can look out at the view and it is worth the climb. Rob holds me from behind and then wants to take pictures with his camera that seems to have lots of different lenses. I have a point and shoot basic camera and am a bit embarrassed but take some pics too. The view is spectacular and I can make out some more Parisian landmarks. I notice an elderly couple that remind me of Margie and Graeme in Bridport, they turn round and I am now pretty sure it is them

"Hey" I say "do you remember me, in the summer in Cha Cha's pub?"

They look at me and both smile and ask how I am. They are having their golden wedding anniversary in Paris and re-visiting some old haunts of theirs. They recommend we go to the Musee D''Orsay and see the Monet's and Renoir's. Rob is uncharacteristically engaging and they coo over him telling me he's lovely and telling him that he is lucky to have me.

They ask us to accompany them to lunch and then stroll along the river, it is a crisp afternoon and the reflection of the sun glinting on the water invites you to linger. We have a most enjoyable time with them, Margie is just full of good cheer and Graeme has a dry wit that has us in stitches. Their chemistry and banter is undeniable; we discover that Margie used to be a singer in a six piece group and had a glamorous time going from various venues around the country. She met Graeme at a gig they did for the Army and he hotly pursued her afterwards, showering her with gifts, turning up at her concerts and sending her love letters. Margie largely ignored him, telling herself he was only after one thing and couldn't possibly be interested in her a lowly showgirl and him so esteemed. Graeme was a senior officer and even got a group of his soldiers to escort her home from a local gig, each holding a red rose for her to take from them at her door. After that she wrote to Graeme and told him she would go out with him if he stopped all the attention seeking behaviours. They went on their first date to Paris, she loved the romance of it all and he told her he was bewitched by her and wanted her as his girlfriend. They never looked back after that. Dated for a year, wed and have been happy together always. No children but content in their love for each other. Rob tells me after they have gone that they remind him of his own grandparents that adored each other until the day they died. They died within a week of each other, first his grandmother and then his grandfather of a broken heart.

We decided as the day was so lovely to buy our lunch and we had a picnic of bread and cheese washed down with some wine by the Notre Dame Cathedral. Graeme pretends to be a hunchback ringing a large bell; Margie hits him playfully. The pretty garden is full of gorgeous flowers and statues. We take lots of photos and talk about art, poetry and museums; there are people with artists easels and rainbow colour palettes of oils and acrylics; capturing the history, beauty and ardour of the place. Some are set up to paint tourists to sell to them for several Francs and Rob wants me to pose for one. I decline and he buys me a little print of the cathedral I like instead; it is on a canvas of five by five inches square and captures the majesty of the building, the ethereal atmosphere and the lushness of the gardens. It is a perfect gift. He holds my hand as we walk along the river and we stroll slowly with Margie and Graeme chattering about so many different topics. I am really impressed by how well Rob gets on with them and they make us promise to keep in touch.

We arrived in a soggy Paris last night and our hotel room was small but lovely; so far we have been getting on well and the sharing of a bed for the first time was surprisingly 'nice'. When we return after our sightseeing Rob pulls out a bottle of bubby and chocolates for us to share. We are giggling over something and his eyes meet mine,

"I think I am falling for you."

He says and I blush but don't tell him it's mutual. Instead I lean in for him to kiss me. And he strokes my hair as he lightly kisses me without sound and without tongue. I just start to feel a zinging in my stomach when he pulls away and says,

"I've booked us a table for dinner downstairs, we have ten minutes, did you want to change? You don't have to, you look lovely, but I thought you may want to."

I of course now run off to the bathroom to freshen up and change into a dress.

"Oh bugger! I need to find my necklace; can you rummage in that green bag of mine and see if it is in there? It is a string of fake rubies, just some red cut glass really."

I ask Rob to help me. He appears with my necklace in his hand and he reminds me I have one minute.

As we enter the restaurant, I feel eyes turn towards us, but I am admiring the décor and furnishings, I feel like I have entered the 1920s, it is so decadent and exorbitant. I completely love it; Rob watches me drink it all in and smiles at me. He nudges the menu over to me to look at and I snap out of my trance. We order some traditional French cuisine although avoid des escargot. The experience seems a bit lost on Rob but he is charming and although chats about work stuff I am enjoying it all. He comments on the piano player as being a bit lounge music and safe and I just wish I could play an instrument.

I love it, the whole atmosphere of the 20's and the piano music playing in the background of idle chatter was sublime. Rob also doesn't like his food and is grumbling, but he doesn't make a scene which I am grateful for. I never like to see people abusing waiting staff over their meals not being quite how they wanted it. I have done my fair share of being a waitress in the past, so I am always very polite and kind to them.

Rob asks me about whether I want to have children and what my dream house would look like. The subjects are making me feel uncomfortable.

"I would like at least four children" he says, "I don't mind what gender they are, but would be good to have four of them. you have a big family, I don't have any siblings, its lonely sometimes. I envy you. Do you want a big family, lots of children Tovu?"

My reply is not completely honest,

"Oh yes of course I love children, I want at least five."

In truth, I would love to have lots of children, but I don't know that I will be a good parent, I can barely keep myself safe and organised. Rob is stroking my hand on the table; he is pleased with my response because he squeezes it tightly.

"And what about your dream house? I want to live by the sea with no-one else around for miles."

I decide that I needed to be really truthful about this one in case he brought somewhere remote and then held me captive there for the rest of my life with just four ragamuffin children I'd have to keep secret and home school.

"I love the sea of course, but I need to be near people. I just find people fascinating and I like the convenience of being near the town, the amenities. I wouldn't want to be isolated from my family or isolate my children".

Rob sees my point and says,

"I guess there are places you can have the best of both worlds."

I joke with him saying that he has been enchanted with Margie and Graeme's story and maybe we had better see how the rest of the weekend goes before talking about these things. He laughs and fortunately changes the subject.

The piano player is now playing a jazzy little number and a few couples are now dancing around him; I would love to join them, but Rob is not a dancer. He does to my relief stop chatting and watch the others whirling around in beautiful synchronicity with me. Who wouldn't fall in love with Paris and maybe the person they are with because of it? I don't think I want to leave this bubble I feel I am in.

An elderly man who holds himself very dignified stops in front of me and holds out his hand to me to dance with him, tells me his name is Jean. I glance at Rob and he smiles and nods. I get up and hope I don't make a fool of myself, I smooth down my skirt and he takes my right hand in his and rests his other hand in the small of my back. I am rotated round and round, first one way and then the next and I manage to stay on my feet. I'm quite breathless when Jean lets me stop and returns me to my seat. The music changes down to a slow tempo and the dancers pull each other closer and nestle into each others necks. Jean places my hand in Robs and tries to pull him up to dance together. Rob gets up and takes me back to the dance floor. We dance as though in a trance.

Yes, the romance continues and it really has been a most perfect day and evening. I certainly feel warmer and closer to Rob and he is giving me puppy eyes a lot this evening; it might be the amount of wine we've drunk. In fact, where previously slightly distant he is now rather intense in his manner and can't stop touching me. When we get to our room he kisses me more fervently than before and his hands are stroking, grabbing, squeezing and caressing me in equal amounts. I am quite turned on and I reciprocate; we get out of our clothes and get into bed to carry on and he gets on top of me. He pushes into me without any foreplay and within five strokes he has come. He rolls off me and kisses my cheek,

"I love you."

He says, rolls over with his back to me and falls asleep.

Great!

6 a.m., I have slept badly. I manage to sneak out of bed, dress in my jeans and a tee shirt and grab my bag. I have decided to take a little walk as it would help clear my head and I reflect on last night. I find there are not too many people about, and I decide I will just walk a circuit so I don't get lost. I hadn't accounted for the morning being as cool as it was, and I ponder going back for my coat but don't want to wake Rob. I hug myself, arms crossed over each other and stroll down the street looking across the road at the buildings which tower ahead, and the architecture is fascinating. So absorbed in this and I crash into a lamp-post. I hit it hard with my elbow and stand there holding it trying not to cry and trying not to curse. A hand rests on my shoulder and a male voice asks me,

"Est-ce que ça va? Puis-je vous aider?"

I nod that I am fine as I am guessing they are asking if I am okay. I turn to look at the stranger and am looking at a gorgeous man dressed immaculately and sporting a briefcase and umbrella. I almost think he could be a French Avenger. He realises I am okay and goes on his way without looking back at me. I watch his back, his poise and confident air. I decide that maybe I am not that attractive and should be grateful Rob is going out with me.

I get back to the hotel and see that Rob is in the shower when I enter our room. On the bed he's laid out his clothes for the day and seems to have half packed his case for the trip home. I notice some pink, lacy fabric in his case. Just peeking out from under a pile of shirts. I am nosy so I have a peek by lifting the pile gently. It is as I suspect a thong. I put the shirts back down in a way that hides the thong better. I get my case and am busy packing and sorting it when Rob gets out of the en-suite.

"Hello, are you okay. Where did you get to? I was getting ready and then sending out a search party"; he says to me.

I explain I couldn't sleep and had a little walk and managed to walk into a lamp-post hurting my elbow. He wants to see if I have damaged it and inspects it. I am thinking about whether he likes wearing lady's thongs or was going to give me a pair as a gift and then thought better of it. Either way it is weird. He is attentive and sweet all morning, getting my breakfast in the buffet downstairs, taking my case as well as his own, buying me an English magazine and some sweets for the trip home. In return I keep a steady stream of conversation going. Nothing too deep or contentious. All good humoured and light.

The trip back is pretty uneventful, no disasters and we are comfortable enough with each other to have an easy silence fall between us at times. Rob drops me home and kisses me goodbye, he says as I get out of the car,

"Thank you Tovu, I loved every second of being with you and I will remember this trip always. Can I see you Wednesday as usual? I was thinking maybe we could just chill out at yours, I will bring a take away with me, what do you think?"

I agree and he leaves. I am so relieved to be home, the weekend away was amazing. I loved Paris, Rob was great most of the time but I was shattered. I lie down on my bed with my case in the lounge sat unpacked, and close my eyes. I hope that I get no interruptions this evening as I just want to veg. Although, I have much to catch up on. I am reminded there was some post when I got in that I had shoved on the side. I go and retrieve it. There is another letter from Tom, I recognise his handwriting now. I am in half a mind to rip it up but I am too curious and read it:

"Darling Tovu,

You didn't reply to me and I know I wasn't expecting you to but anyway I had to write to you again because I wanted to be the first to tell you that our acute care project has won a prize in the National Best Practice Awards. You will get a proper invite but I wanted to let you know. The awards are on the November 23rd in London, you will just have to attend!

I hope you had a great time in Paris and know that I am still devoted.
I love you,
Tom x"

This letter riles me less than the previous one because it does bring good news. Then I think about the fact I will see him at the awards and that he seems to know my every movement. How did he know about Paris? I am mystified. Then I think about his opening words and I am livid; how dare he expect anything off me. Well now I have two letter to discuss with Mary, Belle and Larissa. We need an urgent pow wow, so I am glad we have arranged to meet up at The Tap tomorrow night. The letter has jolted me into action and I get sorted, unpack and put some Bee Gees on so I can dance around the flat.

"I know your eyes in the morning sun
I feel you touch me in the pouring rain
And the moment that you wander far from me
I want to feel you in my arms again
And you come to me on a summer breeze
Keep me warm in your love, then you softly leave
And it's me you need to show
How deep is your love, how deep is your love
How deep is your love?
I really mean to learn
"Cause we"re living in a world of fools
Breaking us down when they all should let us be
We belong to you and me....."

I wonder which of the men in my life would ever sing this to me and mean it; I fear none of them. Tom is unfaithful, untrustworthy and his timing is completely off. Rob is lovely, but there is something wrong, something missing. I do completely concur that we live in a world of fools and I wonder if I am one of the biggest ones. Am I being stupid about Rob, maybe that something will appear over time, but deep down I know I want the connection that me and Tom have. The passion and the fire, however dangerous it may be. I also think about Dan, I have shoved it to the recesses of my brain, the deceit of the man. I also wonder about that pink thong. Why are men not more straightforward, they are supposed to be. The whole Men are from Mars thing is a falsehood when it comes to the men in my life. Only my brother Evan seems to be a decent man and golly does he suffer because of it. I decide to spurn all men and resolve to let Rob know that it's not going to work between us. I am determined that no matter the possible prestige of going to the awards I was no way going. Later in bed, I realise that as always, I will probably renege on these decisions.

Chapter 10

"We're are over here!" Belle is yelling at me, even though The Tap isn't very busy and I can see them clearly. I smile and ask them if anyone needs a drink on my way to the bar, "we have a bottle to share and you can get the next one." Larissa is grinning at me holding up aforementioned bottle. There is a little bit left for me, they are so kind. I sit down and am immediately asked about Paris. I tell them how much I loved the place, about spending time with Margie and Graeme and my reservations about Rob. They come up with a few more options as to why Rob had a pink, lacy thong in his case. This includes, he brought it as gift for his mum when I wasn't looking and it's his lucky thong, he doesn't wear it just needs it nearby. Of course we giggle and then I tell them I need their advice; I have their attention. I bring out the letters from Tom and let them read them one after the other.

"Wow! Tovu, what is going on you little man magnet", Larissa is first to speak and then Mary says, "He is so trying to play you Tovu, you know that right?"

"Both letters made me so angry, I want to rip them into shreds but needed you lot to tell me what you think. Should I go to the awards night? Should I tell Rob about the letters? Am I better off without both of them? Help!!"

Larissa is protective and says I should just ditch both of them once and for all and leave space for the proper Mr Right comes along.

"Tovu, they are not worthy of you and they both have something seriously afoot. Mr T the Player and Rob the pink knicker man can both go hang!"

Mary thinks this may be rash,

"Well I think they both adore you Tove and why wouldn't they. You need to give the both a chance to see if they are what you want and anyway, have some fun with them and see where it goes. Ultimately, they both fancy you and want your company at times".

"It's the 'at times' bit that alarms me a bit, surely Mr Right wants to be with you all the time, wants to share everything with you?" I say.

Mary laughs,

"And then you would be saying they are too needy and too clingy, I know you!"

I shrug,

"Yes but there is surely some position in between distant and suffocating that is what love is about? I observed Margie and Graeme for instance and can see that although they love each other's company they are their own person and not just one being. It's like Kahil Gibran says about love;

"..stand together, yet not too near together: For the pillars of the temple stand apart, And the oak tree and the cypress grow not in each other's shadow." I just don't feel either would stand together with me for the hard times".

Belle chips in,

"I love that Tovu, I think though that perhaps you need to give them both the chance to see whether the soil beneath your feet is compatible with theirs and vice versa. Why don't you give Rob a chance and ask him about lady's knickers? I am less inclined to trust Tom, but he says he is single now and of all people he is making a beeline for you. What harm would it be to see him at the awards and see how the land lies. You certainly seem to have the 'spark' between you."

Of course, we have a good old debate and in the end we agree I had better have more wine and as I have now heard the views of my esteemed peers; I need to make the decisions myself.

"Great! Thank you my dearest friends and sister!" I say softly sarcastically.

I want to catch up with them and find out how things are going with their relationships; two glasses of wine later, I wonder whether I should have taken notes because I am rather confused. Here goes! Larissa has been sleeping with Raj her lodger, Raj keeps going back to see his wife and children and tries to keep the peace. Larissa worries he will eventually go back to his wife and kids but admires the fact he hasn't walked totally out of his kid's life. He apparently caught his wife half naked in their bedroom with his cousin Bhanu, who was kissing her while caressing her breasts. She keeps telling him it was a one off, they are not in any sort of relationship and were just experimenting because they got talking about a lesbian couple they mutually know. Raj does not believe her because he suspected there was someone else on her mind before he caught her. His cousin refuses to talk to him and is scared he will tell her parents. He is kind to Larissa but he is falling behind with rent and she now suspects she may be being used. We tend to agree. Mary is still single and not in contact with Bob anymore. She is focussing on her career and trying to meet her targets consistently to get chosen to do the next level of training and promotion. Her boss is making promising noises and she let slip that the new mortgage adviser in her office is a black man who plays rugby. Larissa and I gasp and ask her whether he came from Hartlepool. She laughs and says no he's called Giles and he is the one who was nice her when she had the awful boss in her previous job. We try an see if Giles has a thing for Mary but she quickly dismisses it.

Belle has been quite quiet throughout the conversations of the last half hour, she seems pre-occupied which is unlike her. I touch her arm,

"Are you okay honey bun?"

She smiles and gives herself a little shake,

"Oh gosh yes, sorry. I was just thinking about work tomorrow".

We look at her puzzled, Belle is a dental hygienist, she knows she is always going to have a list of customers wanting her to clean, polish and scrape at their teeth. It isn't a particularly varied job and one we admire her for but tease her that she must have a sadistic streak. She looks at us a bit blankly, swears us to complete secrecy and then tells us about the weirdest situation. There are three dentists in the practice and two hygienists and two receptionists. All of them are women except for the Lead Partner, Max Schwartz who founded the partnership five years ago and built it up using his inheritance from his parents who died in a plane crash. Max seems to be asexual and has never tried it on with any of the staff team although seems to have employed a very attractive female team around him, who he treats kindly, respectfully and generously with extra bonuses all year round. He is generally quite private and seems to live to work and yet is sociable with his clients and they say he is the best dentist in the locality. Always considerate and respectful, always helpful and apparently so obliging that he is big trouble. One of his colleagues had to cover for him last week and this never happens because Max is never off work, never ill. Last week he was returning from the shops with his arms laden with bags when a cyclist crashed into him, neither he or the rider saw each other, collided and Max has managed to break his right leg as it took the impact of the crash. He was taken to hospital and they kept him in as he developed a temperature and suspected infection.

The colleague who covered for him was shocked to find out how much his clients asked for pain relief, mostly gas and air for procedures that didn't even hurt. One client clearly had a mental illness and asked for the rest of his teeth to be extracted as they were rotting in his mouth and causing poison to seep into the rest of his body. The fact that seven of his healthy teeth had been removed without need, was of grave concern. Max is now of course being investigated for gross misconduct. The whole team have been rocked by this and had no idea. Belle feels very concerned for him as she visited him at his home to check he was okay and has never seen him so depressed and thin. The rest of the team also feel devastated by the revelations and investigation because they also have to be investigated in case the whole practice had been operating unprofessionally. Their clients have been cancelling left, right and centre and Belle is not looking forward to seeing everyone tomorrow and her sunny disposition is challenged.

The last orders bell rings and they are reluctant to leave but get into taxis and Larissa decides to stay at my place again. I of course let her, although resolve to not let her talk me into visiting the family again. It's far too soon. This doesn't seem to be on Larissa's mind thankfully. She wants to continue to unpick our respective relationships with men we probably shouldn't be having relationships with. The taxi drops us at the Annexe and I see a piece of paper on the floor when I open the kitchen door. I place it on the side and we get our shoes and coats off and I make us a cuppa. As I am waiting for the kettle to boil, I pick up the piece of paper and read,

'Tovu, please call your mum urgently, come to the house, anytime and use the phone. Janice x x'

It's late, I am sent into panic and shove the note under Larissa's nose.

"Go see if there's a light on next door"

She says. I can see the hall and lounge light are on, so we both run over to the house and knock on the door. Janice lets us in,

"I stayed up for you, I thought you would be home about now. Your mum rang and basically asked me to tell you to ring urgently. Just use the phone over there"

She pointed to the side table. Larissa picks up the phone and dials,

"Hello mother, its Larissa, I'm with Tovu and we have been asked to ring you urgently."

"Oh Larissa, your father's died. He just keeled over in the pub and they rushed him to hospital but then he never made it. They say his heart just stopped."

I can hear what our mother says and tears prick my eyes. Larissa is crying,

"Do you want us to come home mother?"

"No, no, just wanted to let you know. The boys are coming over tomorrow to help me and then arrange the cremation and everything so I..... I...."

Her voice trails off and she is crying. Our mother never cries!

"We'll come tomorrow evening and check on you"

I say and then we say goodnight.

Janice offers to get us a drink, we decline her kind offer and trudge back to the annexe both trying not to cry for the sake of the other because we both know that once one starts the other will follow. I pour us an emergency Baileys and Larissa says,

"I don't know why I am so sad, he was not much of a father to us lately. Always grumpy and often absent."

"I know, but he's our father and he could be so funny and clever. He taught us our strong work ethic and our sense of honour and drive; yet he also taught us not to trust and to be sceptical or everything and everyone. I know there was some bad stuff Rissa but let's just remember the good things tonight."

"Come here Tove, let's snuggle. I agree. Remember the time we played hide and seek with him and climbed up high in the apple trees and he had no idea where we were and was stood shouting and swearing right underneath us?"

I snuggle in,

"And the time he went streaking down the road for a dare and the neighbours complained?" We giggle and because we know it's probably a bit inappropriate both burst into tears and eventually fall into an alcohol and grief infused sleep on my bed.

In the morning we both cancel work; we know we cannot concentrate and we are both emotional. We need to be with our family, whether mother likes it or not; we head over to our parent's house. It strikes us both, that now it will just be 'mother's house'. We get there and see Evan and Landon's cars in the drive. Our brothers are sat with mother in the lounge, the door is left unlatched, so we have just walked in and announced loudly we have arrived. Landon calls out where they are. Mother gets up and says she will make us a coffee; we go to protest but Evan gestures to say 'let her do it'.

When she leaves the room we sit with Landon on the big, floral sofa and he says,

"Can you go up and see Faye after your coffee? She's refusing to come out of her room this morning. It's hit her hard."

We of course agree and ask them both how they are and how mother has been.

"Evan's more cut up about it than me, you know father and me didn't see eye to eye on my "lifestyle" and Evan being the oldest feels he has to sort everything now and has to be the strong one, don't you bro"?

"He's already organising the cremation arrangements, apparently all father's old cronies want to do some sort of eulogy for him together."

Evan does a half smile and nods.

"Well Landon here is going to sort out the wake aren't you with your business contacts and innate charm, he's going to get us a special offer. I suspect he'll flutter his eyelashes at a few of the saleswoman and we'll be "quids in. Isn't that right?""

Our brothers love each other and love ribbing each other. They are chalk and cheese and share a black sense of humour with their sisters, who they pretend not to understand. We try not to laugh because mother walks back in with a tray of drinks.

We find out that the cremation date can't be set until the coroner has issued the death certificate, that it is likely father had a massive coronary and also cirrhosis of the liver. His GP divulged this to mother, not knowing she had no idea about the liver issue. Larissa and I go up to Faye's room and knock on her door saying our usual,

"Little pig, little pig, let me come in…"

Faye opens up, her hair bedraggled, dark circles under her eyes, which don't detract from her beauty. Even in grief she is stunning, and her green eyes still shine bright, lifting her face to angelic proportions. She sobs and between breaths she says,

"I can't believe it, one minute he's there the next he's gone. Why my daddy? He was too young, it shouldn't have been his time."

We cuddle and comfort, stroke her hair, make cooing 'there, there' noises and let her cry. We tell her about the things we remember about our father before she was born, and she shares her fondest memories of him. As the youngest child she was mostly protected from his tempers and he favoured her so much that he was rarely cross with her. Faye eventually stops crying and wipes her tears from her face,

"I don't understand why mum isn't a wreck."

She says and looks at us openly expecting answers. Larissa provides it,

"Well mother is very private and probably cries in her sleep but not in public, not even in front of her beloved Faye."

We both secretly suspect that mother is somewhat relieved now he has gone, his bullying tyranny thwarted by his heart packing up.

"Come on, you must be hungry"

I say to them both,

"Let's join the others and get some food."

Of course, there is no food in the kitchen, mother had neglected to get anything in so I nip out and get some fish and chips from the shop on the street corner. The owner there knows my parents well as they had a regular order every Friday. He asks after my mother and wonders how she is coping. He tells me that my father will be sorely missed and what a character he was. I nod and smile and look forward to being able to exit the place. He says he will throw in some extra pickled eggs and pickled onions. The smell still makes me feel so nauseous. I try not to breath too much so I can't smell too much. I wish I had bought one of my siblings with me to help, but as usual I had volunteered and said I would manage perfectly fine on my own. I hadn't thought it through, six portions of battered cod and six portions of chips was heavy enough without extras we probably didn't want. I struggle with the bags but it's not far and the portions seem to have reduced over the years.

We all realise how starving we are at the aroma of vinegar and deep-fried cod and eat practically in silence. Faye is a slow eater, as is mother; the rest of us eat like the food is going to be stolen from under our noses if we don't consume it immediately. We decide amongst us that Landon will stay at the house with Faye and mother. Larissa and I will come over at the weekend and he can have a break. Evan will do all the sorting and arrange the cremation, deal with the solicitor / bank, invite guests to the sermon, wake, etc. Mother is quiet throughout the conversations and looks bleakly into the bottom of her tea cup. She suddenly says,

"You know the silly old fool wanted to go up I a firework don't you? He saw it on the TV and told me he wanted some of his ashes shot over the football ground."

Landon chuckles,

"Excellent, I can see what we can do!".

I can see his brain whirring in his skull, he loves a challenge like this and it appeals to his twisted sense of humour that some of his father's will be jettisoned via rocket over Oxford City Football Club grounds. How he will get around the FC and council regulations on this will be interesting.

Chapter 11

Work was very supportive, and I managed to do very little last week. The day of the cremation arrives, and we have all congregated at mother's; she looks suitably miserable and anxious. Faye looks stunning in a black dress that is the epitome of style and the rest of us are ordinary standing beside her in our boring cremation clothes. I feel a little disappointed because I had taken ages choosing my black dress and I had made a real effort to wear a hat too. Larissa catches my expression,

"You look adorable as always Tovu, stop comparing yourself with our incredibly beautiful sister."

I nod gratefully.

Evan organised three cremation cars to collect us all in, they pull up like a trio of beetles seeking something they are unsure of and realise they need to stop and decide what it is. We clamber in and fill them with their purpose, to take us to the crematorium. It is a surprisingly sunny day although crisp and cold, a cold that gets into your bones if you let it. There are about hundred people at the service, half of them relatives, a few of father's ex work colleagues and a large number of his drinking cronies and friends of the family. Mary and Belle have come too as they have been my friends a long time and met father at some occasions. Mostly they are there to support me, for which I am grateful. I know I am going to need it, especially after I have read out the eulogy I have written. I am worrying already it isn't gushing enough, but I can't lie. I hope I have captured his good points and skimmed truly over his worse. I was chosen by my immediate family to compose and speak on behalf of them all; why me? I of course agreed. Now I am panicking and can hear my heart trying to beat out of my chest. I am as ever, sweaty! Fortunately I don't feel windy but that could change at any moment.

As we enter the sterile, cool room I notice Freya and she is with a swarthy and exotic man who seems to be paying her a lot of attention, I am pleased for her and nod hello as I pass. She gives me a small smile and then turns her face to look into the eyes of her new man. Joshua and Lucas were running around the grounds like the tearaways they are, but as they enter the room they seem to sense the gravity of the occasion and seem subdued, they grip Jan's hands and sit quietly. They sit near to Bertie, one of father's drinking friends. Jan knows him from work as he used to work for the same council as her and they chat in hushed voices. The room buzzes quietly and then the music gets louder and our attention is brought to the entrance of the room which is now filled with coffin and pall bearers. Evan and Landon lead the way and two of our uncles (his brothers) and two of father's best friends assist them as they carry my father to the front and lay him on the conveyer-belt that takes him to the furnace to be cremated. The tears come silently, and many people are dabbing at their eyes. Mother is staring straight ahead, trying not to show how she feels but I know is close to tears. The music played as he goes off is The Ride of The Valkyries by Wagner, one of father's favourites and not at all sentimental but quite uplifting.

The service is a blur until I am invited to get up and read out my eulogy; I am so nervous but remind myself that no-one here will be judging me, just awaiting a tribute to the man who was George Jenkins. I face the audience or is it a congregation? Or just a gathering?

"George Jenkins was my father, he was also dad to Evan, Landon, Larissa and Faye. He was my mother's husband, Lucas and Joshua's grandfather, a work colleague when he was in the army and a friend to many. He was born in Lancashire, son to Hubert a miner and Molly a seamstress and was their middle son of three. Uncle Archie and Uncle Sid who honour him today and will deeply miss him. George was the life and soul of the party and as an ex-soldier could down his drink like no-one else. He exuded charm and eccentricity, and this made him popular with everyone. When he retired you would often find him in the company of his friends who play golf, snooker and darts. At home he was always the father who fooled around but also the disciplinarian. He used to chase us and pretend not to find us and then fake a rant about how terrible as little human beings we were, knowing we knew he knew we knew. Father was careful with his money; I know his friends teased him about getting rounds in at the pub; at home we teased him to get him to spend money on our latest hobby and holidays. He would always make a big thing of it, stating we were greedy, and that money didn't grow on trees but eventually he would renege and indulge us. We know that Christmas Eve is upon us and it was always father's favourite day of the year. He was such a music lover and enjoyed Midnight Mass immensely, it will forever be family tradition to attend and light a candle for loved ones missed; and now I will light an additional one just for him. I will always remember one Christmas Eve when he bought us sparklers and Christmas Hats to wear on the walk home from the church and his hat had a festive axe with the words, 'my chopper's a whopper' written on it. We did have to persuade him not to wear it in the church."

I pause to check that no-one is frowning at this tale and see that people are smiling and I have their attention. A few youngsters are giggling. I carry on.

"My father was also someone who did things wholeheartedly, he didn't like a short cut or doing things impulsively. Maybe it was from his military training, but everything had to be planned. Maybe to the extent that his offspring are mostly chaotic and take short cuts and do things half-heartedly, because father was always there to put it right and organise and get things done. How will we manage now he is gone from us? Above all else, we will miss his ability to talk to anyone and everyone. He would stop a stranger in the street and ask them what their star sign was and ask to see their palm to read them their fortune. He would always have something to say and was a nightmare passenger in your car because he never stopped talking and telling you when the next bend was coming up or the next traffic lights about to appear. I used to switch off a bit, but you know what, his rabbiting was comforting. I recall the times he looked you straight in the eye and said "well done" with a twinkle ; they were like being showered in diamonds. The times he sang along to one of his operas he so loved and played the one tune he had learnt by rote despite not being able to read, or want to read a single note on a sheet of music; it was utterly awesome. However, the one amazing thing we all, and many others, remember him for because it was in the news on TV and radio; was as the man who saved the lives of ten children who were out on a trip in a mini bus and a car swerved in front of the bus, cutting in too early back into the first lane, causing it to crash into the hard shoulder. Father was driving just behind them, braked and stopped on the hard shoulder and managed to pull out all the children and their teachers to a piece of land away from the mini bus out of harms way when it exploded into flames. He was praised by the emergency services when they arrived because his actions were so quick and brave. A hero who thought it was just the right thing to do, he taught us so many good virtues and we will forever remember him with love and gratitude. Life without our father will be as lonely and tragic as one of his favoured operas."

As I finish, they play "The Flower Duet" from Lakmé an opera which ends with the heroine poisoning herself and I see my mother weeping, in fact there's not a dry eye in the house. The service continues for a further ten minutes, ending in them playing more Wagner, this time a section of "Tristan and Isolde", as we walk out to receive condolences from the attendees. One by one people shake my hand and say kind words about my eulogy and my father and drift away to look at the tributary flowers lined up and clamber into their cars to take them to the wake venue.

Being as dilatory as ever, I hadn't fully realised where the wake was being held. I had been told it was fairly local, the cars would take us and pick us up at the end of the evening, so I didn't need to ask where it was. Imagine my dismay as we pulled up the driveway to the venue of Uncle Sid's 60th. I told myself it was fine; Dan wasn't there and I didn't have to go outside except at the entrance where you couldn't see "that tree". Nevertheless, I couldn't stop my palpitations as we drew nearer and nearer and the flashbacks made me shaky. Larissa, similarly hadn't realised where the wake was being held and noticing my shakiness, held my hand. To anyone else observing they would have just thought I was upset by my father's death. Larissa whispered in my ear,

"Tove, don't worry; between Mary, Belle and me we will not let you out of our sight."

I lean into her and squeeze her hand gently,

"Thank you, Larissa it still seems so recent still".

I am not sure how I get through the next three hours of people wanting to make chit chat, but after they had eaten and started to leave, my siblings and closest friends gravitated towards each other and me. We sat in a corner with mother at Evan and Landon's sides, we made bad jokes about the potatoes being slightly burnt and remembered more stories about our father. Mother asked to be taken home and Uncle Sid kindly offered as he was tired and leaving with his wife. Faye turns to me when mother has left;

"Are you okay? You are very pale, what were you and Larissa whispering about in the car?"

I don't want to tell my innocent sister and if I tell my brothers, Dan may well gain a face full of cuts and bruises and they would be in trouble.

"I'm okay thanks, just been an emotional day. Did you see what Mrs Halberry was wearing? It looked like she was going to the theatre not a cremation."

I divert the attention to Mrs Halberry who was at the cremation but not the wake. She had worn a scarlet shawl over a sparkly green dress and her red shoes had sequins on them so she positively twinkled. Mrs Halberry was one of our father's darts partners; she had an aim as good as Robin Hood. My siblings take great delight in then wondering whether he might have had a fling with her. This is much to Faye's horror and we tease her rotten about the possibility that her precious dad was a rogue with the ladies. The truth is, he possibly did have affairs when he was younger, and we recall a strange lady friend of his who came to stay with us a few times and then disappeared off the scene. After her, we can't remember a time anyone was allowed to have anyone else stay over at our house.

"Tove, why isn't Rob here with you?"

Landon asks. I was hoping no-one would ask me; I had basically told Rob too late to get time off work which was sort of deliberate. I didn't want him here and I didn't want to address the dilemma I felt about him.

"He had to work today, and where is Tia? Are you still seeing her?"

Ha ha, touché I think. Landon explains Tia is also immersed in work and their relationship remains fairly casual. I survive the re-visit to the place where I was sexually assaulted and hope that if there is a next time it won't feel so awful.

The following morning, we all take a walk together through the woods and decide we ought to try harder to see more of each other, especially Faye before she disappears off to university. Yes, she also has brains as well as beauty and wants to be a scientist. Evan suggests we have a holiday together in the spring, we all agree that this would be amazing. Mother doesn't come downstairs until 10 a.m. which is really late for her, she is usually up at 6 a.m. She looks completely neat and tidy in her usual uniform of blue slacks and plain short sleeved shirt; hair tied in a bun and her mule slippers.

"Good morning all, how did you sleep?"

She asks and then,

"Oh breakfast looks good."

She sits down and takes a slice of toast and reaches for the marmalade. Our mother is no longer sad and subdued looking but quite perky. She starts to ask about us all and our lives, work and partners and things planned. She also asks us what our plans are in terms of going home and back to our jobs. We are a little stunned but take the hint and say we can leave whenever she wants us to. We explain we were all thinking she would want some space but didn't want to abandon her if she needed us at all.

"I think I will be okay; I have Faye at home and she can always get a message to you if we need you."

We are all quite relived as we have bosses wanting us back at work and we miss our homes. Larissa and I hit the road at midday, and I drop her off at her place an hour later. When I get back to mine there is a vase of flowers in the kitchen with a note from Janice,

"Hope you don't mind, thought these needed water. Love J."

The accompanying card says, 'Condolences Tovu, love and hugs always T x.'

I thought they were going to be from Rob. There is a card from Rob, it is a small card bordered in gold and background beige. It says, 'So Sorry for Your Loss' in gold on the front. Inside he has written, 'Sorry I could not be there, I hope it went okay. Rob xxx'

I can't help but compare them and sets me off worrying about what I should do all over again. I decide to go for a walk in the shops to divert me, after I have popped into work to let them know I will be back there tomorrow. There is another card, but this is a card that invites me to the National Best Practice Award Night.

I give Janice a hug and thank her for sorting my flowers, she is kind but not overly so and tells me that everyone will be happy to see me back and to be sure I am ready. Uma rushes up to me,

"Tovu, how was it?"

She hugs me tight and I reassure them both that I am fine. Vanessa then appears,

"Oh my darling! So good to see you. Are you okay? Come and see everyone, get it over with. You know, all the 'sorry for your loss' stuff? Then you can come back and get on with it tomorrow."

Vanessa is just what I need right now, and I get through seeing everyone and know she is right; tomorrow I can get back to work and focus on it. So an hour later I walk to the shops and seek out a new outfit for the award night. I feel it should be black but then I think of Mrs Halberry, I wonder if red, green and sequins might be a better colour combination. I scour the secondhand shops for inspiration and in the last one I find a size 14 black and emerald green knee length dress that is perfect. It is just too big, I decide I can alter it and buy it for two pounds, the dress could probably be enhanced with a few embellishments, so I hunt down something in the haberdashery. I am looking at the range of novelty buttons and sequins when a lady says to me,

"Excuse me love but are you Tovu?"

I confess that yes I am and she says,

"I thought so, my name is Charlotte, I'm Rob's mother. He showed me a picture of you when you went to Paris."

I am embarrassed and then consider why it was I hadn't met her before and what on earth was I supposed to say.

'Sorry, I didn't mean to embarrass you, I know what Rob is like, he doesn't bring his girlfriend's home until he's absolutely sure. I know it is early days for you two but he does talk about you a lot so that is a good sign."

I ask her if she would like a coffee or something in the café, as it seems the right thing to do. Thankfully she declines and says she will tell Rob she bumped into me and she leaves the shop. I decide on a few embellishments for my dress and pay £8 for them. My little shopping trip helped initially but having met Rob's mother I feet even more confused about whether to give Rob more time to grow on me or to finish it now. Then I think about my father and my mother and their past relationship and know that truly I had to finish with him and the sooner the better.

I phone Rob at teatime and thank him for his card; before I can tell him we should stop seeing each other he says,

"Mum said she bumped into you today. It makes it a bit awkward, but I don't think we should see each other anymore. I was thinking about it and much as you are a gorgeous girl, I don't think we quite click together. I'm sorry Tovu."

I tell him that I understand and that I was thinking the same. When I go back to my annexe after the call, I should have felt relief and thanks to him but instead feel a bit aggrieved that I didn't get to dump him first. I spend time wondering what I did that turned him against me and what he didn't like about me. I reflect on how we were in Paris and try and see if I had done anything wrong there or whether I had really offended him about not telling him about my father's death and cremation immediately. Maybe he didn't really fancy me and took pity on this PE Knicker Flashing fool. I wish my friends were here to talk it over with. I start to cry, feeling sorry for myself. I have an early night and know that tomorrow things will look more positive.

Chapter 12

I have been back at work for a week since my father's cremation, it has been so busy and has completely distracted me from thinking about anything but work. I have been asked to start a new group for Assertiveness Skills and have taken on two new 1-1s. Vanessa and the team have been amazing, so supportive and treated me just the same and not like some fragile doll you had to manage with kid gloves. It's a fun music session this morning and I grab a tambourine to shake and organise the group with different instruments. Music Group is always fun, and the patients love it. We play along to requested songs and so long as it is in our collection of records and cassettes we can oblige. Our collection ranges from 50s to current 80s chart music, with the occasional golden oldie. Today they seem to want to play along to a lot of Queen and The Beatles songs.

The group cheers me up and I have the na,na,na,na,na,na's of Hey Jude looping in my head. Dr Ade has asked to see me today; I wonder what that is about so I go and knock on his door having checked with Janice he didn't have a patient in with him. He says in a drawl,

"Come in,"

And then beams when I walk in at me.

"Hello Tovu, how are you?"

"I'm fine thank you. How are you?"

He waves his hand to the chair next to his and tells me to have a seat. I sit down feeling a little nervous and curious as to what this is about. "I heard about your father that is very sad for you. Did you know both my parents were murdered? I lived in Lagos and they were the principality, King and Queen; they were assassinated, shot whilst they were sleeping in their beds. They didn't shoot me or my brother but a few of the servants died trying to protect them. Luckily, we were in quarters far away from my parents. I just wanted you to know that I know what it is like to lose a parent and I am always here to support and be there for you if you needed to talk to someone. Grief is a complicated thing and it can come to you in waves, it can crash to the floor and consume you."

He is looking at me intently as he is saying this; I can feel myself blushing.

"Um thank you Ade that is very kind. I am lucky I have a large family and so many friends to support me but I really appreciate your kindness. I am so sorry about your parents, how old were you when they died?"

Ade replies to me,

"I was only 6 years old, barely knew my parents as we had nannies and they were very busy. I had great nannies who provided for us well and tutors that taught us anything we wanted to learn. Thank you Tovu. Now just let me know if you need a shoulder to cry on any time."

I feel dismissed now, so I get up, thank him and leave the room.

That seemed a little odd as I don't know Ade very well, but a kind gesture. I go and grab a coffee before my next group. It's Anxiety Management, which is ironic as I battle with my worries every day! Today there are seven women and two men attending. The gender split is often misleading I think, I am sure proportionately more men suffer from anxiety too but just don't like to admit it. We are focussing on breathing exercises and the physiology of anxiety and how you can change how you

119

physically feel. I am pretty useless at breathing I decide, too shallow and often hold my breath without realising it. I join Debbie and Charlie with my coffee;

"I so love the Music Group, how were your sessions?" I ask.

"The Men's Group was quite tough, Jacob was really low and very negative, we couldn't lift the atmosphere for at least half an hour, we were gradually able to pick them all up."

Charlie said in a hushed voice.

"Nothing much to report from the Art Group" Debbie said, "Are you okay?"

I tell them about the group and also Dr Ade. They think his gesture is kind.

After lunch I have a one to one with Madelaine, a lady of twenty-five years old, who is desperate for a baby but not able to fall pregnant after two years of trying and she is getting more and more anxious. I had assessed her last week and this was our first session.

"How has your week been Madelaine" I open with.

"It has been okay, I guess. I keep having nightmares and waking up and not being able to get back to sleep. It's been so bad, Martyn has gone to sleep in the spare room so I don't disturb him."

Madeleine talks in a quiet voice, looking down at her feet,

"I don't know how he puts up with me. Do you think he has stopped loving me?"

"It sounds as though you are both feeling the pressure; does he tell you how he feels about things?"

I reply.

"He is so understanding, he says he just doesn't know what to do to help. He tries so hard, runs me nice baths, massages me to help me relax and helps around the house. He just needs his sleep or he cannot function."

"That sounds very positive then. Can you tell me a bit more about your nightmares and what you think they are about?"

"I dream that I am giving birth and there is just so much pain and then when I give birth and look, my baby is dead."

Madelaine is distraught at sharing this and starts to cry.

I let her cry some and then hand her some tissues whilst softly saying,

"Often we dream about our worst fears and it is not a premonition or a sign that what you dream is going to actually happen. Sometimes dreams tell us that a belief or worry we have held has died rather than a loved one dying. Sometimes, our dreams are processing feelings we have. How does the dream make you feel?"

"It's, it's because I had an abortion isn't it? I killed my own baby and now I am being punished!" Madelaine says this despairingly.

"What happened?" I ask gently.

"I was seventeen, I had a boyfriend from school, and we got drunk one night at his house and ended up having sex. I didn't take any precautions; he didn't have a condom. I did it with him one time and fell pregnant. I didn't tell him or my parents, just my best friend Sara who was two years older than me. She got me an appointment at a clinic for the abortion, she came with me, but they wouldn't let her in the room when they gave me drugs and I am not sure what they did. All I remember is the physical and emotional pain I felt. I was really weak, and Sara got worried about me, I had lost a fair bit of blood. She called my mum and mum came and got me. She wasn't furious but I could tell she was angry and upset. She smuggled me into my bedroom and said she would tell everyone not to disturb me as I had a virus and was highly contagious. She came in every two hours in the day to check I was okay, brought me food, drink, magazines, etc and didn't discuss the termination at all."

"Was the clinic not an NHS one?" I enquire.

"It was a back alley one, you know the ones you should avoid, but we didn't know we were young, and I was desperate. When I walked in, I wanted to run out and it was only my parents fury that made me go ahead with it."

"Can you tell me a bit about your parents?"

"Dad's a lawyer and mum's a midwife, can you imagine? They are both strict catholic and generally have been pretty strict parents. My brothers are twins, younger and can do no wrong. Jordan and Joe; they are both studying at Cambridge a Law degree!" Madelaine looks anguished.

"And does Martyn know about this?"

"No! I feel so ashamed! He is so desperate to have a child and I am a baby killer!" She starts to cry again.

"From what you have told me about Martyn, he sounds like he loves and cares for you and would understand. I am sure he would rather know the truth and it would be better for you not to have to keep a secret from him. What do you think?"

I hand her some more tissues. Drying her eyes she nods and tells me she will try and I advise her to be kind to herself and not do too much this afternoon and we arrange to meet again in a week's time. She thanks me and tells me I am very kind. I feel good about the session.

After work I have agreed to meet up with Mary and Larissa; Belle is busy with a 'work thing'. We decide to have a Chinese meal and so arrange to meet there at 6. 30 p.m. when it opens. I have time to go home and have a freshen up and change. I have

122

a lie down for a half hour and regret it as I now don't want to move and make the effort to go out. I make myself a coffee and open my post. One is a bill, one is trying to sell me insurance and the other is a card from Rob saying maybe he had been too hasty and missed me. Wanting to see me again. I am confused but think it is probably best to ignore it, so I chuck it in the bin before I change my mind. I have a wash and drag on some clothes whilst blasting out some OMD. I am now running a bit late, so I rush out the door and manage to catch a bus into town at the end of the road.

Inside the Chinese, there is a distinct glow of red and gold which is everywhere. The effect is oriental and gaudy, the tables and chairs are cheap and cheerful and today there is just Mary sat at a corner table and no one else when I arrive.

"Hi Mary, how are you? I nearly didn't make it; I had an accidental nap!" I say.

"Hey Tovu, well you beat your sister. I have only just got here myself."

She gets up to give me a hug and air kiss.

"Ooh I like your top, very fitting for the occasion".

I am wearing a mandarin collared, silky, emerald green top with a dragon embroidered on the back. As I take my coat off she admires it. Then excitedly says,

"Guess what? I have a new man!!"

She is beaming from ear to ear and before I can ask her to tell me more she says,

"I met him through work, I have been helping him sell his house. It's a newish semi with three bedrooms. Parking and an easy sale. Then last week he wanted my help to find an investment property, he had already brought a detached five

123

bedroom executive home and now wants to look at maybe a small two bedroom flat he can do up and rent out. "

"Whoa there, how old is this man? Why does he have so much money? What's his name?" I interrupt her.

"Oh his name is John and he's working in some technology firm that is starting to really take off. He's only thirty-two."

"He's not married is he? Got a girlfriend that works away or a bundle of children?" I quickly ask.

"No, he's single and no kids and no ties. Only thing is; he seems to have a rather over involved mother. I am not sure about that but apparently she still does his washing and cleaning for him!"

"Sorry I interrupted you; how did the 'I want to go out with you' conversation happen and where did you go?"

I am keen to know more when Larissa walks in. She is calm and collected, breezes in and heads turn as she enters the restaurant. She looks so beautiful in her jeans and tailored jacket, her blonde locks tumbling down over her shoulders. The restaurant has already filled up with other customers and most are now looking in her direction. She is of course oblivious and walks over to us smiling.

"Hey you two, ooh love your top Tovu. Mary you look absolutely glowing, what's going on?"

We catch Larissa up on Mary's love life and ask the waitress to return as we haven't yet read the menus.

"Tell us more Mary."

Larissa is leaning in wanting to know the details I had asked Mary when Larissa had walked in.

"Well he asked me to set up a day of looking at two-bedroom properties and in between a couple we had a some spare time, so he asked me to have lunch as it was the least he could do commandeering my time. Midway through lunch he just casually said to me; 'I really like you Mary, you make me smile and I feel good when I am near you. Do you think you could come on a proper date with me? Tomorrow night? Seven in the evening and I will take you to a gorgeous Italian I like?' I of course said yes. We just get on so well and he looks at me in that hungry way. We haven't had sex yet before you ask. I am a strictly, no sex before the third date gal!"

Larissa and me smirk at each other because we know that she's broken that rule before.

"You don't think that once you have had sex he will lose interest and dump you then?" Larissa sagely asks.

"No but you never know with guys do you? Any way enough of me, what's happening in your world you two. I promise I will keep you updated on the John situation."

Mary is tight-lipped now so after we have finally ordered; I tell them about my day and the throwing away of Rob's card and they agree it is probably for the best. Larissa then tells us about the latest on her and Raj while we eat.

"Well firstly, sex with Raj is sublime, he really knows what he is doing and secondly, I think he's going to end up back with his wife. I get the impression he feels a bit torn but ultimately she has five years and the kids on the plus side. I somehow can't let him go though and pretend I don't realise what is going on."

"Are you sure Larissa? You know you can get a bit paranoid" I say.

"He is spending more and more time there and even less time trying to get me into bed. I know that wears off after a while but not this soon surely. I know I should confront him but if he tells me he is going back to her; I lose my boyfriend and my joint tenant."

We discuss the merits of knowing the truth and being in blissful ignorance for the next hour and tease each other about our taste in men and the ensuing disasters of most of them to date. This is a common feature of our get togethers, and I am grateful to them that they never judge me but always have my back just as I have theirs. We agree that Larissa needs to bite the bullet and talk to him about things as we are sure there are plenty of other men dying to be with her and plenty of people in need of some accommodation should she get the answer she is expecting.

"Oh, and guess what is happening the day after tomorrow?" I say, now rather tipsy from the house wine.

"I am going to that Awards Night. I have to get the train into the 'Big Smoke' and find this grand hotel where it is taking place. They have paid for me to stay over as well, it's so exciting. I have a new dress and shoes to wear."

"And some new undies?" Larissa interjects, "Just in case Tom is there and gets into your boudoir?"

"I have a matching set in case of an accident my dearest sister, not for a Tom Cat that wants to prey on innocent mice like me!"

I laugh and they laugh too.

"Come on, we better pay up and go, I have work in the morning and so have you two."

Mary and Larissa share a cab and I get the bus back. On my doormat in the kitchen there is a note from Janice. It asks me to pop over if I am not too late and ring my mother who wants to speak to me. I glance at the wall clock and it says five minutes past ten o'clock. I look and see the lights are still on, so I trudge up the path to go and speak to my mother. Darren opens the door to me and tells me Janice has gone up to bed but he is watching the football. He gestures to the lounge and I tell him to get back to it as I know where the phone is and can let myself out. I also promise I won't be long because I know my mother doesn't stay on the phone very long at all.

"Tovu, hello Flossy. I wondered if you could do me a favour and let Faye stay with you next week? I am going on a coach trip with the Morrisons from Henley to Dorset and you are so near to Faye's work it would work perfectly."

Faye is now working in a salon in the town, the local stylist she used to work with has expanded her salon there. She is very loyal and although it costs her to get into town on the bus, Faye has stuck with it. I of course agree that it is fine she stays, and then my mother says when I ask her about the trip,

"Oh, it's been planned a while dear, I will tell you about it when I am back. Faye can come to your work Monday after the salon closes and if you could give her a lift home on the following Sunday that would be good. I better go, it is very late."

She says goodbye and I wave at Darren as I am leaving, and he nods briefly before going back to the T.V. I am now worrying about next week. I should have asked mother to send me some money as I don't know if I will have enough to pay for food for Faye. I didn't ask Darren if he minded her staying then and there, and now I will have to ask Janice tomorrow. I am worried the sofa won't be comfortable enough for her and wonder if I should give up my bed for her.

I get back and start making lists of things I need to sort in my head instead of sleeping when I lie down in my cosy quilt. I also replay the evening's conversations we had in the Chinese and then feel nauseous with too much food and wine. I wonder about mother and her trip away. Who are the Morrisons? I can't remember her mentioning them before. Maybe they are a couple of swingers who have adopted mother to corrupt her, maybe they are old friends she just hasn't ever mentioned. It is a puzzle, but then mother tells you very little about her life and what she gets up to. Always giving the impression she keeps the house in order for our father and Faye and keeps the family together by keeping abreast of us all. That was all she did, or so she led us to believe. Now father is no more, maybe she has branched out or maybe she had secret activities we just didn't know about.

Well maybe Faye could enlighten me a bit more when she stays. Right now I think my mother is an alien.

Chapter 13

Award night has arrived, my ability to get lost in a paper bag has proven to be evident today. I am very skilled in this feat. I have taken an hour and a half longer to get to the hotel than I had originally planned. It's a good job that I know myself well and had planned for this possibility. At least the hotel is expecting me, and I trudge up to my room, which I discover is on the topmost floor and furthest away from anywhere at the end of the longest corridor. However, when I open the door my marathon trip seems worth it; the quality and offerings of this room are divine. I discard my bags, take off my coat and boots and jump into the middle of the bed and sigh large delighted sighs. I enjoy myself for about five minutes which is a lot for me and then I start wondering about what time I am supposed to be where in the morning and retrieve the papers with these details on to check for the hundredth time. I have been caught out before, my memory plays tricks. It tells me that my appointment is 2 p.m. and I am sure of this and turn up at 2.p.m to be told I am an hour late. Or I arrive on the wrong day or too early. It's happened before and it will no doubt happen again so, I feel I really do need to check.

The invitation states clearly that I need to be in the Jubilee Room for drinks at 7.30 p.m. and then onto the Regency Ballroom for the ceremony and presentations at 8.00 p.m. I have a seat reserved for me at the front and it will have my name on a card to indicate which is mine. It's now 5.00 p.m. and I decide to have a soak in the bath. I set my travel alarm clock to 5.30 p.m. in case I fall asleep and put it at the side of the bath.

Next I hang my dress up, put everything I need for the evening in my clutch bag and go to put out my undies and shoes. I find my shoes and bra but can I find my knickers? Where are they? I have some greying Tanga Briefs on and nothing else. I unpack and repack my bag several times and the knickers continue to elude me. It's too late to go and hunt down a shop for some new ones, I decide I will have to go commando and wear my greying ones tomorrow inside out. I get in the bath, splash about quickly and get out, I have lost valuable getting ready time looking for knickers.

When I enter the Jubilee Room with no knickers on, I am struck by the fact that this situation is not known by anyone else and I can absolutely just relax about it. My dress clings to my curves and so the lack of a VPL is actually a bonus. I take a breath, look around the room and enter the fray. People dressed up and gathered in clusters, sipping at their wine glasses as though it was something they did every night of the year. My little self decides it is best to go and head for the tables with wine and go and smile and be nice to the servers. Someone might say something to me. It's probably been four hours since I opened my mouth, I do hope my voice still works and doesn't come out in a squeak or grunt. I decide I can practice on the servers. Only the servers are very tall and handsome young men who I flush in embarrassment at and do squeak a timid, 'white please' and thank them in a grunt.

Well that's got that over with, what next? I am about to seek out the lone woman to go and say hi to because I surely cannot be the only one? When a shadow falls upon me, a Tom shaped shadow that says hello and takes me by the elbow to steer me to the side of the room. He tells me how sexy I look and how glad he is I have got here. He melts me, he excites me. I can't help but fall into a natural chat about the world and life in it with him. It's like putting on my favoured 'snuggle cardi' knowing I have only a Basque underneath it. He looks straight into my eyes and tells me I have no knickers on and he is very hard at the thought. I don't blush, I brazen it out and tell him he's being ridiculous.

We are of course placed seated next to each other in the Regency Ballroom, a large round table at the front, near the stage. Accompanying us at the table are seven other award winners who seem very assured and pleased with themselves. We exchange the usual pleasantries and enquire about each other's projects that have been successful in the awards. Everyone seems pleasant enough but Tom whispers that the man three seats to the right of me is hot for me and keeps trying to get my attention. Tom thinks this is hilarious. I tell him that I rather like the look of this man and was only a little concerned by his thick moustache whose ability to store food would be monitored throughout dinner. We giggle like naughty children. Then our compere calls us to attention and proceedings are started.

Tom places a hand on my thigh under the tablecloth and I am very aware then that I have no knickers on. I concentrate on trying not to exude any moisture sweat and otherwise. Such is my concentration I have no idea what the compere is saying but regard his appearance with curiosity. It is a good distraction. The compere is Sebastian Connelly, he is an ex politician who is portly, bald and rather dapper. He wears a monocle, a tweed jacket with a bright yellow hanky peeking out of his top pocket and cowboy boots. He has the most extraordinary voice; it exudes confidence and power yet humour and sexiness; it is most interesting. He has little tics, some barely perceptible, others are exaggerated as if to reinforce something funny he has said. In fact, as I study him further I see that the tics correlate with certain emotions he is trying to convey. Rather than detract from what he is saying they enhance it. Something about him is entrancing, I am absorbed in the look and the sound of him and know that the audience is laughing and engaged by what he is saying and I am too. It's in a different way though, without the detail of his words hampering my observations. Tom's hand leaves my thigh to drink some wine and I am snapped out of my daze. Sebastian calls for the first CEO of the NHS, Victor Paige to come to the stage to start to present the awards. I really should know this person, but I don't. He seems pleasant enough, confident and engaging.

We pay attention now, teams are called up to the stage, announced by Sebastian after he has given a brief summary of what category they have won and why. We are the seventh team to be called, Tom and I get up and I manage not to trip up on the way to, on the stage or on the way back from it. I decide my only role is to try and look pretty and happy about the award and accept the applause. Fortunately Tom also sees this as my role and thanks everyone for the award and accepts the small trophy and certificates from Victor. We shake hands, pause for a photo and then leave. I can relax now that is over. I can also have more wine and look forward to some food. Moustache man leans across the table offering his hand for us to shake and tells us congratulations and well done. His palm is sweaty, and I am glad mine is cool. Although I suffer with sweaty pits my hands are usually cold due to poor circulation. Tom's hand has reunited with my thigh. I gulp down some wine and listen to the rest of the awards, clapping madly at the appropriate times.

Fortunately, there are only another seven categories and dinner is declared as being served. I ask Tom why there were so many people here when only 14 teams won awards. He laughed and said that the others were teams nominated but who didn't win, runners up. He enquired why I hadn't been listening as this had been explained and runners up applauded every time. I assured him that his distraction techniques had worked and how fascinating I had found Sebastian. He concurs he was indeed an interesting man and pours out some more wine for us both.

An hour later I am pretty drunk and everything is completely wonderful and I love everyone in the whole world. Even moustache man who can't believe his luck when I dance with him and tease him gently about his hairy face. I also get to talk to Sebastian and exchange addresses and phone numbers so we can correspond, he is so fascinating and although I am getting to slurry speech stage, we have an in-depth conversation about the merits of advance directives. Tom rescues the poor man from me and suggests we leave. He works out that his room is much closer than mine and steers me off to the lift to take me there. I don't honestly recall how we get there; I am just now grinning inanely on the edge of his bed while he uses the bathroom. When he returns he is suddenly on top of me kissing me intently in the way he does. My body responds even if my mind is hazy and Diana Ross is singing in a loop, 'Let the music play. Just a little longer'. He is delighted to see I do not have knickers on. We have a wild night, it is most pleasurable even though orgasm escapes me, Tom thinks I am multi orgasmic and says I have turned him to the multi orgasmic man. I bet he says that to all the gals. I don't get much sleep, but when we do sleep he wraps me tightly into his chest and kisses my head from time to time. He murmurs romantically, I only hear half of it as one of my ears is squished tightly against him.

In the early hours of the morning I do the walk of shame back to my room. I get into my bed and mess it up as though I had been there all night. I am not sure why I am bothering to be honest, who cares? I guess you just don't know but I sort of know it's not required. I have a soak in the bath and get ready for breakfast; my train home is early as I must run my Women's Group in the afternoon, I didn't want to let them down and cancel it. There is something else I am supposed to do, I am sure of it, but I cannot recall the details. My head hurts a lot, I didn't bring any paracetamol. I gulp down some water from the bathroom taps by cupping my hands and slurping out of them. I am a wreck, I need to do something with myself, food is required and maybe a couple of fags. I go over and over my route back and whilst looking for my hairbrush find my two pairs of knickers I just couldn't find yesterday. Oh well, at least I have clean ones for the trip back.

The train journey home is pretty uneventful, I spend it musing about the evening before. My review of it all brings a smile to my face and a dull feeling in my heart. Life is complex, I don't think I will 1 ever understand it and I definitely will never understand men. When I am with him I think that Tom is just perfect for me but before I left him this morning he made no mention of keeping in touch or wanting to see me again soon. I hadn't even had the guts to discuss whether he was definitely not seeing someone else. He fancies me I suppose but this is not in love and despite all his amazing wooing techniques there are undoubtedly other women in his life. I know Larissa thinks he's a liar and a cheat and I should stay away, and Mary says I should see how things go and try not to overthink it. It probably isn't worth discussing with them again. I make a decision to tell them about my knicker panic, moustache man and Sebastian and downplay any questions about Tom. I don't want to regurgitate the debate. I won't probably bump into him again. Just a little guilty secret liaison no-one needs to know about.

The day centre is busy, two doctor clinics going on as well as the usual programme of groups and one to ones. There is clearly a situation going on because there is both a police van and ambulance in the car park. My heart sinks and I stride in and am immediately beckoned to go into the staff office. The door is shut behind me and Debbie, Jim and Janice look at me pensively and Debbie tells me that Gina; one of my Women's Group ladies has cut her wrists in the toilets and the police and ambulance men are trying to get her to go to A&E. Gina is currently refusing and her wrists are pouring with blood. They have gathered all the other patients in the large activity room upstairs and they have three staff members with them. Vanessa is trying to persuade Gina to go with the ambulance men. I just know I have to go and help; Gina trusts me and I think she will talk to me. Debbie reluctantly agrees and I rush out to the toilets after I have grabbed some absorbent pads, a paper towel roll, plastic bag and gloves from the clinic room.

"Miss you can't go in there."

The policeman blocks my way and so I tell him I am her key worker and she might respond to me. Vanessa spies me and confirms with him that I should be allowed to see if I can help. The ambulance man seems to be getting a bit exasperated with Gina and I ask if he can leave us alone for five minutes.

"Hey Gina, it's Tovu here. I have sent them all out and I have some pads to soak up some of the blood can you let me in the cubicle?"

"You promise you are alone?"

"Yes, let me help you, open up!"

"I don't want to go to A&E!"

"You might not need to go if we can get you cleaned up. If you do need to go, I will come with you if you like."

We talk in this way a little more and she finally lets me in the cubicle to clean her up. I did my best with the materials I had collected and held the pads on her wrists firmly to stop the flow. Gina is crying and she is now feeling some pain. I shout at the ambulance man to give us a bit longer when he calls through the door. Gina is looking ashen, I keep holding her wrists and talking to her gently and reassure her we can sort this out. She is shaking and swaying, I get her to come out of the cubicle and ask her if I can get a wheelchair for her to sit on.

"Don't leave me Tovu, I do need to sit down though. I feel faint, I want to lie on the floor."

I tell her it is better to get her a chair and I shout through the door for a wheelchair to be brought to us urgently and one appears. I let her sink into it and tell her that we need to go to hospital now as I think she has lost too much blood and the wounds need dressing or will get infected. She has quietened and seems resigned to this and makes me promise to go with her. I agree and wheel her out of the toilets and out to where the ambulance is. I refuse to discuss anything with anyone and just order the ambulance man to get us to A&E as quickly as possible and ask Vanessa to cover my group for me if they still want to go ahead or just let them talk about the incident and debrief them if that is what they want to do. She agrees and says she can cancel her meetings as this is more important. The police can wait.

I clamber into the ambulance after Gina, we are both covered in her blood and look rather macabre. I forgot to get aprons. I feel weak and a bit shaky myself but I comfort Gina whilst the paramedic wraps some fresh padding around her wrists and secures it with tape. They press firmly but not too hard on her wrists and have the sense not to ask Gina any questions except to get her permission to take her vital signs. She is meek now and is apologetic. I talk to her about what is likely to happen next and tell her I will be there every step. If she wants. She nods compliantly and I also agree to ring the day centre to make sure they tell her mother where she is because Gina is now worrying that she will be wondering where she is and wants her to come to A&E. Gina's mother has no phone, so they will have to ring a neighbour to go round to her house. Neither of us can recall the neighbour's number. When we get to A&E she gets put in a side room and a doctor is paged to inspect her wounds, which have finally stopped bleeding. While we are waiting for them she starts apologising again and then starts to explain why she got in such a state.

She slept badly last night (I know the feeling) and then this morning she remembered it was her son's birthday and she started to weep, her mother told her she had to go to the day centre and when she got there she just felt overwhelmingly sad. At lunch she couldn't eat and started yawning and one of the other patients who is paranoid shouted at her for getting in his way and stealing his food. She knew he didn't mean it, but it upset her and she went to hide away from him in the toilets. Somehow, she remembered she had razor blades in her handbag, they were a comfort to her and she just cut her wrists. She said she didn't feel anything, she is numb with pain for the loss of her son and then she started sobbing and the blood was spilling onto the floor and someone raised the alarm and there was lots of banging and shouting. She was scared and until I came to help, she just felt paralysed. She said that my calm voice and my reassurance seemed to jolt her into the reality of her situation, and she started worrying about her mother and how she would not be able to cope without Gina. I tell her she was amazing and the doctor walks in. He doesn't take long and doesn't ask too many questions. He says he will ask the mental health doctor to see her in case she needs to be admitted. He has asked the nurse he is with to cleanse the wounds and close it with Steri- strips, bandage the wrists and get Gina something to drink. He wants her to take some iron tablets and antibiotics. Her mum arrives in a state of distress and looks like she has been put through a mangle that creases you up not evens you out. She also smells of fried fish and fag ash. She thanks me before wrapping herself around her daughter like an old blanket, or maybe like the cod and chips in their newspaper wrapping. She tells me I should go and get cleaned up myself and suggests I could do with a sleep as I look washed out. I am grateful for this and Gina tells me to go also. Her mother will call into the day centre on Monday and let us know how she is doing.

I get up from the hard chair I was sat on and in walks Dr Greg. I can hear the two ladies positively gasp at how handsome he is, and it makes me smile inside. We have a brief exchange of what has occurred, and he dismisses me as he agrees with Gina's mum. I look a state and need to get some rest. I'm not sure how I am going to get home as I came in the ambulance, but I wander down to the front entrance of the hospital and to my greatest relief see that Janice is waiting for me. She has covered her car passenger seat with a bin liner and gives me an old but cosy blanket that smells of bonfires to wrap around me. She may not have trained as a mental health nurse but she is intuitive and caring and just quietly tells me to have the water she has thrust into my hand and she will get me home and take me to work in the morning to pick up my car if I am up to it; we have all weekend. I drink the water and thank her.

I have a shower and throw away my bloody top and put the rest of my clothes in the washing machine. I crawl into bed and my last thought before I fall into a deep sleep is that I have left my case in my car at work and I need my makeup bag.

Chapter 14

Faye is singing in the car along to a Queen song, ever since Live Aid she plays their greatest hits album over and over again. She's been with me two days and it has been a welcome joy; Faye is sunshine on a rainy day and the moon and stars at night even when mourning our father. We are going over to Larissa's for a meal and Faye is excited. I have sworn myself to stay sober so I can get home tonight and have a clear head for tomorrow. I am not sure if we will be meeting Raj or not, it doesn't matter either way to me or Faye. Larissa's flat is pretty non-descript on the outside, but my sister has a style all of her own. Part groovy hippy, part 80's glam rock and part African Safari, there is colour, clutter, patterns and textures everywhere. So different to my uncluttered minimalist approach and Faye's fuffy pink and glitterball bedroom. I recall my conversation about our father Faye and I had and his apparent love of ethnic clothes which mother had vetoed him ever buying let alone wearing any. Apparently, he had told Tovu in confidence his friend Alfie had a stash of these clothes, which he used to put on for evenings watching the sport and drinking lager with him. He said he felt his comfiest in them and he also liked joss sticks but another item banned from his home.

I survey the kitchen which Larissa is stood in amid flour dust and a steam bath of spicy smells; left hand stirring a saucepan and the other pouring spinach into a colander in the sink.

"Just wait a moment whilst I get things under control here; sit in the lounge, I promise I won't be long!"

"Can we help?"

"No, no, I have it sorted!"

Faye shrugs her shoulders and we retreat back to the lounge and sink into the only sofa which practically swallows us whole. We giggle and Faye whispers to me,

"Do you think it will be edible? I don't think I have ever eaten anything she's cooked, have you?"

I can't remember a time either.

"It's deffo a first. I don't know how you persuaded mother to let you use the kitchen, she always ushered us out. I took Home Economics at school but Larissa did Needlework instead."

"Hence all the fabric and draping in this place!" Faye giggles.

Larissa walks in as she says it and laughs too,

"Are you two taking the mick out of my penchant for materials? Let me show you my latest creation!"

She pulls from a box on the floor behind the sofa a massive patchwork quilt. It is amazing. Faye and I fight over who she has to give it to for Christmas.

"I'm actually going to sell it my dear sisters, I can get about £150 for it. I met this woman at work who does them too. I shall buy you a little something with the proceeds. Anyway, I'm glad you like it. I also have something you will like better"

She dives into the box and brings out a bottle of Wine and three glasses and I remind her I'm staying sober and she puts one back. Ten minutes later we are eating a prawn and spinach starter. The starter is a bit bland although we don't care because we have a much spicier topic to discuss which is Raj. Larissa finally confronted him last week about his situation with his wife and kids; he admitted he was going back to them, before Christmas but didn't know how to tell Larissa. Larissa told him to go but they had one more night of hot sex; she laughs at our fake outrage and because we are sisters, we spare her from telling us any details. She is trying to contain herself but there is more,

"What is it Larissa, what else has happened? Have you got a new cohabitee already?" I ask.

"Wait right there ladies, I need to get your main meal."

We are having a vegetable curry and rice; the curry is too spicy but we find some yoghurt , sugar and bread to cool it down. It's really filling so we are picking at it by the time Larissa has told us the rest of her news. Raj was pretty decent and paid a full month's rent, but Larissa was keen to find a new person to share with as soon as he left. She put a card up on the local newsagents and one on the staff notice board at her work's office with the details and sure enough a tall, dark, handsome man came knocking on her door. He was older and slightly greying but Larissa said he was swoon worthy. He didn't want the room for himself, but for his daughter who was starting a job in the town in one of the banks and needed a room to stay as he lived in Oxford. He came in and they had a chat, he was so sexy he made her a bit dizzy. There was such chemistry between them she thought but sadly she finds out he is happily married and just checking out her morality before he lets his daughter lodge with her. She reined in her womanly wiles and reminded herself he was very old. They shared some stories about Oxford and he asked about her work and family. He showed her the spare bedroom and blushed when he asked if he could see hers, only to see if she had bagged the largest for herself. He was joking and she was relieved because she hadn't made her bed.

He asked if he could return the next day with his daughter. They agreed a time and he introduced her to Sonia, a quiet young lady with curly hair and cat like eyes; they got on well with her love of books and music and is moving in next week. Larissa wants to catch up on our news and hands us a Milk Maid ice lolly for our pudding, explaining it was better than her burning a cake and reminded her of the time our mother did the same thing one year as a special treat for her birthday having burnt the Birthday Cake.

I tell them about the lady who cut her wrists in graphic detail because it holds their attention and let them know it ended okay and she is back attending the day centre groups. They want to know about the Award night, I brush over it as being; 'alright'. I tell them there is no new man on the scene but did then tell them about moustache man and Sebastian.

Faye tells us about her university application and a boy who fancies her, but she isn't keen on him.

"Anyway, I agree with mum who thinks I should wait until I am at uni or I may end up splitting up because of the distance."

"Talking of mother, why has gone away with 'The Morrisons', who we don't know anything about? Or do you know anything about them Faye?" asks Larissa.

"She's known them for the past two years sis, they met at the Co-Operative Women's Guild, Mrs Morrison that is. She's called Gloria and he's Bert."

"What the hell is the Co-Operative Women's Guild?" asks Larissa.

Faye doesn't know, so I enlighten them and say they were a women's rights campaigning organisation and Faye carries on telling us that our mother was quite the feminist. Larissa and I are surprised and vow to talk to her about this side of her more. Faye says that the Morrisons seem nice enough and there doesn't seem to be any weirdness going on, but we do wonder if it's a bit soon for mother to be gadding about considering her husband died so recently. It still seems a mystery, so Larissa and I decide we will go over when she is home and spend some quality time with her and Faye.

"What did father have to say about this Guild stuff?" Larissa asks.

"He pretended he didn't know about it so when she went to meetings he snuck off to his mate's and…"

"put on his hippy clothes, lit a joss stick and watched the football!" I finish for her.

Our parents, seemingly led pretty sperate lives under the same roof and especially when they walked out of their home's front door. We try and explore what it's been like being in the middle of it but Faye is fairly level headed about it and reminded us she was still really a teenager and teenagers don't care much about anything but themselves. It hadn't really impacted on her and they were happy with the arrangements. We are just about to get ourselves ready to leave when there's a knock on the door. Larissa has no clue who it could be but dashes down the stairs to go and see.

There stood in the rain is Raj, he has a large bag on his shoulder and asks Larissa if he can have his old room back. She explains her sisters are there and wants to know why he is there. He says that his wife has kicked him out because he confessed to her about Larissa. She lets him in, introduces him to us and we grab our bags and coats thank her for the class food and leave them to it. We manage to get soaked getting to the car and I pray it starts, it can be a bit funny in the rain. It doesn't turn over for three attempts and we hold our breaths when I try for the fourth time. It chugs into action and we breath out with relief. We really had wanted to stay and tell Larissa not to let him back, we know she will do what she feels is right at that time and hope she agrees it is a bad idea for him to return.

Faye is tired, not helped by so much wine and so we don't say much on the trip back. With rain lashing against the windows of the car I concentrate hard on driving safely. There doesn't seem to be too much traffic on the road and visibility is poor. We are nearing my place when I notice Faye is crying,

"What's wrong honey?"

"I'm okay Tovu, honestly, I just suddenly thought about dad and how he used to pop his head in my bedroom door and whisper 'goodnight Angel' whether he thought I could hear him or not. I always used to say 'Night Daddykins' when I was little and then when I got older I'd say it in my head."

"I don't remember him doing that Faye, did he just do it to you or the rest of us only we never knew or was it just something he did for you?" my voice wobbles when I say this.

"I'm sorry Tovu I didn't mean to upset you too. I am sure he used to say goodnight to all of us. I was just missing him I guess."

When we get in, I suggest Faye has the shower room first and I make her a cocoa. We have a little chat about the family, and I make her laugh about my trip to the Awards Night and she was back to her usual cheery self. Before we settle in our respective beds I say in a fatherly sort of way,

"Goodnight Angel. You are still an angel and you have us lot to always look out for you. Love you."

"Night Sisterkins, I love you too. Even though you are a nutter!"

I am woken by Faye with a mug of tea in her left hand and she is prodding me with her right foot. I sit up and thank her. She goes for a shower and tells me she is meeting up with a friend this evening; she had forgotten to tell me. I quiz her a bit and am satisfied it will be safe and tell her I will pick her up at 11.00 p.m. at the pub she's going to. I insist although she says she will get a

145

cab. I must go to the acute ward this morning first thing to do an assessment on a young man who is ready for discharge but needs some ongoing support. The doctor wants him to come to the Men's Group and Anxiety Management Group. Usually this would be Jim's domain but he is on leave, so I agreed to do it instead. It meant I had a little extra time to get ready. I make Faye and me a packed lunch and come across a flyer for a 'Disco Diva' night at the nightclub in town for this weekend. I decide it's time I faced a club again and pop the flyer in my handbag so I can photocopy it at work and send to my friends to see if they want to go. I will ask my sisters too. It might be fun.

Damien is shouting about the apocalypse, he doesn't really know what it is but had watched a film about it recently at his brother's house and ever since has become increasingly distressed, leading him to be admitted onto the ward. He had been terrorising his neighbours in the block of flats he lived in and was threatening suicide because he was so scared. Joseph is muttering to himself as he paces up and down the corridor, rubbing his face with both hands, almost wearing a furrow in the carpet. Melanie is wailing in her bedroom having tried to tie a ligature and hang herself, she has two nurses with her trying to calm her. Lorraine s haranguing the staff in the office, pestering them to let her go for a fag. The scene strikes me as far from the way people with mental health problems are portrayed in films. Yes, it's a bit noisy but the vulnerability and loss is what you feel when you walk into the ward. It isn't the uncomfortable, threatening and tense atmosphere created by film producers.

The slender young man awaiting assessment for the day centre is sat bolt upright on the edge of a chair in a side room, he looks up with dull eyes but when I enter, he smiles at me and his face lifts. I tell him who I am and ask if he knows why I am there.

He says he understands and was expecting me. I ask him about his stay in hospital and what his worries were now he is leaving it. His name is James, he has mousy brown hair which falls lankly around his face and he has been on the ward four weeks. He was admitted due to getting stressed at university, he got paranoid and isolated himself in his room and was discovered when he didn't turn up for any of his lectures for a two weeks and his fellow students in the halls he shared realised they hadn't seen much of him over the last five days. He was undernourished and found cowering in bed. The doctors felt he was schizophrenic at first but during his assessments on the ward it became clear that his issues were largely anxiety related. He was started on anti-depressant and anxiolytic medication and engaged well in O.T., enjoying the arts and crafts and had started a Men's Group and had benefitted from talking to some of the older men about his worries. He had decided he wasn't ready to go back to university and was going home to live with his father, a quiet man himself who kept himself to himself. I really thought the day centre would be great for him.

He agreed to attend three mornings and one full day to keep him involved and continue to develop his skills in relating to other people. He looked pleased that this was available to him and he had started to open up a bit about what had upset him at university. It seemed that every social situation had pretty much terrified him, he had frequent panic attacks every day. He was often lost and couldn't manage to speak to others to ask for directions and help. He was paralysed by his fear. I know I worry but I don't let it completely paralyse me; I accept my fears and make myself do things anyway. I really try to take my worries along with me and stop fighting them because they are a part of me. I talk to James about some of the techniques that may help him and reassure him we will help him master them. It takes practice and support to achieve excellence; this is something I tell myself a lot! James leaves the room after I tell him where the centre is and the time we start.

I walk into the office notepad in hand and nearly bump straight into Tom, I say hi and then seek eye contact with the nurse in charge of the ward, a bubbly lady called Julie.

"Oh hi, I've finished with James, he is coming to the day centre the day after tomorrow and we'll start from there. Can you make sure you fax a copy of his discharge letter for me? I have to dash but give me a call at the centre if you have any questions. Nice to see you Tom, hope you are well. Bye!"

I make a hasty exit and silently applause my performance in the office. My heart is racing so I slow down and decide to grab some cakes for the team before I get to work from a nearby bakery. I love the smell of freshly baked bread and cakes. It reminds me of my grandmother in the kitchen with her flowery pinny on and a full tummy feeling that slows my pulse rate. I haven't ever met either of my grandmothers, they both died before I got to meet them and so I have imagined them both to be the essence of comfort and love. I think it's a good day today and I have my home to myself this evening as Faye is going out. I shall have a night in with Soft Cell and John Irving.

Chapter 15

It's 'Disco Diva' night and both Belle and Mary are round at mine finishing getting ready. They are both staying the night so I am relieved in a way that Larissa and Faye can't make it. One, because, how do I fit them in and two, much as I love them, some secrets kept from family members is necessary and liberating when you want to let your hair down. We have decided to get into the spirit of the theme and have a lot of sequins and glitter between us adorning every item of clothing. We make a colourful ensemble and we are laughing at Belle because her boob tube is rather tight and we are worried her voluptuous bosom may spill out if she flings her arms around excitedly at any point. The false eyelashes are proving tricky to adhere and our taxi is due in 2 minutes. One or two of us may have to go without. I take control declaring I have the steadiest hand and do Belle's for her and then have a go at mine. I just about get them right before there are headlights lighting up the driveway and we guess the taxi has arrived.

The taxi driver doesn't bat an eyelid when he sees us pile into the cab; he just confirms the drop off point and heads off to the town centre. We agreed a few drinks in 'The Tap' would be a good idea, cheaper and less busy so we should get served quickly. As we get out of the cab, there are a group of about ten youngsters standing by and seeing our get up let out a round of applause and wolf whistles. We wave and scuttle into the pub. We are relieved to see it isn't very crowded as we thought, and a few regulars acknowledge us and get back to their conversations or blankness as they gaze at their pint. Rick comes over to serve us and comments that we look very colourful and sparkly, he jokes that at least we won't lose each other tonight. He gets our wine and the pub door opens and in walks a group of five men. They all look about our age, maybe a little older and one of them looks vaguely familiar. We move out of their way and find a table to observe them as they order their drinks. Mary whispers something about thinking one of them is familiar and I agree I had the same feeling. Mary makes eye contact with him when he is looking round and he winks at her and she smiles; then recognition;

"Mary Brownlow? Oh and Tovu Jenkins! It's me Stephen Cross from school; I used to hang out with Frank your brother Mary, remember? I was a few stone heavier then. What are you doing here?"

We explain we are going to the 'Disco Diva' night and I live and work here and he tells us he is on a stag do with a mate from university who lives here. He calls his mates over and there are introductions. They all seem about our age except Sean, who is dark, rugged with an infectious smile. I guess he is a little older and discover he is the 'stag's' brother when he tells his brother he's going to make a phone call to their mum as promised. Stephen is talking to Mary, asking about Frank and her family and Belle is asking me for the low down on Stephen. I am mid telling her about him when two of the guys interrupt us and start asking us questions about the Disco Diva night and we must spark their interest as they now want to come along with us. The only one who isn't keen is Sean, he isn't much of a dancer, doesn't like the crowded, dark and noisy atmosphere in clubs, so doesn't go much. He does renege when his brother pleads with him and is reminded that he has promised his mother to keep an eye on him to keep him from doing anything too daft the night before his wedding.

Belle seems to be getting to know all about Stephen judging from the fact they are snogging on the dance floor and Mary is doing some sort of grinding with Joseph one of the others. I decide I need to sit down, not only have I worn my feet out dancing but the alcohol is going to my head. I slump in a chair and notice Sean staring broodily at the dance floor watching his brother and friends wrapped around various females, circling round and round to the music. Sean is quite good looking but he seems a bit of a bore and above himself and others; his gaze swings round towards me and his glance tracks back at me in some sort of recognition and he strides across the room towards me. Something about his stride is sexy but I don't really want to speak to him. The only thing is I fear I may fall over if I get up right now and try and avoid him. I'm not wearing my PE shorts this evening, but I still don't want to bring any attention to myself. He manages to squidge in next to me and starts talking / shouting in my ear. I can't hear all that he says but I get the gist; which is basically he is a bit bored although he doesn't mind the music, he prefers Rock music. He enjoyed watching me dance though and wonders if I would have a drink with him some time as he would like to get to know me. I of course, agree.

I don't know why I cannot say 'no thank-you'! I am cross with myself already but nod in agreement when he suggests Wednesday night meeting him in The Tap at 7.00 p.m. At least Rick can keep an eye on me and its familiar surroundings for me. I am instantly worrying about having to go on a date with a near stranger, let alone one I don't particularly like. I am already rehearsing ways in which I can get out of it. I am just about to get up the courage to apologise and say I have forgotten but I have to go to a work meeting on Wednesday and just remembered. Maybe give me his number and I will call and arrange something; when there is a bit of a hoo hah on the dance floor. His brother has fallen flat out on it and instead of everyone laughing like they did when I fell, they are cheering him and applauding. Sean jumps up and goes to help him up. As the stag party leaves the club together, half carrying the groom to be; Sean shouts at me,

"See you Wednesday!"

Mary and Belle spot me and come over noting this exchange.

"What's that about?" asks Mary

"How were Stephen's tonsils Belle and how was Joseph's groin coping with your grinding Mary?" I counter.

We laugh and agree to get a taxi home, the DJ is packing up and everyone is trailing out. We hold each other up and when we get back, we make toast and pour some glasses of water before we all flop out in the lounge together. We exchange our stories of the evening and the male encounters. None of us are that bothered about seeing these male specimens again, we can't even recall what they look like that much. I haven't told you but Belle is actually single, she hasn't had a boyfriend all year, her last one dumped her just before Christmas. They don't tend to last, Belle wonders if she just attracts the wrong sort. She can join the club! Anyway, Stephen didn't even ask her for her number or arrange a meet. She isn't that bothered; she did enjoy the snogging though. Mary thinks that he will track down Frank and find out how he can get a date with her; he was always a bit shy really before. She says she will ask Frank for his number if Belle wants. Belle is not keen. 'Mary and Joseph' of course amuses us no end, especially with Christmas around the corner. Mary is adamant that they were only dancing and nothing untoward, she is still seeing John, and all is going steadily with him. She won't, however, tell him about the dancing with the 'not bad looking' Joseph.

When I tell them about what had happened with Sean they are in hysterics because I seemingly describe him in such scathing terms they just cannot understand why I agreed to go out with him. I know nothing about him except he seems to be under his mother's thumb a bit and dislikes nightclubs. Neither are attractive qualities in my view. I consider the potential for him to review his choice of date and cancel on me or just stand me up. He has four days to decide and I have four days to worry. Of course my dear friends suggest I do have the option of standing him up but I just couldn't do that. Having dissected the evening we crash on the floor of my home in sleeping bags as if we were camping. I later retire to my own bed after visiting he loo as that seemed the wise thing to do. My hangover is kicking in but I'm too tired to go and get some water. I know I will suffer all day tomorrow.

Wednesday 7.20 p.m. and I am stood outside the Tap, I have been worrying all day if he is going to stand me up, whether he is pretty horrid, whether he decides he doesn't like me after all, whether he might assault me, whether he is a complete bore and I have to pretend I am really interested and on and on the negative thoughts go round in my head. Thankfully it isn't raining, I don't know whether to wait for him inside or not, or whether to pop my head in to check he isn't there, I don't know how I stay composed with the chaos in my head. I decide to pop into the pub to check he isn't in there or I will look a right prune. I enter and there are a few of the regulars inside who acknowledge me and Rick sticks a thumb up at me as I walk to the bar. No sign of Sean. I glance at the clock on the wall and then have to glance at it again as I don't register what it says thanks to my anxiety. Now I have to watch out for him and check he doesn't stand outside waiting for me when I am inside. It is 7.30 p.m.

"What's it to be Tovu?" Rick asks me.

"Just a coke please Rick"

"Are the others running late? Your mates?"

"I'm waiting for a man Rick, he's late"

"Well he'll be along soon I'm sure, he would be daft not to."

I find a chair near a window looking outside the pub, so I can see the entrance clearly. I am now convinced he has stood me up and decide he has until 7.45 p.m. and then I am walking. I am feeling slightly annoyed now, being late is just rude in my book. Now I am also feeling embarrassed sat on my own with a sad coke. The good thing about The Tap is that punters leave you be and mind their own business. Just when I think Sean is a 'no show' he walks in the door, strides confidently across to me and says 'Hi'. Then says he'll grab a pint and nods at my coke and says that he can see I am alright for a drink. He looks less attractive than I remember, but he is tall and undeniably has some sort of sexy vibe going on. It's his nose that puts his face out of line, it is large and bulbous; he has some sort of rugged charm. He's a few pounds overweight but not horribly so, maybe a bit of a drinker. I am getting sweaty, at least I don't have to get too close to him on a first date, if this is what it is. He might just see it as something else. I am about to find out, he returns to the table and sits down with his pint in hand.

"Sorry I was a little late, I got held up!"

He gives me a full on smile which melts me a little. Before I can say anything he tells me he is a self employed builder and lives in his own house near Marlow. I think he must be a good builder to be living there, house prices are much higher than the town. Then he tells me about his day and the problems he has had with some contractors letting him down by not turning up and delivering poor quality work and customers not paying him money owed. Eventually he asks me some questions about what I do and listens quite intently and without much interruption.

I get up for the loo and feel self-conscious as I cross the room, wondering if he is watching. When I walk back, one of my stay up stocking decides to fall down. There isn't much to do except to go back into the toilet or brazen it out and hope no-one notices; but I am half way across the room and Sean is looking out of the window. I hitch it up as best I can and quickly make it to my chair and Sean doesn't notice.

I ask him about his family and he says he has an older sister, both parents live near him in and he sees them all quite often. He talks about his sister and her children and how he loves children and wants three of his own. He doesn't ask me if I want them thankfully but does ask me what I think about alcoholism and what is the definition of an alcoholic. I tell him it's an addiction and where it impacts on your life that you no longer are functioning and performing as well as you were and relationships start to be impacted on.

He asks about my politics and starts banging on about Margaret Thatcher being as tough as boots and doing us proud. I am labour and think she is doing a lot of harm, so cannot agree with him. He argues pro Tory and essentially suggests I am a bit ignorant and don't understand. He's pretty rude. I decide it's time to change the subject after a heated debate ensues. He evidently agrees because out of the blue he asks me;

"So if I have a couple of pints a day it doesn't make me an alcoholic? Not that I do, I do like a pint but it's not every day" he says.

"You would be classed as a heavy drinker until such time as the level of drinking became a compulsive need which led to increasing amounts and you couldn't cope with work for instance." I try to explain.

"Well I am far from that!"

He changes the subject and we chat until the bell for last orders rings and he asks me if I would meet up again, maybe go for a walk at the weekend down by the river near his place. We decide Sunday afternoon. He gives me the details and a suggested spot to meet. When we get up from the table I have forgotten my wayward stocking and it falls down again having managed to pull it up whilst sat at the table. Sean cannot fail to notice; he laughs and says something unhelpful about my thigh getting flat after my coke. I feel like slapping him at that point.

He has had only the one pint this evening and offers me a ride home in his very nice Ford XR3i, I tell him I have my car and he places a kiss on my cheek telling me he has had a good time. I say likewise and scuttle off to my Mini.

As soon as I have left him, I am analysing the evening, I can't decide if I actually like him or not. He has some good points but there are warning signs. I wonder if Larissa is home and if she'd mind if I came round at this time of night. I decide not to, I am tired now too. When I get home, my lights are on and Larissa is on my sofa.

"Hey Tove, Janice let me in. I hope you don't mind? I went to the cinema on the hill and my friend dropped me off here to save her going all the way to mine and coming back into town. I had forgotten about your date. Do tell!"

I tell her I am actually pleased to see her and ask her to make us a cuppa while I get into my PJs and take off my non staying up stocking. They have given me a rash where the elastic has eaten into my skin. Five minutes later we are slumped together on the sofa and I suggest it's a good thing I wasn't planning to bring him back to mine this evening. I tell her about the evening and her analysis is that he sounded a bit old and dull, possibly an alcoholic in the making but not bad looking, solvent, nice car and house; so worth going on a second date to see if here is more about him. I ask her about Raj and I hope her new homie, Sonia. She confirms she didn't take Raj back and he did grovel and grovel to his wife and is back in the family home. Sonia didn't move in, she decided to go to a place nearer the town in amongst it even though her father had wanted her on the outskirts away from the ethnic areas. Larissa was glad she didn't move in and wasn't going to have to come across 'Rascist Rodger' (which is what we now call Sonia's father) again. There is someone at work who is interested in sharing with her, she is the same age as me and wants to move out of her parent's. She bumps into Raj at work sometimes and he is being aloof, sulking. Larissa is missing him but is also interested in a new Social Worker she met last week.

We are due to see mother tomorrow; we had taken some annual leave so we could have a few days with her. We make plans and Larissa has a bag packed ready to be picked up on the way.

When I get to bed, I can't switch my head off, it is full of Sean, Rob and Tom. I feel that none of them are right for me. That I am not right for them but each have qualities I wish the other had and qualities I don't enjoy and in my confusion I decide that I must cancel Sean. I know I won't sleep if I don't write to him immediately. So I do;

'Dear Sean,

Thank you for a nice evening. I hope you don't mind but I now have to work at the weekend and cannot meet you after all. I am ......'

Dammit, I don't know his address. I am going to have to go or stand him up. I am furious with myself and to prove it I punch myself in the leg. Which hurts and I turn off the lamp and try and do some relaxation techniques to get to sleep. When I wake in the morning it's early and I recall a dream. I am being chased by five bank robbers across a wasteland, nowhere to hide. I am fast, I am focussed, I can see a village in the distance. I am losing ground and when I look back, they have taken off their masks and they all look like Tom. Then I look down and I am naked, and the Tom Bank Robbers are laughing at me. I wake up feeling very traumatised.

Chapter 16

We get to mother's mid-morning and she is looking thinner but happier; a smile dances on her face when she thinks we are not looking. We suspect another man is involved. We are all going for a trip to Bath Christmas Market; I am driving us all in my mini. Mother had a car crash three years ago and refuses to drive anymore. It made her really anxious and she refused to talk to us about it. However, she has at last accepted a trip out with me driving, which is a complete first. I am worried about her worrying about my driving and anxious that she is going to be a nightmare backseat driver. To my surprise she sits calmly in the front and doesn't say a word, even when I clip the pavement when I turn out of her road. I ask her what music she would like on or the radio and she suggests silence so we can chat without having to compete with music. She says she has some things she wants to say to us, now she has all her daughters with her. Her manner is upbeat, but I suggest it wasn't fair of her to drop any bombs on us whilst I am driving.

"It's nothing too major Tovu, don't be such a drama queen." Mother glances at me and then turns to look at the road ahead.

Well that put me in my place. With some unease, Larissa asks her what it is she wants to tell us. Mother says in a matter of fact way,

"I was going to divorce your dad you know, before he died. We weren't happy together and starting to lead separate lives. I didn't hate him and certainly I didn't want him to die. I do still love him in a way. We made all you five children and brought you up together. Now you don't need us to be a couple anymore.

Anyway, we had talked about it and he agreed. If I seem as though I don't care about him dying, it is because I had already moved on from him years ago. Well since the car accident. It just...... well it made me think."

This is not really a surprise to us, and mother says the same, she doesn't want any tantrums, she can see we have all grown up to be independent and free thinking women and she is proud of us.

However, she has found someone special in her life over the last six months and it is starting to blossom, so she wants us to be prepared for that. Larissa comments that if it makes her happy and she does look happy; then we support her. Faye and I agree and ask when we are going to meet this someone special. Mother informs us they are coming over tonight for tea. We all tell her we are excited to meet them. Faye is the most excited, she is sitting behind mother in the car and leans over to hug her from behind. Mother laughs and tells her to put her seatbelt back on. We try and elicit information about her 'someone special'. Is he older, is he working? How did they meet? Have they been on many dates? Is he well off? Mother remains very tight lipped and tells us we can ask them these questions ourselves this evening.

"Tovu put the radio on, I am not talking to you lot for the rest of the trip."

Mother turns her head to look out of the window and suggests we change the subject but leave her out of it. She is going to sit back and enjoy the view. We are on the M4 and all there is to see is other traffic, tells us she is determined not to let us know anything before meeting her mystery man.

"Hey Faye, how are the A levels going, you'll be starting exams next year won't you?"

Larissa obliges mother and changes the subject.

Faye is working hard studying and getting great results in mock exams. She, however, is worried that no-one has asked her to go to the college Christmas Ball and that is what she wants to talk about. We tell her that it is likely that the boys are all too nervous to ask as she is so stunning and maybe she is going to have to make the first move.

"But don't you think that whoever wants to go with me should make the first move, be brave enough to want to?" she asks.

"Yes, but boys at seventeen, eighteen are still just boys and they haven't matured as much as the girls. They all need a helping hand. Besides, the ones that are not shy tend to be very cocky." Larissa is certain of these facts.

"Who would you want to go with?"

Faye laughs and agrees she has a point and tells us there is just one boy who is in her English Literature class that is more mature, and she likes a lot. He doesn't seem interested in getting to know her except as a friend. She has flirted with him a bit. Larissa asks if he has shiny shoes, always looks extremely clean and has a feminine bent. Faye laughs and tells us he is definitely not gay, and Larissa pushes her on her questions being answered. Faye thinks a moment and says reluctantly that yes, all those things you could apply but says that none of them or collectively do these things mean he is gay and Larissa is being homophobic. I side with Faye and mother comes out of her car watching trance, to also side with her. Larissa laughs and says she was just checking the stereotype and in principle she agrees with us but maybe Faye needs to find out if he is interested in her or not and ask him directly if he wants to go to the ball with her.

Bath is packed out, the market looks amazing, little wooden huts, lit up with colourful lights, full of Christmas crafts and trinkets. The mulled wine and cheese smells wafting around us make us hungry and we go on a tasting spree around the kiosks and stalls. Mother is having my share of the alcohol; she says this is only fair as she is the eldest and she needs to be tipsy for the journey home and pats me on the shoulder as she says this. Larissa and Faye think this is highly amusing and have linked arms with me and are chanting; 'you better watch out you better not cry, you better not pout I'm telling you why…' until I join in and mother tells us she is going to look at some stalls without us, as she may buy us something and we arrange to meet under an ivy festooned lamp post with a big red sign on it.

Faye thinks mother is going to buy us some patchwork cushions for Christmas. I think it maybe the festive toilet roll holders and Larissa the personalised cheese boards. We take the opportunity to second guess what her new man was going to be like and whether we will like him. I'm the sceptical one and think he might be after her money; Larissa thinks he is probably just a lonely old man who likes being bossed around and likes mother's penchant for a feminist rally. Faye has the more romantic view and thinks she has fallen in love with her perfect man. Just as she is about to elaborate on this, she spots someone she knows and pulls away from us to go and chat to them. We stop and wait for her and note the tall, red haired, pale faced young man she is excitedly talking to. He is not shiny and clean; he is scruffy and looks apologetic. Larissa surmises he is not the English Lit boy. He is wearing an earring and is fidgeting with a carrier bag in his hand.

"I think he likes her"

Larissa states the obvious and I nod.

Faye returns to us and the blushing red head walks off with some swagger towards the paella stall; she is smiling broadly all over her face.

"That's Gary from Geography, he is good friends with James' brother Fred and he says that he knows for sure that Fred wants to go to the Christmas Ball with me."

We suggest that Gary would die to be able to take her too and tease her about how goofy he was around her. I feel a tap on my shoulder and look around, to see Rob. Now it's my turn to be scrutinised from a distance by my sisters. He pulls me off to the side.

"Tovu, you look great! How are you?"

He is also at the market with his mother and I pray that she doesn't appear. I am convinced it was she who got Rob to finish with me. I sort of need to thank her but feel that would be inappropriate. I tell him I am well and ask how he has been. He tells me he had a recent promotion at work and was looking at buying his own place. He then asks if I got his card and I lie and tell him no. He then has to tell me it asked if we could make a go of it again, that he missed me. I blush and tell him I need time to myself, to be on my own. A lot happening with my father dying and work being hectic. He asks me to give him a ring sometime and checks I still have his number. Then goes off in search of his mother.

Hungry for some lunch we chase down our mother at the lamp post; my sisters are keen to find out more about my exchange with Rob and offer their thoughts on his appearance. I am saved by mother who upon seeing us waves madly and is holding out paper bags full of food.

"I got some lunch for us all and found a nice spot for us to eat."

She looks so pleased with herself; we don't have the heart to tell her we were coveting the hog roast stall. The spot she has found is behind an ice cream van, where there are three bench tables hidden from general view. An older gentleman stands up upon seeing mother and she thanks him for saving her spot. He strolls off nonchalantly and we look at each other as if to say, 'who is this woman?' She suddenly seems more ballsy and out there; it is great. We don't realise just how different our mother has become until teatime.

Faye wants to know what mother has been buying apart from lunch, Larissa and I want to know what is for lunch. We open our paper bags to discover vegetable noodles and a gingerbread man. This combination is unusual but not disgusting and definitely eatable. We dig in and relish the tastes while Faye picks at hers and talks nonstop about stuff at college and tells us stories about Gary and his friends when they went on holiday with is dad to Mexico. Gary's dad is apparently rather well off and spoils his only son a lot, but Gary feels embarrassed by it most of the time. He did however, have a crazy time on this particular holiday and had told Faye every gory detail.

There's about an hour to get freshened up and help mother get ready for our tea with her friend when we get back, the traffic out of Bath was manic and I got a bit lost. Mother is a little tense now and more like the mother we know best. We understand she is nervous. I tell Larissa and Faye to go get ready and I help mother organise the tea, as I blame myself for our lateness. I send her to lay out the table and put the lasagne mother made into the oven after I have grated lots of cheese on top because it looks sparse, I also get the garlic bread and salad ready. With the cakes ready; I go to find mother to let her get ready for her man while I finish off the dining room and tidy up the hallway. She has beaten me to it, and we meet at the bottom of the stairs.

"Kitchen is sorted mother, you can go get ready".

"I was going to say, dining room all ready, you can go get ready" she smiles at me.

Half an hour later we have all congregated in the lounge and wait for the doorbell to chime. It feels a little bit like a doctor's waiting room initially and then Faye puts on some Stevie Wonder and we put some nibbles out. I go and check on the lasagne and pour some wine out for us all and before long we are creased up talking about our brothers and remembering father's parties. The doorbell rings and mother gets up, flushed and we detect a slight tremor as she walks across the lounge. She soon reappears holding the hand of a lady dressed in jeans and a white Tee Shirt that states 'RELAX' in black across her chest. She has auburn curly hair and a fully made up face. She is about the same height as mother although thinner, quite boyish hips. Her name is Teri and she is clearly excited to meet us.

Our mother is now a lesbian? We are very confused, and Larissa burst out laughing in embarrassment at our stunned silence as she dashes over to hug Teri. Faye and I follow and greet her. Mother stands smiling and says,

"Teri, these are my girls, Larissa, Tovu and Faye. Girls this is Teri, I want you to get to know her as I hope she is going to be around more and more. She makes me so happy." She turns towards Teri to look into her eyes as she says this.

Teri in turn states in a soft, welsh accent,

"I am so excited to meet you; Jean has told me so much about you and I feel I know you already. I have brought some chilli and rice in case Jean's lasagne doesn't turn out so well." She jokes.

She seems to know my mother's cooking is not the best. It is fascinating to see the chemistry between them and the easy way in which Teri gently but lovingly teases mother. Faye seems to be struggling the most with the surprise; I suggest we go and check on the food and as soon as she thinks we are out of ear shot she immediately asks,

"What the hell Tovu, we did not see that one coming? Why didn't she warn us? Why the dramatic reveal? Oh my fucking goodness I am really surprised. How are we supposed to feel and think about this? I am so bloody obtuse to not have picked up on this. Where do you think they met? How did they get together?"

I tell her to take a breath, slow down and suggest the following as a response;

"I think she must have been so worried about it and thought it better to tell us all together and spare the interrogation and questions, because we can't ask while Teri is here. It will all come out eventually. I wonder why she didn't invite the boys too and now I know. They will be more shocked than us."

Faye wants answers but is mature enough to know she will have to wait for them, and we get the food to the dining room table; hoping it is not going to be too awkward. Faye goes to tell them the food is served, and we are very polite to Teri as she dominates the conversations. We can see where mother's new found confidence and happiness comes from. She has the ability to hold your attention and make you feel special to her; her joy is infectious and where we had wondered what she sees in our mother, we begin to observe how Jean Jenkins is a witty, strong and interesting woman. We find out that they met at the Guild and quickly found out they shared common interests and thoughts on politics and women's rights. They started going to the pub after the meetings and their relationship developed from there. We find out that the relationship didn't properly become intimate until the recent holiday which Teri was also on with 'The Morrisons' and mother just didn't want to keep it a secret out of respect to us all. She intends to tell Landon and Evan tomorrow as they are coming over tomorrow. We cannot wait for that; we are so glad we had booked a few days not just one.

Mother and Teri are completely unconcerned about what others think about their relationship, the Morrisons think they are just friends. They feel they are too old to kiss in public but want to be able to hold hands. We encourage them to do just as they want, the world is changing and they should let people think what they liked, they had each other.

"I like your girls Jean. They are enlightened and a credit to you!"

Teri is gushing and seems to approve.

"They have their father's inner strength, my inner wisdom and their grandmother's looks. See how beautiful they are?"

Mother actually blushes when she says this. We cannot wait to see how this relationship plays out although something is niggling me about Teri. I am unsure if it is just my usual anxiety manifesting negativity or whether there is some intuitive sense that she is hiding something or it's just too good to be true.

After we have cleared away the meal and reconvened together in the lounge; Teri wants to know all about us, and questions are fired like a machine gun across the living room at us. Fielding them is fairly easy at first; parrying the usual type questions of a stranger wanting to get to know you. The harder ones follow though, and it starts to get a bit emotional.

The phone rings, it is Evan telling mother that Nephew Joshua has been in an accident. He climbed down a drainpipe and it broke. He fell 7 feet off the ground and landed on his head and right arm. He is in a bad way. Mother is naturally distraught, but she takes the details and we all squeeze into Teri's car to get to the hospital in the city. Teri drops us off and says to ring her when we want to be picked up, she doesn't think it right to be involved at this point. The four of us find Evan and Joshua in a side room in A&E. Evan is pale but Joshua looks even paler, almost blending into the starched hospital sheet on the bed he is lying on. He has tubes everywhere and is wired up to a monitor. Evan stands up and ushers us out of the room,

"Mum didn't say you were going to be with her!"

Evan hugs us in turn.

"Look he is in a bad way but not critical, they are going to move him to ICU soon. You don't need to all stay, the nurses won't let you anyway. They want him in ICU as a precaution but expect he can go to the Children's Ward tomorrow once the doctor has checked him over again."

We ask him if we can all just see him in twos and mother says she will stay with him while Evan has a little break. I go with Larissa, he looks so vulnerable, so precious and I look at his observations chart. It looks stable enough. I tell Larissa this. We tell mother we will call Teri to pick us up and I will come and get her when she wants to come home. We will wait for Faye to go and say hello to him first.

What an emotional and challenging evening. Who needs soap operas when you live in one I think to myself? We congregate outside and have a fag, pacing up and down until Teri picks us up and drops us back to mothers. She decides to go home but tells us to ring her if there is anything she can help with.

We don't quite know what to say to each other, so we slope off to be on our own, scattered about the house. It all feels really sensitive and shocking; one minute discovering our mother is a lesbian and the next having our little nephew in a critical condition in the intensive care unit. Faye goes to chat to a friend on the phone. Larissa goes outside for another fag and I start clearing away the mess of the tea stuff in the kitchen. My head is whirring as usual, I can't decide whether I like Teri or not, there really is something just a little off. I still can't place it. I am praying in my head that Joshua recovers well, he is such a character; he is strong I know it. Life can be so shitty.

Chapter 17

After the dramas of last week; I am glad to get into the safe routines of the working week. Joshua is on the mend and mother has introduced Teri to Evan and Landon. They apparently took it in their stride okay and were just a little put out their sisters knew before they did.

It's a windy but dry Sunday, I have my date with Sean. I have done my usual worrying and half hoping he doesn't turn up and half contemplating standing him up but it seems although late again he is strolling towards me. I arrived there fifteen minutes early and have watched people pass by me for the last half hour. Again, he doesn't apologise and just waves at me when he sees me, then upon reaching me goes in for the kiss on the cheek and in my surprise, I turn my head the wrong way and our lips meet.

"I like a keen gal!" he says, whilst I blush.

He takes my hand and we head down the river path and he asks me how I am, and then the shitty stick man; before I have chance to say much, tells me all about his last few days. He has had difficulties at work due to customers not paying their bills and other customers coming on to him. He states this matter-of-factly as if the women all find him to be irresistible and want to make him their sex toy or they think sex is a fair trade for him building them a new wall. His mother has been unwell. He jokes that he has had to help around the house a bit for her as she is on her own and gets lonely if he doesn't pop in and see her.

He really isn't my cup of tea. I am getting the impression he doesn't seem to have a good view about women and is closed off to anything too deep. He has continued to hold my hand as we stroll along, he does hold open gates for me and he stops at almost every dog we meet to pet them and talk to them. I am just about to ask him why he doesn't have a dog as he clearly loves them when he says,

"I feel like I want to kiss you Tovu. I find you so sexy. Can I?"

I don't want to reject him out in public and he has paid his first compliment to me ever; I agree of course. His kiss is deep but not too wet and not much tongue thank god. It does get a pleasant reaction out of me; I kiss him back and feel zinging in my tummy. He lets out a small moan and pulls away.

"Wow, you kiss well. I really want you Tovu. Will you come back to my place? I just feel hungry for you." He growls in my left ear.

When I enter his house, it strikes me as being very male, quite sparsely decorated and painted in shades of white, grey and blue. The lounge has a techy corner of stereo player and TV and a large tan leather sofa dominates the rest of the room. He tells me to sit down and offers me a coffee. I accept, I want to see what the rest of his place looks like. The way he was looking at me, I am not sure we will make it to his bedroom. I suddenly feel nervous but then he returns, sets the drinks down and takes me into his arms to kiss me. We don't make it to his bedroom, in fact I think I have carpet burns thanks to his penchant for doggy style. He doesn't seem to want to cuddle up afterwards, so I feel a bit used and decide it is time to go. He has also managed to get ejaculate over my jeans, so I do get to see his large kitchen as I try and wipe it off. I now look like I have peed myself, so I am glad my car fitted onto his drive beside his Ford. I pray it has dried off before I get home.

He asks if I would like to come round next week some time. I say I have a busy week, he suggests Sunday again. I tell him I will let him know as I cannot remember what I am doing. His phone rings, I shoo him off to answer it and get out of his house and into my car. As I pull out of his road I am wondering to myself what on earth was that about. Did I really want sex with him or did I choose the path of least resistance? In any case, I guess that he seems the sort to go off his women once he has shagged them and I fully anticipate not seeing him ever again.

Wednesday night and I am heading to meet up with my friends at the Tap and I am in my usual rushed state. Yet still I and end up being early for them. I don't have to wait too long though and we soon settle into our usual conversations about the men in our lives. When I take my jacket off, Belle asks if my dress is on back to front. When we all inspect it, we agree that my dress is indeed on back to front, so I have to disappear off to the toilets to right it. I am relieved that my boobs have not suddenly grown and are no longer spilling out of my dress. They are perfectly covered when I put my dress on correctly. Mary and Belle think Sean's a dick and think I should stop seeing him as he is not nice enough for me. They only really recollect him from our night out but also think he isn't treating me well enough. They are probably right, but he does also quite intrigue me. He does have a softer side and let's his guard down now and again. They suggest that this is probably during and after sex and laugh at me.

We are planning a return to Bridport. Cha Cha has written to Mary telling her we all have to go for Halloween, he is organising a huge party and thinks we will love it. He wants us to bring extras, and we decided to ask our brothers Landon, Frank and Belle's older brother Jimmy who is a lawyer and doesn't get out much. Only thing is they don't know each other that well and we were wondering how we get six of us to Bridport for a long weekend. In the end, Frank and Jimmy agreed to come but Landon is busy at work and has something on with Tia. Jimmy offers to drive as he has a bigger car and he agrees to share a room with Frank too. We have booked the same B&B and cannot wait to have lots of baked goods and catch up with Cha Cha, Margie, Graeme and our hostess at the B&B, Mrs Deacon. Neither of us want to take our actual boyfriends. We suggest that this is because we just want to have fun with our friends without having the pressure of keeping them happy and having to pay for extra rooms, etc. Deep down, we all think that our men are not worthy of a weekend away with us and know this is not a good sign.

I tell them about my mother and our scare with Joshua. I am still unsure about her new friend and I worry there is something predatory about her; underneath her evident 'niceness' and eagerness to please and exude positivity. Maybe I am just being cynical, maybe I don't want to confront the fact my mother is a lesbian and what impact that has or has not. I recall the trip back from the hospital with mother when I picked her up. She was understandably upset about Joshua, but all she talked about was Teri, she was almost euphoric, in some sort of hedonistic trance. She mentioned that Teri had had a difficult childhood, abused by her father and neglected by her mother. That she had been a nun for five years from when she was eighteen, but then decided she wanted to help children and trained as a child social worker. That didn't last long, and she ended up joining the police force and then latterly took early retirement and now does part time work in an advocacy service. Aside from her career history, Mother talked about her being an inspiration and guiding light. It seemed a bit weird for my very practical mother to be talking in this way.

My friends think it is odd too but are less analytical about this conversation and suggest it sounded like my mother was just trying to put her in a good light to me. Maybe even trying a bit too hard to reassure me she was a good person, but that I shouldn't dwell and just wait and see how things pan out. We agreed that ultimately, if mother had found love, it was a good thing and I reneged that I was the last person to judge as I had no judgement when it came to relationships.

On Sunday, I meet Sean at his place and as it is a pretty rainy and cold day we decide to watch a video and stay in. Sean has dressed down for the occasion in jogging bottoms and a holey tee shirt; it is a sexy look on him somehow. He has makes us cheese on toast and offers me wine. He wants me to stay over with him. I decline and have a coffee instead. He cuddles me on the sofa while we watch the film, it's a pretty lame film I think. Rocky III, he's seen it before but likes it. Why he thinks I will enjoy it I am not sure. Maybe he thinks all those muscular, sweaty bodies will excite me. I think it's really boring, but endure it. He lies stroking my arm and hair absent minded playing and occasionally kisses the top of my head. It's not unpleasant and I feel comfortable with him for the first time. He offers me wine and opens the bottle for himself to have a glass, he encourages me to have just one glass and I do. He turns off the TV and puts on some music and he talks about his work and mother who is deteriorating. He is intrigued about my mother and suggests that it's a phase now she has freedom from my father. He thinks it is funny and teases about her being a closet lesbian all this time and wonders if it runs in the family; I don't take the rise and feign sleepiness.

Before I know it, I have finished off two glasses and resign myself to the fact I am staying the night after all. He starts to kiss me and stroke me more fervently; I respond and stroke him back. We end up in his bed giggling and playful. We don't sleep much that night. I faked a lot of orgasms over the last 8 hours.

In the morning, I must get up early and leave him to get ready for work. As I leave, he suggests we meet up again next Sunday as he has a busy week ahead. I tell him I am going away, and he is disappointed but we agree to meet the following Sunday instead. He says he will give me a call midweek. I manage to get back to my place in time to shower, get changed for work and arrive weary but clean and clothes all correctly put on. After the morning meeting, Dr Ade asks to see me. Initially he asks about a mutual patient call James Bond, he actually changed his name by deed poll to this name. He has a manic-depressive illness; and he is recently coming out of a manic phase so we are worried he is dipping in mood rapidly. Last time he was low in mood he tried to kill himself by jumping in front of a train; luckily the train driver was slowing down anyway and managed to stop in time. James now thinks he is indestructible and says things like; 'I'm James Bond, I'm not going to die. James Bond lives forever.' Dr Ade suggests he increases his medication and wants my opinion on this. I suggest his Carbemazepine (a mood stabilising drug that also is an anticonvulsant), could be slightly increased but we needed to ask him to come to the day centre daily so we can keep an eye on him. He agrees and then says to me;

"Tovu, I have been watching you and I think we should go on a date. I think you are a good person and I like you. I think you would be a good match for me."

I am taken aback and a not sure what to say. I pause and then say;

"I am really flattered but, I am actually seeing someone at the moment. I am so sorry."

"Does that mean if you wasn't seeing someone you would go out with me?" he counters.

I blush and say that I really don't know him very well but of course I would go on a date with him and see how we got on, but I just wasn't in a position to right now. He smiles and leans back in his chair and says,

"Well I hope it doesn't last and you consider my offer and I mean that in the best possible way."

I make my excuses to leave and go outside for a sneaky fag to calm my anxious soul. I have often dreamed about meeting a nice doctor and how lovely to go out with a wealthy one because you can really tell that Ade is wealthy. He exudes it. Then I think of Sean and his casualness and sometimes rudeness. Yet last night was good and we did have a laugh together. I must pull myself together to get ready to run the Art Group. I must face everyone wondering if they know Ade has proposed we go out with each other. I must face him if he comes out of his clinic room. I am decidedly shaky and Janice, ever vigilant in reception calls me over.

"Did he ask you?"

I now know she knows and nod. She is excited about it and thinks he is such a catch. I explain my dilemma and she tells me that if he is serious he will wait and see what happens. She says this in a knowing way and I haven't time to quiz her, so ask her if I can come over to hers later this evening and she agrees so long as I spend some time with James Bond after the Art Group this morning.

Now I am the least arty person there is, and I am only covering the Art Group for Debbie who is on leave. I get them all doing collages, because this is something I can make look reasonably okay. It's a largish group today, twenty of them. I don't have much time to think about Ade and Sean any more for an hour and half. Sam is one of our patients who has been coming to the day centre for many years; he has Schizophrenia and can paint beautiful landscapes; he doesn't want to do collages, so I let him paint. Martha also wants to paint instead, I set them a theme of 'Joy'. The results are uplifting, except for Tanya. Tanya is in her thirties, recently divorced, no children, parents live in Scotland and had moved here with her husband two years ago for his work. He left her for his PA, such a cliché and she is bereft. Her collage is anything but joy; it is mainly black with in red bits of paper right across the middle stuck to make the word 'Joy' broken up with the O shaped like a heart that has a massive zigzag down the middle of it. In the bottom right of the picture is a small eye with a big tear drop in red coming from the corner of it as if it is bleeding. We talk about it and she agrees it is how she feels but creating it pictorially has helped her. She thinks it helps her understand how she feels and instead of being numb and empty, she realises she is in pain. It is cathartic and she starts to sob. The rest of the group rally round her and tell her all the positive things they know about her. She absorbs their kindness and I reflect how valuable these groups are. Sam has painted a beautiful river scene; the sun is shining and a boat is meandering down it. He gives this painting to Tanya telling her that she must look at it and be happy. That the lady lounging in the boat with a smile on her face will be her in time. She is beside herself with gratitude. A great session. I might do these Art Groups more often.

Dear James is sat in the dining room muttering to himself, I go over to him and ask him if we can have a chat in private. We go into an interview room and I ask him how he is today.

"I asked God to send me a sign this morning, I waited at the window with my arms open wide and he didn't come to me. I stood on a chair for a while with my arms wide and still he didn't come and then got down and had a cup of tea and then I came here."

I ask him what sort of sign he was hoping to get and how would he know when he had got it. He replied a little scathingly that he was waiting for a light of course. A beam of God's light that would show him how to die in peace. I tell him I am glad the sign didn't come because we all wanted him to live and to help him find his peace in other ways. We get onto talking about his family and particularly his father who was still very supportive of him; even though he had had so many traumatic incidents with his son over the years through his ill health. I ask him about his medicines and whether he is taking them, about whether he is sleeping and eating well. He doesn't want to tell me, so I suspect the answer is no on all accounts. I ask him if he will let me help him with his medicines and food to help him sleep and he reluctantly agrees for me to have his medicines for the week and he can have his morning ones when he is at the day centre and also his lunch time ones. I will give him his night time tablets in a pot each day to take home with him to take before he goes to bed. We also agree for him to have three meals with us every day this week and make a plan for the week what he would like. He thanks me after the session and asks me to sit with him at dinner time. I of course agree. He says he will only eat and take his tablets for me, no pressure then I think to myself. I ask him who else he could take them for and he says his dad, his friend Mrs

Beauchamp who lives down the road and is a friend of the family's and of course Mrs Moneypenny. I am not sure if he is joking with me, so I just smile and confirm there are quite a few people he needed to remember cared about him and wanted to help him.

The rest of the day is as busy as the morning and I am shattered by the time I get home; especially having had little sleep the night before. I ask Janice to take a rain check on our chat because all I want to do is lie down and listen to some music and sleep if my brain switches off to allow me. I cannot even do my usual musings about the men in my life. Instead I think about James Bond, not the patient, the fictitious character. I think about his mental state and wonder if he suffers from PTSD and covers it up by having sex with lots of different women or just compartmentalises things and doesn't allow himself to feel. An emotionally constipated Machiavellian sex god? As a consequence I dream about James Bond chasing me across a desert; it's so hot that I wake up sweating and realise I left the heating on.

Chapter 18

Weekend return to Bridport

Jimmy it turns out, is a fast driver and gets us safely to Bridport in good time. He worked out a route that avoided lots of Friday evening hotspots and used some narrow, bumpy lanes and B roads instead. He must have studied and researched the route well. We are full of praise, if a little shaken from the drive. Our hostess is delighted to see us again and fusses over the men even more than she does us. They are sharing a little twin room and we are back in the same room we had last time. It sort of feels like home. Our supper is crumpets with jam and marmite and cheese, followed by home-made mince pies she says she is perfecting for the village Christmas Fayre. We agree to go to the pub for a couple and stretch our legs. We are excited to see Cha Cha and can't wait to see what Jimmy and Frank make of him and he of them.

The pub is festooned with Christmas already, it is red and gold everywhere. As flamboyant as Cha Cha himself who cannot contain his excitement at seeing us and flutters and fawns over the men. They seem to rather like it and play along, Jimmy initially uncomfortable but follows Frank's lead and becomes Mr Heterosexual with a fondness for camp. Us ladies spy Margie and Graeme at their favourite table and go over, they are thrilled to see us too and make space for us getting locals to give up spare seats for us to drag over to them. We leave Jimmy and Frank at the bar drinking pints, Cha Cha has to serve some other punters, so they chat together happily.

Margie is excited to see us and gets various tables nearby to give up seats for us and we gather round to listen to their latest stores. They have booked a cruise and Graeme raises his eyebrows when Margie talks about all the shopping they have had to do for the evening events. Most of them are black tie only. Graeme is not pleased, he is happiest in his corduroy slacks , green holey jumper and gardening boots and says so. Margie gives him a playful punch and then wants to know all about our men we have brought with us and she is slightly disappointed they are related, but keen to meet them. On cue, they appear bearing drinks and offer to get Margie and Graeme one. Belle and I give up our seats for them and head for the bar to get them their whisky and cokes.

Cha Cha serves us and tells us some of the town gossip. There has been a local scandal with a local business man leaving his wife for their cleaner, the wife was apparently a leading light in the Samaritans. He also told us about a sad child death where the parents left a bedroom window open and the child fell out of it. He is outraged by the former and desolate about the latter. He asks us about our love lives to cheer himself up. He chuckles anyway when we tell him to mind his own business and take the drinks off to the others who seem to be having a hilarious time. We discover this is largely at Mary's expense because Frank is regaling them with stories about her when she was younger. The time she wet herself in assembly at school and blamed the puddle on her neighbour, when she farted in geography when the room was silent and she was sat in the front row. Again, she acted as though it was her neighbour, looking at her aghast. He also tells them about her going to the cinema pretending to be older with her best friend and they wore socks in their bras, made their faces up and wore heels. It was a disaster when her friend fell over and a balled up sock got dislodged and went skidding across the carpet. Yes, you've guessed it. I was the brunt of all three incidents. Frank lets this piece of information out when we arrive at the bar, timing it impeccably; so the laughing is at its peak and I have no clue until Mary tells me what he has been talking about. We then gang up on him and recall the time he came home crying from school because he was called a 'nincompoop' by a teacher and he thought it meant he was like a pooh.

Before we launch into other stories, who should walk in the door but Sean.

"Hello, I thought I would surprise you Tovu. I have been in two other Bridport pubs looking for you, so third time lucky. Introduce me then."

I hide my horror and introduce everyone, Sean says hello in a general way to everyone and then says,

"I'm just going to nab Tovu a moment, please excuse us."

He pulls me aside and says he just couldn't wait to see me next weekend and managed to get a room booked in a hotel ten minutes away, in the opposite direction to where we are staying. He wants me to come back with him. I am fuming, this break was about spending time with my friends not with him. He also makes it clear he doesn't want to hang out with my friends, just wants my company. I can just about manage to say,

"I don't understand, I thought I had made it clear this was a friend's only weekend. What are you really doing? Checking up on me?"

"Don't be like that, I like you. I missed you and wanted to see you."

"You should go, I don't want to make a public scene."

His face says it all, he is not happy that am not leaping at the chance to spend a night with him in some seedy hotel. He does however, suggest we meet up tomorrow morning for breakfast and if I still feel the same way he will go home. We arrange to meet at his hotel for breakfast and he leaves, red faced and terse. He does ask me to say that he had to go to the others and says goodbye. He makes a sneery comment about the males in our group and I ignore it.

When I get back to everyone they politely ask no questions and carry on chatting about this and that and the last orders bell rings. The pub empties out until it's just our table and Cha Cha left and then they turn on me. Mary starts it off, sometimes I wonder why she is my friend.

"Oh my God Tovu, why was Sean here? Why haven't you gone off with him? What were you saying to him? You looked cross!"

"He's not as bad as I remember him", Belle says before I answer, "He's still got a sneery look about him though."

"I liked that Rob we met in Paris better Tovu, when did you two finish?" Margie exclaims.

"OOOOH!! Scandal Tovu, tell us all!" says Cha Cha.

I relent and tell them about Rob and Sean, they are all ears even though of course Mary and Belle have heard it all before. The consensus is that I am right to tell him to leave and that it seems like I haven't met Mr Right yet. Frank lightens the mood and says he will go and meet him for breakfast so he doesn't have to have breakfast with us lot. Jimmy agrees that they should both go. I give them a friendly punch each.

The next morning, I have a bad hangover and am not sure I can eat anything for breakfast; I walk down to where Sean said he was staying. It is cold and damp, traffic is fairly busy with people starting their Christmas shopping I guess. The shop windows are full of festive cheer already but I feel very unchristmassy. I get a bit lost, so arrive ten minutes later than we had agreed. There is a frosty looking woman on the reception and I feel nervous. I steady myself and ask if a Sean Herring is staying; she clicks her tongue and starts to look down a register. She pauses and then looks me straight in the eye and tells me in a tense voice, he's left. I ask if there is a message from him, she says not.

I thank her and turn out of the door, hiding my embarrassment as much as is possible. I am puzzled but decide it is probably a blessing. Tracing back to the B and B takes me a while because I lose my way again but Belle and Mary are still lounging about in our room when I get back. They try and reassure me that he probably got called away or he forgot he had something on and had to get back. We head downstairs and see the men are already tucking in; Miss Charlesworth has surpassed herself. The table is packed full of delightful breakfast items. We tuck in and I have to tell Jimmy and Frank about my no show. They also think something must have cropped up. I wonder if he just decided to go and that was the last I would see of him. My appetite has returned though and I consume a croissant while the others discuss the plans for the day. It ends up a toss up between a walk in the woods or a trip up to Yeovil for shopping. Frank wants to pinch some muffins and bread rolls from the table and when we protest, Miss Charlesworth happens to enter the room and tells us to take the leftovers for lunch if we want. Frank kisses her on the cheek and she is flustered but clearly delighted. It was Frank who had managed to extract her full name and she asked him to call her Miss Charlesworth. He told her he will call her 'C' like

Miss Moneypenny is 'M' and she cannot disguise her pleasure. The rest of us are more respectful and less cheeky.

Langdon Hill wins by a vote and we head off to get ready. Belle hasn't bought her walking boots and Mary hasn't got a waterproof coat, they argue for going shopping first so they can get kitted out. We settle on finding suitable attire between us and whilst my boots are slightly large on Mary and her coat is a little snug on Belle, we pull off the winter walking range at a well-known retailer look pretty well. The boys of course have been waiting for us and look suitably smug as they are well togged up and already started on the breakfast goody bag which we are none too pleased about. Then 'C' appears from nowhere with a large bag of sandwiches and home made scotch eggs to give us. She really is the best hostess ever. Frank invites her along but she blushes and says she has to do some shopping. I would imagine she would have had to sit on his knee to fit in the car. The vision amuses me and I supress a giggle.

The route around the woods is not far and as it is just under one and half miles we set ourselves the challenge of getting around it four times. Well at least Jimmy and Frank do. I am thinking that us females will want to quit after two circuits. The woods are stunning and the frost remains on the ground and leaves on the trees, it sparkles as the sun streams through and soundproofs the tree tunnels as you stroll through them. We start collecting twigs and like good boy scouts mark our route; not to keep us from getting lost but to provide markers from when we walk around it again. The woods are quiet and apart from a couple of dog walkers we are the only ones in it; so to them we may seem rather loud as we chatter and giggle. We try to rein in Frank as he decides to climb some trees and make a den; but he wins us over and we have a 'climb a tree' challenge. It is great fun until Belle falls out of her tree, losing her footing and she screams. When we rush over to her I knock heads with Frank as we bend towards her in unison. My eyes water, I lose my balance and fall over and I yelp! Frank is now split between making sure Belle and I are okay. Jimmy and Mary join us and they help Belle up, leaving Frank to check up on me. Belle hobbles but she feels okay. A few bumps and scratches but otherwise we are okay.

Frank is looking intently at my face and then into my eyes, he gives me a funny smile and shakes his head,

"Only you could give a man near concussion and make him wonder if you could ever be in love with him."

I rub my head and said,

"Don't you mean, give a man near concussion so his brain goes soft? Behave yourself!"

He laughs and pulls me to my feet,

"You do look kind of cute though. Come on you'll live to drive another man wild!"

I give him a brief hug and we join the others.

As we now have three injured people in the party we decide to head for a village pub and get some lunch. We decide on Evershott and it is the most picturesque of places, a gorgeous olde world entitled gentry feel to it. The pub is so cosy and food amazing. A few older couples dine alongside us and Frank of course gets talking to them all. We discover one couple live in London and the other locally. They are all retired and just enjoying life. They start talking to each other as Frank loses interest and turns his attention away from them. There is something familiar about one of the men, he reminds me a bit of my father. As I am wondering about this, the door opens and a very dapper couple of men walk through the entrance. Sebastian Connelly and a younger man who fusses over him. I immediately stand up and shout a hello, before thinking that he may not even remember me from an award ceremony. I bet he does loads of them. True to his gentlemanly ways he waves and comes over to the table.

"Well if it isn't the delightful Tovu Jenkins, these all your friends? Meet my friend Bolly, so called because of his love of a glass of the old Bollinger."

"Sebastian, you remember me! I am so thrilled. Meet my friends Mary, Belle, Frank and Jimmy."

After all the introductions, tables pulled together and another round of drinks ordered we listen to Sebastian and some of his stories. He is so hilarious. One time he was playing poker with a well-known actor and a pop singer, the actor was doing well and was being really cocky with it. The pop singer was off his head on some drug as he had completely lost his game. Sebastian was watching and waiting for his moment. Just as he was going to make his winning move a large bosomed lady in scruffy, tight fitting jeans, cowboy shirt and boots appeared at their shoulders and loudly pronounced she wanted to play. She was a bit tipsy and her face heavy with make-up. He wanted so desperately to tell her to go away but he is a gentleman and he decided his best tactic was to give her a chip and ask her to get them all a round of drinks before she joined the table with them. She was incredibly insulted and slapped him around the face telling him he was an asshole and she strode off. The actor looked at him straight and told him he had just pissed off his leading lady and he would never hear the last of it. Sebastian unperturbed played on and won the next five hands of cards, wiping the floor with his companions. The actor declared he would never play poker with Sebastian again and thanked him again for upsetting his co-star. Sebastian just looked him in the eye and told him that fortune favours the brave and the strong and better luck next time. He told us he didn't know how he didn't get a punch that night.

Bolly is also a funny man once he stops fussing over Sebastian who he calls Seb. Bolly was born privileged and sometimes lives indulgently. However, he is an anthropologist; set up several charities and spent time in various third world countries volunteering and checking funds are being spent on the right things. He just loves people and engages us really quickly with his wit and genuine interest. We all have a crush on the couple. We have invited Sebastian and Bolly to the pub tonight in Bridport. They are excited to accept. Cha Cha is going to be more excited than them.

All good things as they say come to an end and we have laughed long, re-fuelled and deepened friendships. We decide to stroll in the nearby Deer Park as we all feel up to it before heading back. Jimmy is unusually noisy as he tells us how much he loved Seb and Bolly; he really has come a long way this weekend with his homophobia. Belle is pleased with him and gives her brother an affectionate hug whilst telling him he needed to hang out with us more often as it was good for him. Mary also gives him a friendly poke in his side and reinforces this. I wonder if a little frisson is developing between them.

I won't bore you with the most amazing fun night ever; you had to be there. It was intensely joyful and immensely awesome in every way. There were no dramas, just good friends old and new having a great time.

Chapter 19

Back home I feel like I need a week off to recover from the sensational weekend antics. We are all pledging to go back next year. My work colleagues are jealous of the fun I have had when I tell them and then we are sobered by some news of James Bond needing to go into hospital. He threatened to jump off a high-rise building. Police managed to persuade him down. I ask if I can go and visit him and we shuffle things around so I can do that and pop into town to collect our petty cash from the bank.

The ward today is noisy and fractious, the staff are busy rushing around and there seems to be a lot of them. I find out that James is on a 1:1 and in a side room as he has been quite disruptive. I agree to do the 1:1 and give the staff member a break for 30 minutes. I know I might well regret this but I do want to see him. James' eyes widen as he sees me and he lets out a whoop of delight.

"Have you come to get me out?"

I explain who I am to the support worker, a bank nurse who is a balding man with a portly stomach and probably one of the prison wardens who sometimes do extra at the hospital on the bank. He shrugs and gets off the chair slinking off down the corridor. How nice I think and then turn my attentions to James. I ask him how he is.

"I wanted to jump, show them I can survive anything! They made me come here and they bundled me into a cage. I was scared and I hit someone. I didn't mean to. I want to go home and they put a guard on me so I can't escape. Get me out of here!"

I talk to him about what he says and calmly we piece it together so it makes better sense to him. I talk to him about his feeling he can do anything and still live and how that worries us because we see him as a great person and we would not want anything bad to happen to him, just in case. We talk about his medication again and he admitted he had forgot over the weekend. I ask him about how his family his and whether they have visited. He doesn't know if they know if he is here and I tell him I will check up for him. Then he asks when he can leave. So we talk through what it would need for the team to feel he was well enough to leave. He is calmer by the time I leave and I do check back to let him know his family know he is there and will come and visit him soon. He wants me to visit him again too.

The bank is also noisy and busy. After all that country air and space at the weekend I wonder if I am becoming a bit intolerant of busy towns and lots of people. It takes what seems ages to be served and then when I leave I see across the road Sean and another woman. She is a petite oriental girl, holding on to his arm and gazing up at him as he chatters away. I pause at the doorway and watch them, he doesn't see me. I don't know what to think. Has he been two timing us? Has he just met her? Has he lost his mind? I don't know whether to feel upset or relieved; I sort of feel both. Part of me wants to run over to them and slap him in the face and the other wants to sneak away. I decide on a version of the first option and dash up the road so I get level with them and then stride across.

"Hey Sean! What happened to you on Saturday? Oh Hey, are you his girlfriend? Funny that, I thought I was."

"Tovu!" he looks genuinely uncomfortable. "Err this is Kiara, she's my best friend from school. Kiara, this is Tovu. You know I told you about her".

Kiara to be fair blushes and offers me her hand to shake, I choose not to notice and tell Sean I was puzzled as to why he hadn't waited for me for breakfast on Saturday. Sean goes on to tell me he had to rush back because Kiara had a health scare and wanted to see him. He tells me he will call me tonight to explain it all.

I tell them I must dash back to work, I had already been held up and was late. I stride off with my head held high and can feel Sean's eyes burning into the back of me. I grab Janice when I get back to work and we have a quick coffee together; she is all ears. The fact that clearly Kiara knew how to get hold of him in Bridport, that she clearly was in love with him from her demeanour and he hadn't had the decency to wait for me to tell me he had to go home anyway makes us both believe he's not worth pursuing. Janice wants me to give Ade a chance and I say that I just want some time on my own without all these stupid men making me so anxious and giving me stomach pains. I reassure Janice when she looks startled at the possibility I may be pregnant when I say this. Thankfully, with all these liaisons of mine I have been on the pill and encouraged condom usage throughout. Janice agrees to tell Sean I am unavailable tonight when he calls and that I don't want to see him anymore. I feel a bit of a coward but chances are he won't bother to phone anyway. He's been caught out and most men are complete cowards.

I write up my report on James and then I work on an induction training pack that Vanessa asked me to do. Just as I think it's time to get home there is a knock on the office door. Ade pops his head in and then without invitation comes in and announces;

"I have tickets for the ballet next weekend, The Nutcracker. Get us in the Christmas spirit. Want to come?"

I hesitate and then decide why not and agree. I wonder if Janice has spoken to him this afternoon, but Ade leaves me as abruptly as he arrived saying,

"Excellent! I will write down the itinerary for you."

I end up being last out and do the locking up and alarms. The car park is deserted except for my little mini and to my surprise Sean. He tells me he has been waiting there for ages and is desperate to talk to me and explain the weekend. I tell him I am in a rush and have to go. I tell him I don't think I want to continue to see him now anyway. He tries to tell me about Kiara and her health condition. I had some of this sort of thing from Tom and his ill ex girlfriend and I really don't think it should be my problem. Sean tries to tell me how good we are together and how he has fallen for me. I am blunt and say I don't feel the same way. He seems rejected and eventually puts his hands up and says slightly aggressively;

"Okay Tovu, okay. Just know we could have been amazing." He walks off.

When I get in the car I am shaking, why do men think they are so fantastic and never think about what they can really offer us women. All they seem to care about is how good we make them feel. I decide I must go and see my sister and tell her the latest. Larissa should be home, I recall her telling me she was on early shifts this week. I decide to chance it and drive over to her place. The lights are on and I can see she has company. I hesitate to interrupt but at least I should just say hello and if she looks like she needs space I can rearrange another time. I knock on the door; she takes no time in answering and surprised to see me gives me a whoop and envelopes me in a sisterly hug. She welcomes me in and then I see the other person is Faye; I am delighted. Larissa tells me they were going to come over to mine and surprise me and then I seemed to have beaten them to it. The family jungle drums must have been in tune and drawn me in. Faye hugs me tightly too. I am so happy to see them both.

Larissa makes me sit down, Faye hands me a water as requested and then they launch into a bunch of questions about the weekend. They are attentive, laughing and nodding in all the right places and want to come to Bridport next year. They agree that Sean is to be avoided, that I have made the right decision and give me extra hugs when I tell them of our car park meeting this evening. I of course want to hear the family news, catch up on both my little nephew and my mother but everyone else too. Faye starts off by telling me that mother is out most of the time with her friends and seems happy enough. She is verbally affectionate to Faye although treats her like a favoured niece rather than a daughter who needs her in anyway. Little Joshua is mending well and back running his parents ragged. Evan has been given a promotion, he wasn't keen but he felt the extra money would be helpful. Landon seems to be laying low; always working. Faye herself is still studying hard and plucked up the courage to ask Fred (English Lit Boy) to the Christmas Ball and as predicted he said yes.

Larissa grabs some wine before she launches into what she has been doing. I take this as not being a very good sign. Apparently, Raj has started flirting with her again at work and hinting he wished he never left, the colleague who was going to move in has let her down so she is worried about rent. I tell her she can live with me if need be and to not let Raj back into the flat. She then tells us of a speed dating event she attended with a woman called Aggie, one of the home managers who was recently divorced. The event was held in a village hall last Wednesday night and she has been dying to tell us about it. There were four men to every woman, which is unusual by all accounts. The organiser was a tall, lean, pale man called Ivan who had an unfortunate winking tic. He was nice though and had everyone at ease making little jokes and keeping people moving. As there were more men than women he sat the women on one side of a long table and the men had to queue to sit with each lady in turn. They then had three minutes to make an impression and then the lady could score them before meeting the next man. Larissa thought it was all very mortifying and funny at the same time.

Larissa couldn't remember the real names of the men she met so she renamed them; most memorable were Pirate Pete and Slim Jim. Pirate Pete had an actual wooden leg and a large bushy beard. He claimed to enjoy sailing and eating meals out. Slim Jim, almost disappeared when you looked at him sideways on. He was very agitated and kept apologising for anything and everything and nothing, he made Larissa feel so edgy herself she knocked a glass of water all over him. The poor man was soaked but kept apologising still and ran out of the room never to be seen again. Ivan was upset about this incident as he lost one of the men and blamed Larissa. He was charming still most of the time but also spent the last hour intermittently scowling at her. At the end of the event Ivan made the women choose their men and all the men choose a woman. Those who chose each other could go on a date and those who did not were given passes to return for another session. Larissa didn't choose anyone so no matches and she threw her return voucher in the nearest bin as soon as Ivan was out of sight. Her friend was chosen by Pirate Pete which she thought was hilarious. Larissa's friend was not pleased and did not want to have a date with Pirate Pete and told Larissa she wished she had been as moody and uninterested as Larissa had been.

Faye and I cannot stop laughing until Faye says;

"I don't have such a funny story to tell you, but I do have a romantic one!"

Faye grins from ear to ear, so we pour some more wine and she tells us not about Fred who turned out to be very boring but Jake, a boy who she met at the gym. She was running on the treadmill next to him and they ended up chatting when they both took a break at the same time. He is a university student studying Geography but home for the holidays early. Jake is tall, blonde, green eyed and looks a bit like Landon. He is funny and sweet and asked Faye if she would come to a concert with him. It was the Eurythmics which she completely loved. After the concert they went for a drink and he told her he felt completely enchanted by her and asked if he could give her a kiss. When they kissed she said it was electric, they have agreed to meet up again tomorrow evening. We are excited for her but keen to give her advice on taking it slow and not letting him go too far. She informs us she is not a virgin and we are shocked. Faye is laughing so hard.

"Your faces! I am not a kid anymore you know? I have had some experiences that may make your hair curl!"

Faye is delighted with the reaction she is getting from us. She gives us some more details and we are slightly shocked but also share some of our embarrassing and funny sex stories.

We agree that we really were none of us that lucky in love and put on some female empowerment music to dance to. We find hairbrushes and wooden spoons to make into pretend microphones and laugh some more at each other. You know the song choices include Gloria Gaynor, Pat Benatar, Kate Bush and Annie Lennox. When we stop, we crash in the lounge, a heap of drunkenness.

In the morning I find myself cuddling Faye's legs. Larissa is nowhere to be seen so I assume she has found her way to her bed. My head hurts so bad and I go in search of water. I have to sober up and get ready for work. I get in the shower and pinch some clothes from Larissa's room, she is snoring her head off. Faye stirs as I go to leave, and I blow her a kiss and tell her I have to get to work. She smiles and wraps herself in the blanket she pulled off the sofa and says she loves me. That makes me smile and I say I love her back. I realise not for the first time that I have two amazing sisters.

The roads are busy, the sky is grey and my head is pounding. I try and recall what I have to do at work today. I think I have groups in the morning and a couple of assessments this afternoon. The day will probably go really quickly, and I must get an early night. My poor liver is crying with the amount of wine I have consumed over the past few days. I seem to have hit a traffic jam, I am going to be late, I hate being late. My anxiety starts to increase, my mouth is so dry and I am sweating everywhere. I try the power of positive thought and ask the higher good to help me and get me to work on time. My signal to the law of attraction must be off because I end up fifteen minutes late. No-one seems that perturbed, the morning meeting hasn't started yet. I grab some coffee and sit ready for the meeting to commence.

Jim starts off the meeting with big news, his wife is pregnant and he looks like he has grown a massive mane and is king of the world. We congratulate him and he blusters saying he never wanted children because they make mess and are noisy. We know he is really delighted though. Debbie then tells us she has a new job in Liverpool as her husband wants to move back there and they have both got jobs and plan to move in a month's time.

It's all happening and yet I feel a bit gloomy. I wonder if I will ever have children or a husband who I want to follow across the country because I love him that much. I rather suspect I am unlikely to have either in the next year or so judging by my disastrous love life. I don't linger on these thoughts for long. I have a group to run. This morning it is my Women's Group. It has grown over the past weeks and I am looking forward to seeing how everyone is.

One of the newest ladies is Lottie, she is struggling to cope with being raped. Her anxiety levels are high and she rarely leaves her flat, the Women's Group feels safe though and she tells us this. She just doesn't feel safe anywhere else. The rapist was a friend of one of her brothers and her brother does not believe that she didn't consent to having sex with him and has taken his friend's side. She feels completely betrayed by him and knows that whilst they have never really gotten on as she thinks he is a pig, he should have been on her side. Uma is sat next to her and looks her straight in the eye and tells her she will help her and be by her side if she wants to go shopping, or the pictures or even to help her get to work. Lottie hasn't been to work since the incident and is starting to waste away as she hasn't been eating much. She smiles at Uma and thanks her. Then a couple of the others also tell her they will make themselves available to her to get her out more and acknowledge this will help them too. This leads to a planned group walk in the woods together for some of the group and one of the ladies invites everyone to her house for an American supper. Lottie asks the group how they handle being around men as she knows that most of them have had difficult experiences with men. After there is a lot of discussion about this, I ask them to think about positive men in their lives or they know through family, work or friends. They can all find at least three positive males in their life and we celebrate them. I remind them that in our group a positive relationship with men is difficult to see where many of them have had recent and past abuse but that there are good men out there and many who are not abusive. There are a few nods and I am just thinking I must remember my own words when Uma says,

"I used to think that all men were complete bastards but now I just see through them, they don't exist to me. Well they do, only the nice ones I see as non gendered, almost female. It helps me, I don't feel that fear or shame when I don't see any men."

Maybe I should take this approach, but I say;

"Uma, I think that is a great strategy for you if it works as well as you say. I wonder if it may be difficult for others to achieve. What do you all think?"

Naturally there were a range of views and mostly the women applauded Uma for developing a strategy that worked for her. It was a great session. Really positive. I grab a coffee before the 'Current Affairs' Group I have next. It is much more low key than the Women's Group. There are five men and two women who attend. Most have been coming to the day centre for many years and enjoy discussing the latest news. They tend to need some prompting and encouragement to discuss news items that lurk in the smaller columns of the inner pages of the papers. We try and steer clear of politics, war and news of murder. That's the challenge, but of course these are the topics they mostly gravitate to.

"How was 'Current Affairs' Tovu?" asks Jim

He knows full well it is the same as it always is but I just tell him it was great. He then asks me if I might be open to babysitting. I tell him that of course I would and wonder whether I may regret this.

Chapter 20

The following day at work I have to go on a joint assessment with Dr Ade. I am puzzled as to why, but we have to go to a secure unit in Aylesbury. Dr Ade has another meeting there first, so I meet him there, which is better than driving there together. I manage not to get too lost and find a parking space. The reception has an air lock entrance, you can't pass through one door until the other one is shut tight. They read you a list of forbidden items and check that you have your ID with you before letting you enter. I explain why I am there and the security man asks someone to collect me. The tall, dark haired and bearded escort is one of the other security men. He is a man of few words and leads me down a myriad of corridors and through numerous doors he has to unlock and re-lock with his bunch of keys. I get put in an office to wait for Dr Ade and then a petite, curly haired lady who smells of musk appears in the doorway and asks me if I want a drink. My mouth is dry so I eagerly accept and ask for a cup of coffee and sit down on a hard plastic chair. Her name is Paulette, she is one of the medical secretaries and has worked there for years. She is warm, chatty and completely puts me at ease. Ten minutes later she takes me to the ward to meet with Dr Ade for the assessment.

The ward is calm and a few of the staff and patients are milling about and I join Ade in a small interview room. A staff nurse called Pete is also there and the patient we are assessing called Bill. Bill is 45 years old, has been known to the mental health services for all his adult life and has a diagnosis of Schizophrenia. He originally came from Norfolk but entered forensic mental health services when he was 22 years old following an assault on his father who subsequently died after hitting his head on the corner of their dining table when he fell from Bill's blows. He has been in this particular hospital for eleven years. He now wants to settle in the area and recognises he will need support. He is delightful, he tells us he loves poetry and art and show us some of his work. One of his poems nearly makes me cry it is so lovely but I manage to compose myself. He says he is worried about living in his new group home and hopes he gets on with the other four people there. Ade asks him gently about whether he still hears voices. He tells us that only when he is worried, which is quite insightful. He says they don't scare him though and he tells them to go away and that helps subdue them. The rest of the assessment meeting goes well and Ade and I reassure him that he will fit in well at the day hospital. He leaves smiling but rubbing his face. Ade turns to me when we get out of the hospital through the air lock and asks me what I think. We have a quick discussion and then he asks me on a date. I am caught by surprised I had pulled out of the last invite out. I decline again, saying I don't want a boyfriend right now but thank him again. The poor man looks really dejected but accepts my answer with grace. He asks me if I will write up the assessment and of course I say I will.

I get home a little late and decide I am going to write my Christmas shopping lists and write out some cards. I can put on some music and make some snacks after a nice shower. Mid making my snack there is a knock on my door. It is Janice who asks if it's okay to have a chat. She looks a bit upset so of course I let her in and forget my plans for a quiet evening. Janice tells me her mother has been diagnosed with breast cancer, she is of course distraught. He face crumples when she tells me and she asks for my advice on whether she should accept her mum's wishes to go untreated. Her mum sounds scared and naturally in denial. I talk to Janice about her knowledge of cancer and the treatment options. She knows people lose their hair, that they are very sick and that after drug treatment they may have to have a mastectomy and wear prothesis. I talk through the different things that she mentions and that it is different for everyone and dependent on how early they have detected the cancer. We chat about what might reassure her mum and whether she will accept a visit from someone else who has been through the treatment to chat to her about what it was like. Janice is very grateful for our chat and the colour has returned to her cheeks. I tell her to keep me updated and I offer to chat to her mum if she wants; rather hoping she doesn't want to talk to some young stranger.

Janice appears at my door the following evening, she had had the day off work and spent time with her mum. Her face is drawn and lined more than yesterday and her hair is uncharacteristically greasy and matted in a tight pony tail. Her tired eyes reveal the pressure and strain of the last two days. She almost collapses into me when she comes in and is unsteady on her feet, I grab her arm and lead her to the lounge to sit on my sofa.

"I'm okay, sorry. Just exhausted. It's been a long day and mum has been such hard work."

I tell her not to worry and to have a moment of quiet while I make her a cup of tea. She nods and gives me a thumbs up. When we are nursing our mugs of tea, she tells me that her mum had been stubborn in her wish not to accept treatment, that she was prepared to die when her time was up and if it was a little premature she would rather go in peace than have to endure drugs and being 'messed about with'. Janice, her brother and father had pleaded with her and cajoled her to at least try the drugs. Her mum refused. They tried to guilt her and that didn't work. They got angry and she only dug her heels in. In the end they had to accept that they were not going to get anywhere. Janice offered her my services and she declined. I suggested that maybe her mum was entitled to have the dignity she sought and that no matter our views hers should be respected. She had a good point; being 'messed about with', going through treatment was a tall order in itself and there were no guarantees it would work. The medical team had not been able to give any clues at this point as to how long it had gone undetected. Janice was in agreement, she realised that it was selfish of them to keep asking her to have the treatment. She was coming around to her mum's view and ultimately had to respect it. She gave herself a little shake and then asked me about Ade.

To cheer her up I told her about the assessment and how good he had been with the patient, but I just didn't want to go out with him. I didn't fancy him and whilst I admired his approach with the patients, I didn't feel the least bit moist around him. Janice laughed and said it was fair enough, she told me that he never failed to ask after me when I wasn't at work and he was. He was obviously keen on me. She pointed out that he must be dirty rich and agreed that wasn't the best reason for going out with someone. I told her that he did have an irritating way of calling himself The Doctor like he was Doctor Who. We giggled a bit and Janice said she needed to get to bed and left me. I had a sudden urge to talk to my mother and Janice completely understood so we went over to hers so I could call.

"Mother, It's Tovu. I just wanted to say hi and check all was okay." I say.

"Yes dear, all is good as far as I know. You only recently saw Faye. Are YOU okay?"

"Of course, yes, I am okay mother, I have had a busy week at work and just had an urge to say hi to you."

"Well that's nice dear. Are you coming to the Christmas Party on the 20th? Talk to Larissa and get her to come too won't you? She says she has to work but I'm sure she could re-arrange things. Mary and Belle coming? I do like your friends, they always bring fun to the party"

"Yes, I will be there. I will check with Mary and Belle and let you know. Are Landon and Evan coming? I haven't seen them in ages."

"I think so Tovu. My darling Teri spoke to Evan yesterday, she bumped into him at work and they had a natter. And before you ask, yes she is fine too and you have nothing to worry about this end."

I take that as mother telling me she has had enough of the chit chat now. I say goodnight and tell her to give Faye a hug from me.

The works Christmas Parties have fallen to me to organise. Both the one for all the staff and patients and the evening do for all the staff. The latter was easier to organise, we are all going to a local restaurant for a Christmas meal and then those who want to go on clubbing can and those who do not can leave after eating. The former however is more tricky. I have worked hard to consult with as many people as possible as to what they want to do and it is fair to say, the diversity of opinion has driven me crazy. I wanted to make it better than the usual turkey and tinsel affair but what it boiled down to was that most people like tradition and then some added weird extras. One lady wanted a Santa Stripagram, one gentleman wanted us to have a snow machine so we could have a snowman competition, and another wanted us to have a famous band that lived not far away from the centre. None of these were achievable given the budget I had. However, I had organised the turkey buffet, the centre's decorations were already up and some of the art sessions had created a whole load more. I had brought lots of art materials for people to make paper snowmen and I had rented a karaoke machine for the day for some entertainment.

In addition, I had arranged for Belle to attempt her latest Guinness Book of Records attempt at the centre with the official assessors present. Belle was attempting the world record for the fastest time to eat three mince pies. Two of the patients also wanted to try this record as they fancied their chances. The rate Goran and Francis ate anything, at the speed of a starving dog; we thought they were definitely in with a good chance. Belle had been practising a fair bit but at the risk of her detesting mince pies she had changed it to different foods that she felt were equivalent. Goran had stuck to mince pies and was happy with that. Francis didn't really like mince pies so had like Belle been practicing with other foods. We had decided that the Day Hospital Party would be early as many of the patients were spending time away at relatives for a couple of weeks and some of the staff were taking holiday leave to travel up to their families too. So Friday was the day and I had yet to organise the karaoke song lists and test out the machine. I had elected for Mary and Belle to come over to mine to help me tonight. They brought wine and snacks and Christmas hats to get us into the spirit.

Belle is the only one of us that can really sing and so she was elected as the one to try out the songs and Mary and I would create the song lists. Although the company that rented the machine had its own folders, we needed to reduce down the number of songs to make it easier on the day. Having run the Music Group a few times now, I know what sort of music the majority like. The staff like most pop hits and suggested a sprinkling of the oldies like Tom Jones and Frank Sinatra. There was of course a selection of Christmas songs. Before we get started Mary tells us she has news;

"I have been dying to tell you both and I know you will think it crazy and you may beat up a certain someone Belle; but….."

She pauses, we pause and then we tell her to go on. She reddens slightly and chews the inside of her cheek so we know she is nervous about telling us her news.

"I have been seeing Jimmy this week, we went on a date. It was lovely, we didn't realise how much we had in common. He said that Bridport made him see me differently. Like a grown up, not his little sister's mate."

"And how do you see Jimmy?" I ask.

"I suppose similarly, before he was Belle's geeky brother, but I saw another side of him at the weekend. He was funny, charming and sexy. He just came out of his shell so much. I loved his bromance with Frank as well."

"Yes, well Frank brings out the mischief in everyone"

I say and Belle is nodding and mocking me.

"Especially petite little best friend of his sister."

She says and Mary laughs.

"Oh yes, was there not a little spark between you two?" She asks.

I divert the attention back to Mary and ask,

"So have you two snogged yet, gone further?"

Mary blushes at this question and says that they had kissed a lot and it had been very lovely. She said she was not going to share any more than that but we were not to worry all was absolutely divine.

Belle and I are delighted. We thought there was a bit of a spark between them when we were away. Belle is not surprised that Jimmy has kept this from her, but they haven't been in touch since the weekend away. We suggest we don't need the gory details but want to know when they are seeing each other again.

They have arranged to meet up on Saturday to see a film and have a drink. They talk every day as well and Mary's dad had been cross with her for being on the phone so much, especially when he is on call. Of course, Frank teases them both so much and loves that his sister and his 'Bridport Bro' as he calls Jimmy, are a budding couple. He wants us all to have an annual visit to Bridport as he enjoyed it so much and loved all our friends and the adoring Miss C. Miss C had given him extra muffins for our trip home, clear favouritism. We all love her.

We then get into singing and typing out songs on my electric typewriter I treated myself as an early Christmas present. The machine work well and we have a lot of giggles at our attempts at being Madonna, Britney and Cher. Belle's trousers split when she attempts a few high kicks and we can't stop laughing and then there is a knock on the door. It's Janice holding a small package.

"We're not being too noisy, are we?" I enquire.

"No, no, I just thought you might like this and rather than forget to give it to you tomorrow at work I thought I would pop it round."

Janice looks pale and drawn. I tell her she must come in for a drink and properly meet Mary and Belle. I think this might cheer her a little.

After introductions Belle asks Janice how her mum is, and we sympathise with her about how hard it must be and how stressful. Janice is grateful to talk about it a bit and even more grateful when we rope her into helping us prepare the karaoke as she is such a quick typist. We are soon giggling again until I remember I have a small package that needs unwrapping in the kitchen, I ask for everyone's drink requests and start to unwrap the package. I find inside a brief note from Tom and a small purse with £100 in it. The note says:

'Dearest Tovu,

It's been too long since I saw you and I miss you very much. I might not get to see you before Christmas, so just wanted to send you a little something beforehand. It's just to either treat yourself or help out with the expense at Christmas time. Don't get mad, I wanted you to know, you are forever in my heart!

Tom x'

I am furious, what does he think I am? Some sort of prostitute? Is this paying for services rendered? I thrust the note into Mary's hand and alarmed she asks,

"What the hell! Is this what was in the parcel?" she reads it and looks at me puzzled.

"What's wrong the note is quite sweet?"

"It's the £100 I am most upset about, I don't need his money, he is an ass!" I declare and dramatically throw the money onto the floor.

"I want to put Gloria Gaynor on at this point." Belle says

"Who's Tom?" Janice asks us.

Mary and Belle look at me as if to say, 'You say? Does she know him?' I realise this and before I can come up with a possible 'Tom'; Janice picks up wine glass, takes a swig and tells me it must be Tom from work, he never used to pop into the day

207

centre as much as he has over the past six months and he always seems to be looking for someone but never says he is.

"Oh my, its so clear now, of course. Doesn't he have a girlfriend?" she looks at me directly as she asks this.

I tell her the whole tawdry tale and tell her to please keep it private. Janice is of the opinion that I am best not being involved with him at all. She tells me that there are always rumours about him and different woman.

"He is a heart breaker and trouble with a capital T!" she says.

"He doesn't seem to be able to stay away from Tovu," Belle tells her.

"Like most of the men she meets, they all fall in love with her!" Janice laughs and shakes her head at me in a way that says, 'some people have all the luck'.

"Oh yes it was always the same at college, school not so much as she was a late developer!" declares Mary.

I tell them they are all delusional and ask them to focus on the dilemma in hand. Do I acknowledge the note and money as good, bad or ugly?

It is unanimously agreed that I have to decide for myself but with caution. Great help this lot, I give up and put on some Abba to sing along to and choose 'The Winner Takes It All' to start with. What a belter. We then play 'Dancing Queen' and have a good dance as we sing, 'See that girl, watch that scene, digging the dancing queen.' We all point at Janice at these lyrics because she is a dancing diva.

Chapter 21

The Christmas Party at work is a joyful occasion, the excitement and fun we had together staff and patients is just indescribable. The mince pie eating competition is hilarious, there is pastry and mince flying everywhere as the line of five contestants in the end stuff their faces. Belle wins but sadly the adjudicators hadn't turned up due to car problems earlier that day. We decided to go ahead anyway and everyone agreed it should become an annual event because although a little messy made us laugh so much it hurt. The highlight being Vanessa having a go and getting it all over her usually gorgeously made up face.

The Karaoke was also a huge hit and we had several moments when we just didn't think life could get much better. A few of the patients just had amazing voices and completely had the staff's rendition of jingle bells into the lower ranks of the talent pool. Jim and Charlie were serenading each other as Elton and Kiki, when in walks Tom. He walks straight over to Vanessa and says something that immediately makes her laugh. I can feel the heat rising in my face from my neck and my heart is racing, I have to get a grip. Belle must sense something as she has arrived at my side and drags me away to check up on me. Janice also appears,

"Oh my word, Tom is here!" Janice proclaims.

"Wow, is that THE Tom?" Belle asks and Janice nods furiously.

I feel strengthened by their support and start to feel indignant about the money again. That serves to stop the palpitations and I start to flush with outrage. I decide the best thing to do at this point is go and sit in one of the clinic rooms and avoid him altogether. I suggest this to Belle and Janice, who leave me to get a breather and they go back to the partying. I am sitting enjoying the quiet, barely five minutes when the door flings open and Tom strides in. He shuts the door and then pounces on me, wrapping me up in his arms,

"I have so missed you Beautiful! Did you get my present? I hope it helped out; I recall you saying Christmas left you a bit skint when we were talking about it."

He pauses, as I haven't said anything or responded to his kiss.

I pull away and say in my strictest voice, "What are you doing? You have no right to come barging in here trying to kiss me and treating me as if I am your girlfriend as I am not! As for the money you can have it back, I am not a whore and I am not a charity case, just leave me alone."

Tom steps back from me and hangs his head, then looks up with twinkling green eyes and smiles,

"Don't be cross with me, didn't you miss me? I thought you wouldn't mind with Sean off the scene." He says gently.

"And that's another thing, how is it you seem to have tabs on me and know my every move?! Have you got me under surveillance? Do you know how it feels to have someone you like being so distant but evidently knowing all that goes on in your life?" I am on a roll and wait for some answers.

"You know what it's like at work, people talk and the gossip has always been very reliable. I promise you it's no more than that." He says and moves towards me like a panther, quick and smooth. He subtlety touches my arm and says,

"Tovu, I adore you. When are you going to believe that? I am sick with love for you, I can't be with anyone else but you." He is stroking my arm as he says this.

My turn to pull away,

"I don't believe you, you will always have other women, I could never trust you."

Tom, touches his chest as if I have struck him a hard blow and then has the grace to say,

"You are right, I am a rogue. I love you though. Please be mine."

My heart is racing now and I really want to fall into his arms and kiss him but something holds me back and I tell him I need to go back to the party and make my escape.

Belle sees me enter the party room and asks me in a whisper how it went. She saw Tom enter the office before she could stop him. I pull a face and tell her I will tell all later. Vanessa comes over and asks me if I had seen Tom as he seems to have gone missing. I tell her I saw him taking a call and guess he is stuck on the phone. She floats off in search of him.

I get stuck in to helping with the clearing up of food and spend some time chatting to the patients. Una is having a worry about Christmas with her sister and niece who have invited her and she is wondering if they would be better off if she didn't go. Bill, the gentleman I assessed with Ade is worried about Christmas with his mother who at last has got in touch and seems to be forgiving him about his father. Bill thinks the family re-union should be at another time rather than Christmas and he wants to take it more slowly because he knows it will stress him out. I do my best to provide reassurance and listen to what they are saying with compassion and understanding. They are both right in some ways and I can see both sides of their dilemmas. I advise them both to listen to what their hearts and heads are telling them. Instinct is usually pretty reliable. I probably have to practice what I preach because I am already worrying that I won't see Tom again and that I went too far. I am hoping he doesn't reappear and took the hint to leave well alone. Vanessa has probably tracked him down and has caught him talking about her family and work stuff.

Jim appears and asks me about whether I had heard about a spate of burgularies near where Janice lives, I tell him no and pretend to be extra busy before he asks me too many questions about my Christmas plans. I have a dreadful fear that he is going to ask me to baby sit soon and I hate saying no to him as he can be really sweet to me at work. I hurry over to where Belle is talking to Debbie and ask her if she is staying around or leaving soon. Belle asks if its okay if she leaves and Debbie uncharacteristically suggest I go too.

"You go too Tovu, you did a great job today and it's been a real hit. Let us finish tidying up and we'll see you in the morning."

I initially try and act the martyr and say I will stay and help clear up more but then realise it would be a really good idea to leave with Belle. Belle is also looking at me with a fierce glare which says, stop it and come with me now.

Making our escape we decide to have a little shop and then go our separate ways. Belle still has some Christmas shopping to do and I have cards to post. I am also hoping she will give me some clues about what she wants for Christmas as I haven't got her present yet. I also have to check on the restaurant for the works staff do I have booked and am preparing a joke award ceremony. Dr Ade has also left me a note asking if they do a nut roast option as he a strict vegetarian; so I think I had better check. There is no sign of Tom when we say our goodbyes and leave; and my worries start again. Belle knows I am lost in thought as I drive out of the car park onto the main road and digs me in the ribs.

"Oy you! Stop it!" she growls comically.

"Stop what?" I laugh because the look on her face says it all. "I am driving Missy; I need complete silence from you and no more poking!"

"I won't poke you if you stop worrying about Tasty Tom!" she chuckles, and I tell her to tell me about her love life and leave mine alone. She denies any action in the boy arena for her, so I ask her if she has spoken to her brother Jimmy and whether he has revealed his feelings for Mary. Belle hasn't had a chance to speak to him properly after Mary's revelation yesterday and is hoping he will be around in the town as he works nearby and often takes a break. She thinks they are well suited and would love it if Mary became her sister in law. I suggest it was bit early to be getting new hats for their wedding and she concedes.

We spend about an hour walking around shops and then go for a coffee, no Jimmy appearance but of course; to make my day, who should be in the café but Sean. He nods in acknowledgement when he sees me and says hi. I reciprocate and try not to ogle too much at the girl sat opposite him. Belle of course makes sure she gets a good look at her though. She is a slender redhead with big eyes which are framed by the longest of lashes. Her lips are blood red and she has perfect teeth. Her clothes are designer and she looks so poised. Not Sean's type at all I think to myself. By the time we have sat down with our coffees they seem to be making an exit. Belle whispers that he isn't holding her hand. I shrug nonchalantly. I do not care.

"Oh my God Tovu, we just need Rob to walk in and we'll have caught up on all your men of 1985!" laughs Belle.

"Don't forget Sebastian, Cha Cha and Rick the Barman, I think I have had more time with all three of them than the men in my life! There is also some of the year left to meet my soul mate" I joke.

"So any heart flutters for Sexy Sean? Seeing him again stir up any juices?" Bella grins at me.

"I swear now that 1986 is going to be a man free year!" I proclaim,

"Oh, turning lesbian are you?"

"I wish I could, women are so much more grown up, but it's just not me. Mother seems to be enjoying having a girlfriend though. You just never know." I say.

We finish off our coffees reflecting on the day and Tom's entrance and advances towards me. Laughing at the best bits and laughing at the not so good bits. Friendship feels like my strongest support and asset right now. We head out to the restaurant to check out their nut roast. The manager is very swarthy and Italian looking, he has the most gorgeous smile. He tells me they do a vegetarian option for the Christmas menu but it isn't nut roast, he describes a mixed vegetable rice dish. He goes through options for me and checks numbers, he seems to be flirting with Belle who is lapping up the attention. His name is Luigi and his parents own the restaurant; he tells us he is helping out in the holidays and the usual manager has gone home to Scotland for a break. Luigi is studying in medical school in Manchester. Belle immediately starts to talk about her job as a dental hygienist and I am left on the side-lines, looking out of the window.

I watch the elderly couple arm in arm chatting lovingly to each other as they walk by and the coolest mother with designer kids stroll hand in hand with them as confident as if she had diamonds embedded in her thighs. I wonder if I will find such perfection and confidence one day. Belle nudges me out of my daydreaming and we say goodbye to Luigi. She hugs me. We go our separate ways and I am glad to get home. Except on my doorstep is Tom with a bunch of flowers.

"Have you been waiting here all this time?" I ask.

"Of course, you are worth waiting for," he flashes me a smile. "Actually, I haven't been here that long. I wanted to apologise; you were right. You were brutal but right. It was unbelievably clumsy of me. Will you forgive me?"

"Tom, thank you for saying that but I know you just can't give me what I want. I am in love with you and it hurts me when you keep me at arms length. One minute I am wrapped in your arms and it feels like we should never be apart and the next you are gone and I don't hear from you for weeks and then everyone tells me you have lots of different women and to stay away. My heart breaks a little bit more. You are always honest with me and I know it's unrealistic of me but I want more than the odd shag, the odd flirtation and the occasional cuddle. I want it all."

Tom looks at me intently, scanning my face and doesn't say anything in response to my outburst. I open my door and step in, I look at him a moment and then sadly turn away and close the door on his handsome face. He walks away and my heart feels like knives are piercing it repeatedly, I break down into tears on my bed. I know he can't give me what I want. I know I won't hear from him for a while now but think he will never be totally out of my life, he and I are destined to be so. That much I know.

Wearily, I wipe my face and pull myself together. I wonder if Larissa is working this evening or whether I should go round and see her. I need my sister and her unique view of the world to sooth my troubled heart. I fight with myself as to whether to bother seeing if she is in or not. I wish my telepathy was working and wonder whether to phone my mother instead as she may know what Larissa is up to tonight. I decide to have a shower and then see how I feel and decide. I feel so drained that I wonder if I should go to bed early instead. I am still not sure what to do after my shower when there is a knock on the door. It's Janice,

"Hiya, have you recovered from the party? It was awesome! Anyway, your mum rang and wants you to phone her back."

I thank her for the message and tell her I will come across to the house when I have made myself decent.

Half an hour later I am in my car driving over to Larissa's. My mother told me that Larissa had been to the hospital for blood tests but didn't know what for. She told me that she only knew because her neighbour's son had seen her at the phlebotomy department when he was there having a routine blood test for his diabetes. I was worried and needed to make sure she was okay. I pull up and park, run up the steps to her flat and bang on her door. Larissa appears looking absolutely radiant and she gives me a huge hug.

"Tovu, I am so happy you are here! I was going to try and get to yours as it feels like ages since you were here." She beckons me inside and then looks at my face. "What's up? You look worried."

I tell her about my call with mother and she tells me not to worry she is just having a routine check-up as she is considering donating her blood. I am so relieved. She asks me what else has happened, she knows me so well. I relate my day to her, and she tells me how proud she is of me for being so honest with Tom whatever the consequences. We dissect his lack of commitment and crass gestures; I mean flowers! Such an easy option, maybe if he'd turned up with my favourite CDs and a book of poetry I might have let him in. Larissa wants to know what I would have done if he'd come bearing a diamond ring and I joke that if it was big enough I would definitely say yes.

Larissa wants to have a karaoke night with me at my place and wishes she had been there when Janice was dancing to Abba. I want to catch up on her love life and see if she has had anymore hilarious speed dating nights. She laughs and says she is a male free zone and as I was now one maybe we should get a ticket to the Swan Princess New Year's Eve Ball. I think it's a brilliant idea.

We make plans for the family Christmas Party and talk about what we are going to wear both at that function and New Year's Eve. Larissa wants to go fancy dress as someone glamorous, but I don't want to do glam. I'd rather go in something lower key. I ask her if Faye would want to come, whether Mary and Belle and Larissa's friend Sharon would want to come too. We decide we will open invite all our friends and Faye, who Larissa tells me is in love. I feel pleased for her, at least someone in the family was loved up. Mother seemed less enamoured about Teri when I spoke to her earlier. I tell Larissa that Teri apparently hadn't invited mother to her work's do (no partners allowed) and couldn't go to mother's club one as she was on shift. Mother saw this as a huge snub and wondered if Teri was falling out of love with her. She also divulged that Teri had an annoying habit of moving mother's furniture and ornaments around when she stayed at the house which upset mother.

"Mother would hate that; do you remember her telling father off about moving a coffee table nearer to his chair in the lounge? She was always moving it back and telling him off. She thought it looked out of place. He insisted it had a much better functionality where he placed it"

Larissa asks, "Do you think the honeymoon period is already over? The cracks starting to show?"

I laugh at the innuendo and Larissa joins in. We agree that whether mother was a true lesbian or not, we didn't think Teri was the one for her. Something about her didn't seem right. Apparently, her family were going to be at the party so we would be able to find out more about her then.

I decide to return home as Larissa wasn't dying of an incurable disease and she had made me feel better about the Tom situation as I thought she would. What a crazy day. I needed a long sleep.

Chapter 22

Saturday afternoon and I am driving over to mother's with Larissa for the family Christmas Party; it's a bright, cold but dry day and the traffic isn't too bad. Larissa is in a jolly mood, she is such sunshine sometimes. We put some Soft Cell in the tape deck and have a good old singalong. We agree that the best of their songs is a toss-up between Torch and Say Hello Wave Goodbye; we both love the angst and drama of them.

When we pull up to mother's our youngest brother seems to be there as his flashy car is in the drive. We think this is a bit odd as he is never early for anything and we were expecting him to arrive late as usual. He opens the front door to us and looks a bit pale.

"What's up Landon?" Larissa is straight on it. "You look ashen, has something happened?"

Landon gives a wry smile, ushers us in and says,

"Guys I am so glad you are here. I need my sisters to give me some love." We wait for him to continue and tell us more.

"Well it so happens that ...." He pauses for dramatic effect; "I am truly hungover! That Teri can put the booze away!"

Larissa thumps him and tells him he's a dick. He explains that he decided last minute to take the week off as he felt he deserved it and came a day early to have dinner with mother and Teri. He wanted to treat them and find out if Teri was as cool as she seemed at face value. They had so much to drink that mother had to be half carried home and she was still in bed claiming she had the flu. Teri had left for work fairly early and so Landon had dragged himself out of bed to greet us. At this point mother appears in her dressing gown looking even paler than Landon and apologises for her feeling ill. We don't as a rule tease our mother, she is too sensitive for that. We just go along with her and tell her to sit down while we make her a cup of tea and get her some toast.

When I return with tea and toast mother is complaining that she is worried she will not be able to get everything done for the party and blames Landon for taking them out in the cold last night. Us siblings exchange knowing looks and smiles and of course tell her we will get it done and all she has to do is rest and tell us what she wants. She palpably flinches at the thought of us taking over and it seems to stir something within her so that she rallies.

"No, no, no! I will be okay. Let me get in the shower after this toast and I will get ready. I have done most of it any way, the food is mostly done and the house is clean and just needs a bit of organising. I just need you to fetch the drinks and the fresh fruit I need for the fruit trifle this morning and organise the music. That's your job Tovu, but none of that electronic stuff."

True to form, mother is more interested in whether the party prep will be done to her standards than whether Larissa and I are well and okay. She even seems to have forgotten about Larissa's blood test and doesn't enquire. We have grown to expect this from our mother and don't bother to get upset.

She gives some more details to her requests for help, gets up and is off up the stairs, suddenly the thought of not being the greatest hostess in the world galvanises her. Landon makes a snide comment to this effect and suggests he also gets ready and sends us off to get the drink and fresh food.

By the time the night skies filter though, everything is ready and mother and Landon look much healthier. Faye also returns from her friend's house and we catch up with her as we are getting ready. The rest of the family and also Teri's are arriving from 6.30 p.m. and so we leave the last preparation tweaks to mother as she always likes it. It gives her the chance to make it look exactly as she wants it. She's already dressed in her usual party attire, plus a pinny. Landon has gone off for a 'drive' which probably means he's gone for a fag and chat to one of his ladies in a local phone booth.

Faye tells us that all is going well with her boyfriend and she stays around at his quite a lot. She agrees that mother and Teri seem a little less enamoured with each other but nothing too bad. Her studies have suffered a bit because of her boyfriend, just because she prefers to hang out with him to studying. We give her a gentle lecture about the need for her not to let a man get in the way of her success. She mockingly retorts that she would of course follow her sisters' example and laughs. Her only bit of gossip is that one of our neighbour's daughter's has decided she wants to live life as a male and is changing her name from Beth to Barry. We wonder why Barry. Surely, she could have chosen a better name than that. I suggest Bertie and Larissa Byron. Barry is however, a very good macho name. we talk about transgender a bit more because I have come across some people wanting to transition genders through work and know how depressed and anxious, they have been because of the bullying they get. Some have been disowned by their families and communities. A lot have left their workplace due to them not allowing them to use the female toilets and other discriminations. One man who changed from being female was still sexually harassed and excluded from nights out. It's not an easy choice, it isn't a choice and it brings great hardship but everyone of them said they thought it was better than living a lie. Faye wants to know the difference between a cross dresser and someone who changes gender. We explain and she gets it.

I change the subject and ask her if she wants to come with us to the New Year's Ball; she declines as she already has plans. She suggests we cross dress and go as men when we tell her its fancy dress. She is going as a flapper girl to her party. We just know she will be the most gorgeous flapper girl ever. She is currently standing before us in a little red dress and small fur bolero, she looks like a sexy Mrs Santa. Larissa is in green and has a sparkling coloured beaded necklace and we decide she is a very beautiful Christmas Tree. I am then the chimney sweeps brush because I am in black frilliness. My sisters laugh at me and tell me that at least I'm good luck to whoever passes me tonight. I retort that they can pass on by because I am sneaking off to bed alone at the earliest chance I get. They promise to keep me up all evening.

The house is full of people, the noise level is at an acceptable level for the neighbours who are sat on the couch pissed on Glenfiddich and feeding each other Maltesers. I have no idea whether they brought them with them, or mother actually provided chocolate. Larissa and I have been helping mother keep food and drink accessible to all and everyone seems happy. Then father's brother Raymond asks mother in the loudest voice,

"So where's your lesbian lover I've heard all about?"

All eyes dart to him and then mother, Samantha his daughter tells him to shut up and drags him out into the kitchen to berate him. Teri's parents are standing just off to his left and look angrily at him. Mother is flushed and Landon comes to her rescue by suggesting it was time for the family tradition of a sing song and he sits at the piano and bangs out 'We wish you a Merry Christmas'. Others start to join in, and a few family relatives bring out guitars and percussion to accompany Landon. I study the room wondering if this family of mine are for real. Someone is tugging at my sleeve, Larissa by my side says,

"Bloody hell, it's like a scene from the Waltons! You better hide from mother or she will have you spouting some of your poems next!" We giggle and sidle off to the garden to escape.

As we are huddled together having a fag when a man seems to be coming down the garden path towards us; it is Teri.

"Hey girls, how's it going?" She goes to hug us and plants a kiss on each of our cheeks. "I got off early and wanted to surprise your mum, is she in the kitchen panicking?"

We say we are not sure and follow her in, wanting to see how this plays out. Mother does not like surprises.

Instead of the expected whispered row, mother takes one look at Teri and almost gleefully embraces her and kisses her full on her mouth. More than half of the people in the room have their mouths open in surprise. No-one has seen mother displaying affection in public before, let alone so brazenly showing she doesn't give a damn about what people think about her and Teri. I sort of want to applaud her. She is introducing Teri to everyone and we watch their reactions and are disappointed because most people seem drunk and the awkward embarrassment, we were hoping to witness isn't there and people greet her as though she was a good friend. We find ourselves chatting to Teri's parents. Joyce, her mum is a square shaped lady who blinks three times as much as most people and has been interrogating us and asking questions about everyone at the party. Herb her husband works in a bank and is now waxing lyrical about interest rates and Landon joins us. We wonder if her dad is attracted to Landon as he cannot get enough of him.

I feel the need to hide and tell them I am off to the loo. I shut Faye's bedroom door behind me and climb onto her bed to have a quiet moment. I must have fallen asleep because when I awake, I can hear shouting. It must have infiltrated my psyche as I was dreaming that Tom was shouting my name over and over again, but I couldn't see him. Larissa is shouting at me,

"Tovu, Tovu! You have to come downstairs now! It's all gone crazy!"

"What? What do you mean, what's going on?"

Larissa tells me that an almighty row broke out between Teri, her mother and our mother. I tell her we should leave them to it, it's nothing to do with us and I'm tired. She pounces on me and I can smell pickled onions on her breath, and I flinch. She doesn't notice and starts to tell me all about the row. It had started with Teri flirting with several members of our family including Landon and cousin Samantha. Teri said she was just having a bit of fun and was upset that mother had told Teri's parents that she thought Teri was commitment phobic. Mother said it wasn't like that she just said that she didn't feel Teri was ready to think about moving in with each other. Teri said she was 'too right' and challenged mother with saying that maybe she should look at all her two oldest daughters who are hardly in committed relationships. They both burst into tears and mother ran off saying she had never been more humiliated. At which point Larissa decided she needed to remove herself. Just as she was winding up the story Faye burst in and flung herself across us both on the bed.

"I've just been with mum; she is really upset and rather tipsy so I gave her a cuddle and told her to take some deep breaths. I just left her when Teri arrived much calmer and sorry for what she had said. I think she has a drink problem because that got way out of hand too quickly, it seems calmer now but mum was saying to me she thinks the relationship has gotten weird and she wants to end it." Faye is wriggling herself between us and looks to each side of her to see our reaction.

"Well maybe it's for the best?" Larissa comments.

"It might just blow over if they are both drunk." I say.

Before anyone says anything else Landon bursts through the door.

"Fucking hell, here you all are. I've been looking everywhere! Did you see the drama? Everyone is leaving, including Teri. She said she's completely embarrassed and mother has told her to leave. Mother is not coming out of her room and has locked herself in there. I'm not sure what to do. Fucking drama!"

Landon is upset but more because he wanted to carry on partying, he doesn't seem that concerned about mother and then as we expect he tries to get us to go out with him.

I try to suggest we try and tidy up for mother and have a couple more drinks at home while we do it but I am shot down and they plead with me to go out to the local pub.

"C'mon Tove, it's only 10 p.m. we can clear up tomorrow morning!"

I go and check up on mother, she lets me in after a little while and looks rather grey faced and says she has a splitting headache. She tells me she is okay and that she is fine with us going out and tidying in the morning. She asks me to get her some water and a few snacks and she will try and get some sleep.

When we get to the pub it is heaving, with a very convivial atmosphere and music playing out Christmas songs. A few of our relatives had snuck off there too, so we had a repeat of joyful hugs and family banter with no mention of the drama that unfolded nearly an hour before. Landon soon latches onto a pretty brunette with green eyes and an Irish lilt to her accent leaving us girls to chat to a group of cousins who had been to a family party also and escaped to avoid the tension. Their mother was an alcoholic and always had a row with their father, so they made the tiff at home earlier seem rather petty and small. They were quite interesting and James, the tallest, most attractive of them was particularly entertaining. He described things so uniquely. I wanted to steal some of his phrases, like 'she acts as though she's too posh to piss' and 'he rammed his words down her throat as if they'd been shot through a pistol'. I guess people would be a bit aghast, which brings me pleasure as I like the element of surprise. Most people expect me to be sweet and never swear, truth is I am far from it and I like to shock. Anyway, James is also looking rather attractive the more I drink, and Larissa seems more interested in his cousin Merlin whose mother was a believer in legend of Arthur and his round table. He's got beautiful sparkly blue eyes but James' brooding, slightly dangerous look appeals to me more. Faye is talking to his sister whose hair is ebony and she has the same jarring features which fade like shadows when she smiles and laughs.

The pub has a lock down after closing time and because we have been buying bar staff drinks all night we are a few of the locals they allow to stay.

"Tovu, that's an interesting name. Why did your parents call you that?" Oh dear, this question is usually followed by some cheesy chat up line, I like him, I am a bit drunk but really I don't want to go there. A little flirting is fine and he is interesting. From what he says about his parents I wonder how much he may be harbouring some mental illness. I am doing a complete 180 degree turn in my head and say,

"Something to do with the Moomintrolls I believe" and laugh. Which is my own code response to block further questioning unless they want to know what a Moomintroll is. Which then only leads to conversations about cute creatures and whether you prefer one type of cute creature to another. Then James has other ideas, he grabs my arms, looks intently into my eyes and says,

"Fuck me, I don't give a shit about that really. I do really want to snog your delectable face off though!"

His actions shake me inside and I feel panic but hold it together and put on a plastic smile. Then say in a firm voice,

"Please let go of me. I need to go to the loo."

He lets me go and starts talking to his sister and Faye about a quarrel he had with a customer who hadn't paid him for a painting job he'd done. I walk away hearing him say,

"The bastard not only had the nerve to tell me 'it's Christmas have a heart' but he then had the cheek to say the paint was too dark. He chose the bloody paint not me!"

By the time I return I have got my composure back and have told myself not to be daft and have a bit of fun. Snogging never harmed anyone after all.

Chapter 23

The day after Boxing Day and I am home in my little annexe. Things had been quite civil for the rest of Christmas after we had recovered from the party and pub. Mother and Teri had decided to call it a day but to remain friends. Mother wisely decided it was all too soon after father had died, and she didn't need the intimacy of a relationship right now. I had a very nice snog but that's where it ended. We exchanged phone numbers knowing we were never going to use them. I gave him my work number and goodness knows whose phone number he gave me. I won't be trying it.

Larissa was working today, and I said I would pick her up later to plan New Year's Eve outfits and get something to eat. Meantime, Mary and Belle were coming over and wanted to catch up about all the family gossip. When they arrive, I am full of joy, they look fantastic and both have the glow of being completely adored by another person. Mary and Jimmy are going strong and Belle has finally got into the Guinness Book of Records for the fastest time to eat three mince pies. Fortunately, she has been running every day to compensate for the amount of mince pies and other food she has had to practice with. She has enjoyed running so much that she now has her eyes set on a race. They both look so amazing and when I tell them this they laugh at me because I only saw them a week ago.

We decide to go for lunch in town and end up in MacDonalds feasting on our chicken sandwiches and fries; having had so much Christmas food it almost seems decadent. I joke that we are going to regret this decision and we all feel pretty bloated afterwards. Mary tells us she and Jimmy have booked a weekend in Nice over Easter and thinking about a summer holiday too. This sends us on a discussion about where we wanted to go abroad and why. Which then leads to questions about who we would want to go with. Belle tells us about her fantasy of going to a mountainous region with Jeremy Irons who is her secret crush. She saw him in a film called 'Betrayal' and thought he was brilliant. Belle turns on me and says,

"So who would you choose, the Sexy Sean, the Troublesome Tom or someone else?"

My heart pounds when I think of Tom and say as much, but tell them I would go with Anthony Andrews and he and Jeremy could re hash Brideshead Revisited with me and Belle starring. Mary says I'm a 'silly tart' but she loves me and whether Tom deserved it or not she understood that when there is chemistry there is chemistry. We universally agree that both Jeremy and Anthony were welcome at ours.

The cold day is biting through us, so we don't linger about the town for long and we soon get on our way to pick up Larissa. We have to wait half an hour, so the engine is running when she appears.

"Sorry guys, I had Meryl weeping about something and I couldn't leave her until she had calmed down".

Meryl was one of the residents with a learning disability and she had had a meltdown over the TV not working when she wanted to watch it. Larissa had managed to sort it all out but said she was keen to get home to shower. I said I would detour as she was supposed to be staying at mine. She did kind of smell a bit weird, we took her back to hers and regaled her with renditions of Elton John songs.

By the time we get back to mine it is sleeting, dusting the land like icing sugar on a sponge cake. It looks pretty. There are large footsteps up to my door, a man is standing there in a large duffle coat. It's Tom. I let the girls in and then turn to speak to him.

"What are you doing here?"

He looks strangely nervous.

"Can I come in? It's freezing out here!"

I reluctantly take pity and let him in and suddenly feel nervous with him standing in my kitchen so agitated. He is shifting his weight from one side to the other and is looking at me.

"I will cut to the chase, will you live with me? Can we move in together? I don't really do marriage, but I want to show you I love you and I am committed to you". He blurts this out.

He touches my shoulder and starts to stroke it. I pull away and say,

"No Tom, it's never going to work. I can't."

He looks so wounded and sad. I want to jump into his arms and tell him how much I love him but I just know in my heart that he isn't going to stay. He is too much of a free spirit, he wants me because I am saying no. He'll get bored with me. I say as much to him and he stands there shaking his head telling me I am wrong, that he loves me. My chest feels as though my heart is going to burst out of it, but I find the strength to ask him to leave. He wraps his arms around me and it feels like heaven and I nearly melt. I gently push him away and say,

"Goodnight Tom, take care always."

It seems to take an eternity for him to let go of me and I feel the imprint of his hands on my body, I cannot look at him for fear give away how my heart is shattering into little pieces. He turns away from me and as he opens the door he looks over his shoulder and says,

"Just send me the key back Tove, I need to return it. Bye"

I don't have a clue what he means but I just nod and say "Okay".

Mary is first to get to me when they hear the door close and then Larissa and Belle,

"Oh fuck, what did he want?"

Before I can say anything, the door knocks. We freeze, has he come back? I open the door and Janice is on the doorstep.

"I thought you were back, Merry Christmas! And thank you for my pressie Tovu. I wanted to drop this off to you, it was on the doorstep yesterday when I walked by and I rescued it in case it got wet. Oh hello girls, so lovely to see you too!"

Janice hands me over a small package, I recognise the writing immediately as Tom's. I thank her and ask her if she wants to come in for a cuppa. She declines and says she has to get back as her mother is staying and being rather demanding. I ask her how her mum is, all the time thinking I want her to go so I can unwrap the parcel. She tells me that her mother is frail and tired but also calm and trying her best to be upbeat. It is the family that is struggling but they have had a nice Christmas. I give her a hug and she scuttles off up to the house.

Belle and Mary eagerly want to see what Tom has sent me; I gingerly start to open up the parcel and Mary rips it from my hands and tears it open. A silver key and a note fall out. I suddenly realise that I have misjudged Tom. The note says;

'Darling Tovu, I just want you forever. Live with me. Please say yes xx Tom xx'

Then in small text it says, 'if it's a no then please return this key to ….and then an address'.

I feel a fire in my belly and I pick up my car keys. I have to go after Tom. I am not sure where he would have gone, I don't know where he lives and whether he is staying anywhere tonight. I realise he does love me and that I can't let him believe I don't love him back. I need to find him, but where would he have gone?

Everyone takes a guess at this question and I realise I have no clue where he lives these days. Larissa suggest trying the address where the key is supposed to be sent back to. I re-read the note and it says to return to an address in Amersham. I wonder if the sleet is turning into snow and whether it will be too dangerous to drive out there for a split second and decide it will be okay. The girls want to come with me and make sure I am okay. I am worried we may all get stuck in a snowstorm and tell them I will be fine without them. My darling sister takes charge and says she will come and Mary and Belle need to stay at the annexe in case they are needed later.

My heart is pounding and Larissa asks me if I want her to drive. I am not prepared to die, so say I am fine and we get in the car. Half an hour later we find the address on the note, there are no lights and it doesn't look like anyone is home. We get out of the car to check. The small, modern house looks empty and we walk round the back to see if there is any sign of life there. Peering through the windows we can see some furniture and boxes, it looks half moved into. But no clues to the occupant. Larissa suggests that it may be half moved out of. We give up and trudged back to the car.

"We could wait around a bit, see if he turns up?" Larissa says as she sees my disappointed face.

I agree we can wait for a little while until it gets too cold, which doesn't give us much time because it is icy. It isn't sleeting anymore, and the moon is lighting up the sky in a quiet glow. I am beginning to lose heart and tell Larissa we need to get home.

I turn the key and the car struggles to spark into action. Thankfully it does and Larissa asks if I want to leave a note, but because I don't really know whether this is Tom's place I decide it would be better not to.

Feeling calmer, I laugh at myself and tell Larissa I read to many romantic stories. I think I was hoping for a happy ending and actually my first instinct had been right. He probably has gone home to another woman and forgotten about me already.

New Year's Eve and we look so funny. We went with a superhero theme; so, we look colourful and puny as superheroes but we love our outfits. Somehow, we have achieved sexy and cute in our capes and outside underpants.

The streets are full and we manage to squeeze in at The Tap having persuaded Rick to give us free tickets for the night as his favourite customers. We get a lot of looks as we weave through the crowd and someone manages to squeeze my arse as I pass them. I ignore it and manage to get to the bar. I feel nervous and hope they haven't run out of vodka. Belle has ordered the drinks and we all have double vodkas and orange. Some Dick, nearly has me over as they move past me to get to the bar and I am about to give them a piece of my mind when I see it is a man dressed in a penis outfit. It's quite awful and I can't bring myself to talk to them. I was right he really is a Dick!

We move to the end of the bar near to the juke box and get a better view of the array of costumed party goers. There is plenty to laugh at and we particularly find the usual group of men dressed in frocks for a joke amusing. There are five of them and they look about twelve but probably just eighteen. Now and again they start dancing like blokes in dresses and then they stand supping lager pretending to be coy ladies but lapse into laddish banter and lewdness most of the time. As the evening moves along a group of young girls dressed as schoolgirls edge more closer to them and the annual cliché plays out as they start to dance with each other.

We down our second vodka and head off to The Swan for the party. We enter the venue and it has been adorned with sparkle and retro shaped décor. The staff are in flapper dresses and suits. We suddenly feel rather out of place and then spy other people in a number of bizarre costumes. Relieved we head for the loos and reapply makeup and sort out tousled hair. The mirrors are unforgiving, and I look pale and panda eyed. Everyone else looks young and glam to me. My heart is racing, I need another drink. I wonder if I am developing some sort of social phobia. I feel sweaty and let Larissa take my hand to guide us down to the bar. I need to dance, lose myself in the music and stop worrying about nothing in particular. Mary and Belle have found Jimmy and Frank who had agreed to come out tonight too. They had just got here and were pleased to see Larissa and me. I suddenly felt safer and more relaxed. Frank gave me the best squeeze and kissed me on the cheek.

"Hey beautiful!" he says in my ear.

We head to the dance floor, Frank can dance. He loves the same music as me and we move well together. The DJ is good and we are barley off the dance floor; I am enjoying myself and Frank teases and looks after me between tracks.

"Hey beautiful, shall we go sit down a while, my feet are throbbing?" Frank takes my hand when I nod a yes.

He guides me through the crowds and up to a terraced area. It's a bit cooler and quieter.

"So, will you let me kiss you at midnight?" he asks me with a big grin on his face.

"Not if you start a sentence with the word 'so' and only if you promise to make it the best snog ever." I reply.

His grin broadens and he tells me I am a pain but still cute. We talk about Mary and Jimmy; Frank is genuinely pleased for them. He thinks they will be long term. He wants to know about Tom as he has heard from Mary about the key and note and my attempt to find him. I blush because I feel a bit silly about this event and I want him to tell me why he hasn't got a girlfriend and why he was leaving to move south for his job. I manage to shift the focus on him, and he tells me he has a promotion but it means moving to Hampshire, he is excited by it. I look down and see Mary and Jimmy with Larissa, Belle and a swarthy Italian looking man and I realise it is the guy from the restaurant in town Belle had been chatting to before Christmas. I see a blonde head and take a double take as I think it might be Tom. It isn't. Frank is telling me about a girl he likes at work, but she is a bit 'drippy' at times. I find myself wishing Tom was with me and wondering if 1985 has been a good year or not. I wonder if I will cry that the year has passed or whether I will rejoice that it is over.

Frank says,

"Hey, Tovu, it's five minutes to midnight. Shall we join the others?"

I agree and we make our way down to where they are standing. They whoop when we arrive and then before I know it, we have the count down.

As we shout out "ONE", we all turn to each other to kiss and hug saying Happy New Year.

Frank snogs me long and hard and I snog him back, there are no sparks, but we feel like a worn pair of slippers, comfortable and loving.

Whilst 1985 has been a packed year with failed relationships with men; I feel elated that I have a great family and the most wonderful friends. As a baby of the 60's I feel the mid-eighties have made me stronger and I have more resolve to move forward with better focus in the next years. I feel I have been dancing about life letting the rhythm take me here and there and I realise now, as the year turns, that I can be a dancing queen for the rest of the century and beyond. Happy New Year!

THE END

Printed in Poland
by Amazon Fulfillment
Poland Sp. z o.o., Wrocław